SORROW'S GIFT

ETERNAL SORROWS, BOOK 2

SARRA CANNON

For those of you who waited.

PART ONE
THE GUARDIANS

ONE

ZOE

The last of the sun's light lingered like a halo above the city.

Zoe hated this time of day. Everything looked warm and beautiful, but as the night came, it turned cold and horrible. It was a betrayal of the worst kind, like giving hope to someone on death row.

She didn't like watching what came next, but this stupid suite had so many windows. When they'd first checked in, she'd thought they were lucky to get a room with such an amazing view of the city and a balcony.

Now, she despised it. She had a front row seat to all the destruction and death. The fires that had spread throughout Central Park. The cars piled up in the streets where desperate people had rammed into each other, trying to force their way out of the city.

And worst of all, she could see hundreds of those things as they shambled and limped along the sidewalks and streets below, their clothes covered in blood and their jaws snapping hungrily.

She shuddered just thinking about it.

It was almost dark again. The small groups that wandered the streets during the day were nothing compared to the large packs that took over during the darkest hours.

Soon the undead would emerge from the shadows, their hungry mouths ringed with blood. The sound of their moans would echo in the streets below. Sometimes, she could hear people screaming.

But the screams were less frequent now.

Zoe wasn't sure if that was because there were no survivors or if the ones who were left were hiding, like her. Waiting for something—or someone—to come save them. Zoe hadn't seen more than a handful of survivors all week.

In the first few days of the awakening, she had seen thousands of frightened people traveling in groups during the daytime, scrambling to escape the city. After the sun had set, she sometimes liked to imagine those people had made it somewhere safe. Somewhere the rotters didn't exist. Someday, those people would come back for her and take her to a city that had running water and electricity. Maybe Parrish would be there waiting for her.

But tonight she didn't have the energy to pretend. She knew it was a fairytale.

No one was safe anymore. No one was coming for her.

Maybe she was the only person left in the entire world.

Every once in a while, she caught the flutter of a curtain in the window of a building across the street. Sometimes she'd wave toward them, hoping they could see her. Longing for some kind of human connection. But she never saw their faces.

For all she knew, it was a trick of her imagination. Maybe she really was all alone in this world.

She hadn't left the safety of her hotel room in more than a week. One of those things was trapped in the hallway just outside her door. She could hear it pacing the floor, roaming from one side to the other in an endless loop. It never seemed to get tired or want to sleep. It just walked and walked and walked.

Her father was one of them now, too.

When he'd first gotten sick, he had locked himself away, only talking to her through the door of his bedroom. He'd told her to stay safe and cover her mouth if anyone came into the room. He'd told her everything was going to be okay.

But a couple days later, he'd stopped talking. He'd stopped coughing.

It was the weirdest feeling to hear nothing on the other side of that door and know there was nothing she could do about it. He was dead and there was no doctor to call. No police or ambulance to help.

There wouldn't even be a funeral. Before the power shut off, she'd seen on TV that there were so many dead now they had started putting the bodies into mass graves. She'd thought maybe someone would come to collect her father's body. But that was before the dead started walking around and attacking people. After that, the TV stopped reporting news and just started showing endless reruns until it finally cut off altogether.

She was alone now, her dead father's hungry moans the only thing keeping her company.

Zoe had moved a few things in front of his door, just in case. Things she could carry. Her suitcase. A chair. She'd managed to push a table in front of his door, but everything else had been too heavy for her to move. She lived in constant fear, plagued by nightmares about her father pushing through that door and coming after her.

She'd seen what the rotters do to the living.

The thought of her father...

A tear rolled down her cheek. What was wrong with the world? How could something like this be possible? Why wasn't someone coming to save them?

She turned away from the brilliant colors of the setting sun and ran the back of her hand under her runny nose. No one was coming, because there was no one left.

Zoe glanced longingly at her violin case on the bar. God, she wanted to play so badly her fingers ached. She needed something to drown out the endless moans. The sorrow and death.

The light was almost gone, and the tears began to flow. She hated the night. And right now, she had the thought that she wasn't even sure she could survive it. Not again.

Her heart ached. She ran her fingers along the rough edges of the black case and wished they'd never left their home in Virginia.

She wished she knew if her mom and Parrish were still alive.

If anyone was still alive out there.

Zoe brought a hand to the silver necklace she wore. Parrish had given it to her the day she left for New York. An infinity sign with both their birthstones.

Parrish promised she was coming to get her, but even that was just a fairy tale. Even if her sister was still alive, there was no way she'd make it through the city. It was hopeless.

Zoe reluctantly closed the curtains as the last of the pink sunset disappeared on the horizon. In the darkness, she walked over to the bar and pulled her violin from its case. It was too dangerous to play at night. Noise agitated them and drew them closer. She needed to stay as quiet as possible and wait for morning.

But the thought of another endless night with nothing to do but listen to the sound of their moans nearly broke her.

Maybe it would be better to just invite them in and let it all be over.

Crying, she lifted the instrument to her shoulder and rested her face against the cool chinrest, closing her eyes as she slid her bow effortlessly across the strings. The sound made her heart soar and expand, hope blossoming inside her for the first time in days. It was dangerous, but she didn't care. She needed something. She needed to feel okay for a little while.

She heard the orchestra in her head and imagined the conductor leading them as an entire hall full of people listened. She clung to the memory of the music.

Sobs shook her shoulders as she played, knowing a rotter could burst through the door at any moment, lured by the sound of her violin. She didn't care. Let them come. All she cared about was this one thing that told her she was still alive.

This one thing that proved the whole world was not lost.

TWO
PARRISH

Rotters flooded the streets of D.C.

Parrish gripped a canvas loop hanging from the ceiling, her body jerking with each bump as the Humvee plowed over the corpses of the dead.

At first, no one spoke. They were all exhausted. Confused. And scared as hell.

What were those things back there?

Parrish had barely gotten used to the idea that the dead were walking around trying to eat the living. Now she was supposed to somehow wrap her head around the idea of super-zombies with magical powers and enormous strength?

It was too much.

Surviving the endless attacks of the regular rotters was hard enough when they were in big groups, but these super zombies? They were impossible. And worse, those things had come straight for them. It was almost like they'd been hunting them. If Crash hadn't shown up when he did, what would have happened?

Parrish closed her eyes and leaned her head against her arm. She didn't want to think about that. She wanted to go to sleep and wake up tomorrow to find this was all some terrible nightmare.

The worst part was that it still wasn't over yet. They still weren't safe.

The truck swerved violently to one side and Parrish slammed into Noah. He reached his hands out to steady her, and the warmth of his fingers brushed across the bare skin at her waist.

Parrish drew in a sharp breath and turned to look at him. A streak of blood had dried across his forehead and his hair was covered in dirt and ash, but his eyes were as beautiful as ever, focused and dark. Her heart raced a little faster.

"You okay?" he asked.

She nodded and looked away, gripping the loop tighter above her head. She didn't want him to see her fear. Or her attraction. She scooted back over on the bench seat and shrugged out of his grasp.

She needed to focus on survival. Staying alive so she could get to her sister in New York was all that mattered now. The last thing she needed was to be daydreaming about some guy.

Still, her eyes traveled back to his.

The problem was he wasn't just some guy. This was Noah. She'd stayed up late thinking of him so many nights she'd lost count. He was the one she'd always looked for in a crowd. The one guy she'd ever wanted to kiss.

But that was before the end of the world.

He was staring at her, one hand gripping the canvas loop next to hers, and the other resting on the bench between them like a dare.

"What were those new zombies? Where did they come from?" he asked, barely loud enough for her to hear over the roar of the Humvee's engine and the groans of the undead clawing at the truck.

"I don't know," she said. She scooted toward the guy in the driver's seat. "Hey, Crash. You ever seen anything like those rotters back there? The ones with glowing eyes?"

Even though he was only a few feet away, she had to shout to be heard.

Crash shook his head. Their eyes met through the rear-view mirror for an instant. "No way, man. What the hell were they?"

"I was hoping you would know," she yelled back. "We've never seen anything like it. If you hadn't gotten there in time, I don't think we would have made it."

Across from her, Karmen pulled her knees up to her chest and buried her head between them.

The new girl sat next to Karmen, her eyes wide and her hands cradled in her lap. Parrish still didn't even know the girl's name. They'd all risked their lives to rescue her, even though they had no idea who she was. How in the world had Crash even known she was up there? A dream, he'd said. She was the fifth. The one who was supposed to complete their group somehow. But what did that even mean?

There were too many questions and not enough answers.

Parrish just wanted to find a safe place where they could try to make sense of this.

"How much farther?" she shouted.

Crash pointed to something up ahead. "We're almost there," he said, slowing down to a stop. "But getting in is going to be a bitch."

There was only one small window in the back of the truck, so Parrish leaned forward to look through the windshield. Hundreds of rotters swarmed the vehicle, their bloodied hands grasping at metal, desperate to get inside. Their jaws snapped like gators, hungry for the taste of flesh.

Parrish searched their eyes, looking for any sign of a red glow like the ones they'd fought in the office building earlier.

Anger surged through her as she studied the monsters on the street. Some of them wore suits, as if they'd gotten dressed for work and died somewhere along the way. Some wore hospital gowns or pajamas. Jeans and t-shirts. But their clothes were the only things normal about them anymore. It was the only thing that proved they had been people once, just like her. Just like her mother.

But there was nothing human about them anymore. Their milky eyes were wide and wild, desperate with hunger. Most of them were already rotting, their skin sagging and gray. Some had been partially eaten, their bones exposed and their clothes covered in dried blood.

As her eyes scanned the group of them, rage pounded in her head.

It wasn't fair.

It didn't make any sense.

How had this happened?

She released her grip on the canvas loop and leaned forward. "Where exactly do we need to go?" she asked.

Crash pointed to a gated garage about fifty feet away on the left. "That's my apartment building," he said. "I have the inside secured, but we have to find a way to hold these things off long enough to get the door open and drive inside without letting too many in with us."

She nodded and tried to estimate just how many were out there.

"Give me ten minutes," she said.

Crash turned around in his seat, one eyebrow raised and a smile playing at the corners of his lips. He was a pretty good-looking guy, she realized for the first time. Asian with long, messy black hair and dark eyes. He looked a few years older than the rest of them.

"What exactly do you have in mind?" he asked.

Parrish glanced at the crowd of rotters standing between them and the gate. She reached back and closed her fingers around the hilt of her katana, carefully pulling the sword out of her bag.

"I'm going to kill them all."

THREE
PARRISH

Noah moved forward to help open the back door of the Humvee. The entire inside of the vehicle had been customized and hollowed out to make room for two benches, one along each side, and a large door in the back. Karmen rushed forward, ready to shut the door quickly, but the new girl did nothing. She barely even looked up. Her hands were trembling.

Was she in shock? How had she survived all on her own?

Parrish shook her head and jumped forward, landing firmly on the pavement in front of Crash's apartment building. There was no time to think or plan. There was only action.

She and Noah raced around the left side of the truck. Most of the zombies had moved toward the front of the vehicle where the lights were shining. A few others stood alone in the darkness, stumbling toward the Humvee.

She only had a breath's worth of time to send up a prayer before she lifted her sword. The blade hit flesh and she winced as the sharpened sword sliced through the neck of a man in a brown suit.

Or what used to be a man in a brown suit.

His skin had begun to decay around his eyes and mouth, and there was a chunk of flesh missing from his cheek.

The man's head fell to the ground with a bloody thud.

Noah moved ahead. He lifted his baseball bat and swung forward with enormous speed. The sound of wood meeting soft flesh rose over the sound of the truck's engine as the zombie's head caved in. Blood splattered out, some hitting the side of the dark green military vehicle.

There was no time to think about what they were doing or who these people used to be. There was only time to kill. To do their best to survive.

The two of them moved forward, picking off a handful of zombies that stumbled around the Humvee.

They killed as quietly as they could, trying not to draw the attention of the larger group of rotters until they moved up near the front where they could be seen in the dim headlights.

She wasn't sure if they saw her or smelled her, but the undead clustered in the headlights snapped their heads in her direction.

Parrish didn't hesitate. She swung her sword with a skill she still had no idea how she'd learned. Or when. She gave into that deep instinct and sliced into the first of the rotters—a woman with dirty blonde hair and bulging blue eyes. Her head landed at Parrish's feet with a thump. Parrish kicked it aside and turned, gathering momentum and strength as she buried her sword into the neck of a large fat man.

A bloodied hand grabbed her shoulder and tried to scratch at her, but she flipped around just in time, first kicking the dead woman away and then bringing her blade down hard on the woman's skull, splitting it in two.

Parrish gagged at the dark blood that spilled down the woman's face as she fell forward.

There was a part of her that just wanted to sit down and cry. To try to make sense of all this chaos. She needed peace and quiet and time to figure out how the world had turned into this horror show. But there were others clawing at her clothes, trying to grab her and drag her down.

From the corner of her eye, she saw Noah's bat slam into another of the zombies, crushing its skull like a rotten pumpkin.

If he can do this, so can I.

She drew in a deep breath, ignoring the putrid smell of decaying flesh, and forced herself to keep moving. She sliced and kicked and killed until a pile of bodies lay in a circle around her. She turned and looked for Noah.

He was on the other side of the truck, fighting off a group of four or five.

She scrambled over the bodies of the dead and ran through the headlights toward him.

She drew in a breath and cursed. A huge crowd of rotters was making their way over from one of the side streets. There were too many of them. A lot more than four or five. There had to be dozens more. Hundreds, maybe. There was no way to kill them fast enough.

She glanced at the Humvee. Should they give up and just go back inside and wait this out? It looked sturdy, but would they survive until morning?

Parrish sheathed her sword and lifted her pistol into the air. Maybe she could kill them faster with a gun than with a sword. She took aim on one of the zombies in the middle of the crowd and squeezed the trigger.

She missed and bit her lip. Her hands were trembling.

Her plan backfired. The gunshot rang out through the empty streets, drawing the attention of the two dozen or so zombies all headed toward the truck. They moved faster, hungry for food.

Noah set his bat on the hood of the Humvee and took out his rifle. He aimed into the crowd and blew the head off the zombie she'd been trying to hit.

"Nice shot," she said, impressed with his aim and steady hand. "But I think we made them mad."

Noah flashed a brief smile and turned toward the group of rotters as they lumbered forward.

Parrish backed up, making sure none of them had moved up behind her. Together, she and Noah slowly drew the crowd away from the truck, picking off one at a time with their guns.

Parrish only hit her mark one out of three or four shots, but Noah was amazing. He never missed. Not once.

She would have told him how impressed she was except for the fact that they had more than twenty zombies heading straight for them.

Crash appeared through the roof of the Humvee and took a few shots with the machine gun he'd mounted to the top. He sprayed the crowd and more than six of the rotters fell to the ground.

Parrish cheered, but then realized that the rest of those still standing were now heading straight for the truck.

"Stop shooting. You're drawing them back to you," Parrish called out to him. "I'll distract them, just get that gate open as fast as you can."

Parrish looked around for anything that might make some noise and get the attention of the zombies heading for the truck.

Just a few feet away, a small red Ford two-door had been driven onto the sidewalk and abandoned, its door still open. She put her pistol back in its holster and grabbed her sword again. She ran up beside the small car.

This was probably the dumbest idea she'd ever had, but if they didn't do something drastic and create a brief window to get that garage gate open, they might all die out here tonight.

"What are you doing?" Noah shouted, taking a few shots and downing two or three rotters at the front of the crowd.

She reached inside and slammed her hand down on the horn, one long bleating cry into the night. The sound echoed against the tall buildings and every rotter in the area growled and changed direction.

FOUR

NOAH

Noah ran toward the small red car, shooting the heads off two zombies standing in his way. They fell like ragdolls.

"What were you thinking?" he shouted, fear rushing through him. He moved in front of Parrish to shield her from the wave of zombies headed straight for them. "You'll have every rotter in a five mile radius headed this way."

She climbed out of the car and jumped onto the hood, sword in hand. "I know," she said. "But it's the only way he's going to get that gate open. We'll be fine. Just kill fast and don't get bitten."

He cursed under his breath and got to work. She was probably right, but did she have to go announcing their presence to the entire neighborhood? Couldn't she have just beat her sword on the side of the car or something instead?

He glanced over at the Humvee and saw Crash dart from the truck toward the gate.

All they had to do was hold these things off until Crash got the Humvee inside.

Well, that and pray that he and Parrish were still alive when he did.

Noah reached for his bat, then remembered he'd left it on the hood of Crash's truck. He secured the shotgun in the straps across his back and reached for the two guns he'd shoved inside his belt loops. The rotters were too close for any kind of long-range weapon and a shotgun was way too slow right now. He'd never tried shooting with his left hand before, but there was no better teacher than an insatiable need to survive.

He held both guns out, straightening his arms and aiming as best he could. He shot once with his right hand and then with his left. Two zombies fell to the pavement and he let out a surprised cry of relief.

"Switch places with me," Parrish called down to him. "You can pick them off from above and I can slice and dice down there."

He hated to put her in close range with these monsters, but it was a good plan. With any luck, he could kill most of them before they got close enough for Parrish to even need her sword.

He popped off two more shots and climbed onto the hood of the car. Parrish jumped down, her boots landing firmly on the pavement below. She put two hands on the hilt of her sword and spun around, her pigtails like whips. She took the head off a large man with a single slice.

Noah moved to the roof of the car, the metal and plastic groaning against his weight. He planted his feet firmly and started shooting into the row of rotters on the front lines of the attack. Bodies fell, but more just kept coming. The pile that formed near the car slowed the others down. They tripped and stumbled and climbed their way through, but there was nothing that would stop them. Nothing but a bullet or a blade.

Noah glanced at Crash. He'd managed to open the lock and was pushing the gate wide enough for the truck to pull through.

They didn't have much time.

The few dozen that had been here at the start of the fight had multiplied into several hundred. Noah could see them shambling through the streets in clusters, pouring from every alley and open doorway. If he and Parrish didn't move in the next few minutes, they would be surrounded. And he wasn't sure how many bullets he had left in these guns.

Not enough for all of them, that much was certain.

He wished Parrish could blast these things with light like she had done back in the office building, but he had no idea how those powers had worked. Had it only been a response to the super zombies? Some kind of upper-level human evolution that no one had ever had to use before? He wanted to ask her, but the question sounded stupid in his brain. Part of him wondered if he'd just imagined it all. None of this felt real.

Still, when he looked down at her, he noticed a faint blue glow around the blade of her sword. Whatever these powers were, she was using them in some way now, even without the super-zombies here.

A sick feeling twisted his stomach.

Unless they were close. What if there were more of those things heading their way right now?

He scanned the crowd, searching their eyes as he aimed for the sweet spot in the middle of their foreheads. He didn't see any glowing eyes, but he had the uneasy feeling that they were in a lot more danger than they realized. Were they being watched?

The engine of the Humvee revved as Crash pulled through the gate. Noah caught Parrish's eye and took a few more shots before he jumped down from the roof of the car.

"Let's go," he shouted.

The horde of rotters had already formed a circle around the red car and he had to crouch as Parrish swung toward the closest one. Its head made the most disgusting squish as it fell at Noah's feet. He stumbled backward, and before he could catch himself, a rotter seized him from behind. Brittle nails cracked against his skin as the zombie grabbed him and pulled him further back, off his feet. His head smacked against the pavement as another reached him and collapsed at his side, drool pouring from its open mouth.

Noah screamed and closed his eyes as the first rotter grabbed his arm and bit down.

FIVE

CRASH

Crash threw the Humvee into gear and sped into the garage. He jumped out and ran toward the gate, ready to help Parrish and Noah get inside before it closed.

Fear pulsed through him as Noah's scream echoed off the nearby buildings. Crash reached inside the cab of the Humvee for his gun.

"What's happening?" Karmen yelled, her shrill voice filled with terror.

"I don't know," he said. "Stay here."

"Wait, don't—"

He slammed the door on her words. He pulled the gate closed as best he could, leaving just enough room to squeeze through to the outside. If he didn't come back, at least the girls would be safe in there for now.

Crash peppered the area with machine-gun fire as he rushed over to where a mob of rotters had descended on Noah's body.

Shit, man. This was all his fault. He hadn't moved fast enough to get the truck inside. He hadn't planned this whole thing out enough, and now one of their group was down. After all his work and planning to get the five of them together, he couldn't believe he was about to watch one of them die just a few feet from safety.

Parrish kicked two of the rotters off Noah's body, then spun around, sword in hand. With a furious strength, she sliced through five more of the zombies feeding on Noah. Her sword glowed with a dim blue light that left tracers in the darkness.

Crash's heart pounded so hard he could feel it in his throat. Apparently this chick had things under control as far as Noah was concerned, so Crash turned and started spraying the approaching mob with gunfire.

"Help me get him up," she shouted when she'd killed all the ones biting at Noah. Her voice was stern and wild and commanding.

Crash shot off a few more bursts of bullets then reached down to grab Noah's outstretched hand.

He was still alive. But for how long?

Crash had seen plenty of videos over the past few weeks. He knew that even if someone seemed to be immune to the virus itself, a bite from one of those things would kill even the strongest men. And once they died—

"Move. Now," Parrish shouted.

Noah was on his feet and he threw one arm over each of their shoulders as they ran toward the gate.

Growls and moans and footsteps followed them, but Crash didn't dare look back. All he cared about was getting them inside. God help Noah once they got there, though. He wouldn't have much time before he turned.

Parrish was not going to take it well when they had to put him down. Crash wasn't sure what their relationship was to each other, but he could see it in her eyes. She cared about this guy. She wasn't going to let him go without a fight.

They reached the gate and Karmen pushed it open just far enough for the three of them to slip inside.

"I told you to stay in the truck," he said.

"Last I checked, I don't take orders from you," she said.

Crash's eyes lingered on the blonde's long tanned legs. Man, if they weren't all doomed here, he would have liked to stand there a few minutes and appreciate the view. She was hot, and she had attitude.

Just the way he liked it.

He propped Noah against the wall next to the gate and pulled it closed just as the group of hungry rotters reached them. He closed the three locks on the fence and moved back, a dozen bloody hands reaching through the chain links toward him.

He breathed in relief and rested against the bumper of the truck, his stomach turning as he glanced over at Noah.

He'd barely gotten the chance to know the guy and now this. What a shit show.

"Help me," Parrish said. She lowered Noah onto the ground a safe distance away from the gate and tore at his shirt to get a better look at his wounds. "Do you have water? Bandages? What can we do?"

Crash opened the back door of the Humvee and pulled himself into the back of the truck to look for the first-aid kit he'd stowed inside.

The new girl just sat there in the middle of the truck, a blank expression on her face.

Crash eyed her, but she didn't look up. Her hands were shaking.

He motioned to the space below her. "I think I stashed the first-aid kit under that seat," he said.

Her eyes lifted to him and she nodded, sliding across the bench to get out of his way. Something in her eyes caused a strange chill to run down his spine. Crash shrugged it off and grabbed the backpack he'd loaded with bandages, alcohol, and other first-aid supplies.

"What happened?" Karmen asked from behind him.

He tossed the bag over his shoulder and turned to Karmen. She was staring at Noah, her arms wrapped around her body tightly. Her beautiful face was marred with tears, black eyeliner dripping down her cheeks.

"Is he hurt?"

Crash made a face. "Noah's bit," he said.

Karmen gasped and her eyes widened. She pulled a hand to her mouth. "Is he going to be okay?" she asked, looking to Parrish. "He'll be okay, right?"

"I don't know," Parrish said. She held an impatient hand toward Crash.

He unzipped the top of the bag and pulled out a bottle of alcohol and a wad of cotton bandages. He handed them to her. "Look, Parrish, I don't know that there's anything you can do for him."

Her violet eyes flashed with anger and she snatched the supplies from his hand. "He's going to be fine," she said. "We just need to hurry."

Crash swallowed. It didn't look good. Noah's clothes and chest were smeared with blood.

He crouched at Noah's side as Parrish doused one of the bandages in alcohol. He shook his head. Alcohol wasn't going to do shit. It was already too late.

He kept his mouth shut, though, knowing he needed to just let Parrish do whatever she could to make herself come to terms with this. He kept one hand on the extra handgun he'd slipped into the back of his jeans.

Just in case.

Noah's eyes were open, but he wasn't talking. His chest rose and fell with each deep, terrified breath.

Parrish took his arm in her hand and wiped the alcohol-soaked bandage across a bloody spot on his arm. "It's going to be okay, you hear me?" she said. "Just hang in there. We're going to—"

Her voice cut off and she stared down at Noah's arm.

Crash frowned and leaned forward to see whatever it was she was looking at. He expected to see a large bite mark or decaying skin, but instead, there was nothing. It was clean.

"What?" Noah asked, sitting up a little. He held his arm up to the light and shook his head. He ran his other hand across his skin. "I don't understand. I felt them bite into me. Here." He pulled up his shirt on the left side. His clothes were torn and the side of his torso was caked in dark blood.

Parrish picked up the alcohol and poured it over the spot. She used a clean bandage to wipe the blood away.

Crash stared in awe. He sat back on his heels, his mouth hanging open. There wasn't a single mark on this guy. How was that even possible? He'd been covered in rotters. There's no way anyone could survive that.

Noah continued to point out spots where he'd felt teeth sink into his skin, but as he and Parrish worked to clean the wounds, they couldn't find a single bite mark. Crash stared at them, shaking his head.

Parrish threw her arms around Noah's neck and he slowly pulled her into a hug, his eyes dazed as he stared past her.

Crash stood. "I don't understand," he said. "I saw them. They were all over you. How is it possible there's not a single bite on you?"

Noah shook his head and released Parrish so he could stand up. "I have no idea," he said. "I swear I could feel them biting me. Maybe my clothes protected me?"

Crash ran a hand through his long, black hair. It didn't make sense. He'd seen rotters tear a person apart. Normal jeans and t-shirts weren't going to suddenly act like a suit of armor. How was this possible?

A crowd of zombies pushed against the chain-link gate, their moans growing louder. They were going to draw too many of those things if they didn't get inside. The gate was strong, but if a couple hundred rotters started pushing on it, it would cave.

"We should get inside," he said. "The longer we stand here, the angrier those things are going to get. Let's get settled in the apartment and we can take a closer look."

He headed toward the truck to grab the rest of his guns and ammo, but threw a sideways glance at Noah. Was it even safe to let him come inside with them? What if there was a bite they hadn't found?

He would have to remember to keep a close eye on the guy for a while. He'd never seen or heard of anything like this happening before, and he didn't want to take any chances.

Especially now that he had three other girls here to take care of.

Crash turned back toward the Humvee to find the girl with the long black hair just standing there, watching them. She didn't look scared. Not really. She just looked...interested. Curious. When she saw him staring at her, she smiled.

A shiver went up his spine. Who smiles at a time like this?

He raised an eyebrow and reached past her to grab some more of their supplies from the truck. "Grab what you can and wait for me by the door."

He motioned toward the metal door that led to the stairwell and moved up to the front so he could pull the truck into a safer parking spot farther away from the gate. There were still a lot of cars parked down here, but most of the residents of his building had packed up and tried to get the heck out of town a week or so ago. He wondered how many of them had actually made it out of the city. And where in the world they thought they could go to escape all this.

The virus was everywhere by now. In just a matter of weeks, it had spread from coast to coast, country to country. The entire world was infected. No one knew how many were dead. Or how many had come back as those rotting things pulling on the gate out there.

He swallowed and parked the Humvee across four empty spaces on the far side of the garage. All that mattered now was that the five of them were safe. For whatever reason, they'd survived despite everything. He'd dreamed of them before the virus even hit, and now Noah was alive even though he'd been bitten. Something greater was at work here, and Crash was determined to figure it out.

They were alive, and he was going to do everything in his power to make sure it stayed that way.

SIX

NOAH

His hands were shaking.

What the hell had just happened? The moment he'd lost his balance, he had known it was over for him. He'd literally felt teeth sink into his skin.

How was he still alive?

Noah's heart raced. He wanted to get inside and strip down in the bathroom to see if he could find a wound they'd missed. There was no way that many rotters had been on top of him and none of them had managed to actually bite him.

Crash took a keyring full of jangling keys from his pocket and unlocked the door leading from the parking garage to the main building.

"Come on, guys," he said. "Let's get down to my apartment and get settled. We have a lot to talk about."

Noah stood and forced his feet forward. He quickly grabbed his duffel bag from the back of the Humvee and followed the others into the dank concrete stairwell. It was almost like he was only half here. Dead man walking. His heart pounded in his ears and he couldn't seem to catch his breath. The others were talking and rushing inside, but Noah could barely even hear them.

All he wanted to do was make sure he was really okay.

What if they'd missed something? What if he had a bite somewhere under his clothes and he turned into one of those things? He'd end up killing someone.

His mouth opened slightly and he struggled to draw a deep breath, wanting to calm his heart. Even his vision was blurred from worry. Or was it the virus working its way through him?

He shuddered and looked up to the second floor landing. The concrete stairs were stained and covered in dirt and filth. The entire place was dark except for the dim light of some emergency bulbs along the floor at each landing.

The door to the second floor was closed, but the sounds of moans echoed throughout the stairwell.

They'd just stepped into a building full of them.

Crash must have secured the doors, because they were all shut tight, but the sounds coming from behind those doors were undeniable.

Noah did not want to become one of them.

He gripped the railing and tapped his toes inside his boots, waiting for the others to make their way down the stairs to the basement. Crash's apartment must have been down there, and Noah hoped to God he'd been able to soundproof the place. He wasn't sure how they'd survive listening to these moans all day and night.

Once the others had started down, Noah hiked his bag higher on his shoulder and made his way down behind them. He'd dropped his shotgun outside somewhere, but he still had a pistol and a bat. He liked the shotgun, though, because he didn't have to be close range to kill. He wondered if Crash had more guns stashed downstairs.

Crash led them down a dark hallway. Water dripped somewhere nearby, the sound of each drop echoing softly around them. There were only a few doors down here, and most of them were unmarked. Electrical closets, maybe? Supply rooms for the building?

Crash stopped near the end of the hall at a door with the numbers 102 nailed to the front, their bronze surface scratched and dirtied.

He went through a series of locks and deadbolts and finally, after cycling through more than ten different keys, pushed the door open and leaned against the wall with a smile.

"Home sweet home." He motioned for them to go inside and Noah let the three girls go in first before he followed.

Crash shut the door behind them and threw the bolts on all the locks. Noah started to walk past him, but Crash grabbed his arm, holding him back from the others.

"If you find any bites or start to feel strange, you let me know okay?"

Noah nodded. "I will."

The girls had stopped short in the small entryway, but Crash pushed past them and stepped into the small living room. He flipped a switch and all the lights came on. Smiling, he held his arms out to the side.

Noah squinted up at the bright lights. How the heck did this guy have power?

"I know it's not much, but it's safe and it's clean." Crash bent down and scooped a pile of clothes off the couch, tossing them into a corner near a large computer desk. "Well, relatively clean."

"How do you have power?" Karmen asked. "You've got a generator?"

A sly smile spread across the guy's face. "No generator," he said. "I'll explain it later. Come on, I'll show you guys around."

No one seemed to know what to do or how to act. They were all covered in blood and grime, their bodies sweaty and sore. They were in a strange place, still trying to make sense of what had happened to them tonight.

"Is there a bathroom?" Noah asked.

Crash nodded. "Of course. I'll give you guys the grand tour," he said. He stepped about two feet to the left where faded linoleum curled up at the edges of the grey carpet. "This is the kitchen."

The kitchen consisted of a single small stained countertop with a shallow sink in the middle. On one side sat a microwave and a small toaster oven. On the other, a stack of paper plates and a tower of plastic red cups.

There was no dishwasher and only a small mini-fridge, but the whole place seemed to still have power. Without a generator, how was that possible? It had looked like all the power in the city and surrounding areas had gone out.

Crash stepped back to a tattered grey carpet stretched over concrete floors. "And this is the living room and dining area."

There was one long couch covered with a heavy brown blanket. Beside that in the corner was a recliner that looked like it had definitely seen better days.

The other half of the room was completely devoted to Crash's desk and computer equipment. He had three large monitors sitting side-by-side on the top of the desk with three matching ones mounted to the wall above the desk. Noah had never seen anything like it, and the expensive set-up looked incredibly out of place among the ratty used furniture and fading wallpaper.

Did all that equipment still work? The screens were dark, but the large computer unit under the desk had a red light glowing from the case. Was he still able to get online? And how was that even possible? There were a lot of strange things going on in the world, and Noah couldn't even begin to make sense of it.

Karmen cleared her throat and wrapped her arms around her waist. "Please tell me there's more to it than this," she said.

Parrish threw her bag down on the floor and walked over toward the couch. "There are no rotters in here. Be grateful we have a place to stay where we can relax for a little while," she said. She turned to Crash. "Thanks again for saving us back there."

"It was my pleasure," Crash said, a smile twitching the corners of his mouth. "It was actually kind of cool to get out there and test that machine gun."

Karmen sighed and slapped her hands against her legs. "Can we please stop with all the formalities?" she asked. "We don't need a grand tour of your crappy apartment. We don't need to hear about your obsession with guns. I just want to know what the heck we're going to do now? How long can we possibly survive in a place like this with those things out there trying to get in? We're trapped here."

She collapsed onto the couch and let her head fall into her hands. Her shoulders shook as she began to cry. Noah and Parrish exchanged looks from across the room.

Karmen could be dramatic and bratty, but he knew it was mostly an act. She was a lot more fragile and scared than she wanted anyone to know. He glanced down the small dark hallway to his left and sighed. He wanted to find that bath-room, but he couldn't just let Karmen cry.

He set his bag on the floor and sat down beside her. He put his arm around her shoulders and pulled her to him. She placed a hand on his bare chest and rested her cheek against his shoulder, not even seeming to care about the blood and stink that covered him.

"Karmen's right. We do need to talk about what we're going to do," he said. "Even more than that, we need to talk about what in the world we just saw. Fighting a group of rotters is one thing, but whatever those amped up ones with the glowing eyes were? No thank you. Where did they even come from? What if this is just the next stage of their evolution?"

A twinge of fear shot through him. What if he was going to become one? He tried to calm his racing heart.

"I've never seen anything like it," Crash said. He sat down in a rolling chair and pushed against one side of the desk. He skated to the main desk and began typing away on his keyboard. The monitors came to life, their screens buzzing as they powered up. "I've been watching everything from here. Videos, newscasts, forums, blogs. Everything. I can do some research, but I've never seen anyone mention zombies with superpowers."

"What about humans with superpowers?"

Everyone grew quiet and turned to look at the girl still standing near the door. She hadn't said a word since they'd rescued her over an hour ago.

Her dark eyes stared into the room, giving Noah a slight chill. She seemed different somehow. Strangely beautiful with her dark features and pale skin.

"Good question," Crash said. He looked around the room, his hands clasped tightly in his lap. His shoulders were hunched and tensed, as if he were about to spill his deepest, darkest secrets. "Before all this started, I was having these dreams. I told some of you about it earlier, but it was weird. They weren't normal dreams. They felt, I don't know, real. Like I was seeing my own life, only it wasn't a memory. It was the future. Maybe. It's hard to explain. I just knew that it was real. I knew something was coming and that when the time came, I'd have to find the four of you."

"That's how you knew we would be at that rescue center?" Karmen asked.

Crash nodded. "And how I knew we'd find the fifth hiding in that closet," he said. "I dreamed it. All of it."

"I never got a chance to say thank you for that," the girl said.

"How long had you been up there alone?" Noah asked. He still didn't understand what in the world was happening, but this new girl seemed to add more mystery to the whole situation. He wanted to know more about who she was and where she'd come from.

Noah had trusted Crash right away, even if he couldn't explain it. But this girl...

He wasn't so sure.

"I don't know," she said, leaning against the doorway with her hands crossed around her middle. She shrugged. "Days, maybe. My memory's a little fuzzy, honestly."

"What's your name?" Parrish asked.

The girl hesitated and something strange flashed in her eyes. She straightened awkwardly, her lips parting.

"What's wrong?" Karmen asked. She sat up, removing her

warm hands from Noah's chest. "Don't remember your own name?"

Noah bumped his knee against hers. Why did she always have to be so rude to everyone? He knew from the times he'd spent alone with her that she wasn't always so crass and mean, but damn, get her in a room full of other girls and she had to make sure everyone knew their place. It was beyond aggravating.

The girl shook her head and moved to the edge of Crash's desk, steadying herself against it. "I don't have a name," she said so quietly Noah almost didn't hear.

"Everyone has a name," Karmen said.

"Did something happen to you?" Parrish asked. "Were you attacked?"

"I don't remember," the girl said. When she looked up, there were tears glistening in her eyes. Noah felt a jolt of regret. Maybe he'd been too quick to judge her. Something was definitely wrong, but maybe she'd really been through some bad shit. "I'm sorry. I don't know what's happening. I can't remember my own name."

Her head collapsed into her hands, and Noah immediately wanted to go to her. He started to stand, but Karmen placed her hand on his knee and shook her head. Noah questioned her with his eyes, but she didn't say anything.

Parrish crossed to her instead. She wrapped her arms around the girl's shoulder and waited as she cried.

That was two emotional breakdowns in a span of about two minutes. It was understandable considering that everything they'd ever known or loved was gone, but Noah was about to have a breakdown of his own.

He didn't want to put anyone in danger or send anyone

into a panic, but he couldn't ignore it any longer. He had to get to a bathroom so he could check his wounds. If he'd been bit somewhere, he needed to get out of here.

He shuddered, remembering the feel of all those teeth grating against his flesh. He just couldn't believe that none of them had pierced the skin. It didn't make sense.

Noah stood and grabbed his duffel bag. "Is the shower working in this place?" he asked Crash. "I want to wash some of this blood off."

He didn't mention he also wanted to check for bite marks, but Crash's eyes met his in understanding.

"Sure, man. We probably don't have a lot of hot water, so don't use too much, but you're welcome to whatever's in the bathroom," he said. "It's just down the hall to the right."

Noah nodded and headed for the small bathroom he'd seen off the main hallway.

"Hey," Parrish called out.

He turned, his stomach tense. He just needed a few minutes to himself. He needed to get his head on straight. "What's up?"

Parrish's eyes met his, studying him. She was still holding onto the new girl, patting her back, but her eyes were locked on Noah's. He didn't want her to see the fear he carried there, but he knew there was no possible way to hide it from her. Her tight expression softened. She shook her head slightly and turned her attention back to the girl.

Noah took in a deep breath, looked around briefly at the others, and disappeared into the hallway.

The bathroom was small and cramped, every inch of it decorated in olive green tiles, most of them broken or chipped. The small sink had almost zero counter space, so Noah set his bag down on top of the toilet. He yanked off his shoes and stepped out of his blood-soaked pants.

His hands trembled as he turned on the hot water in the shower, letting it run for a second while he checked his legs for bite marks.

He couldn't find any right away, but he was still soaked in blood and grime. He checked the temperature of the water and stepped inside the small shower.

Blood and dirt dripped onto the green tile at his feet. He grabbed a bar of soap and scrubbed his face, arms, hands. He scrubbed until the water ran clear, all evidence of battle washed down the drain.

He switched off the shower and stood there, leaning against the wall of tiles, trying to get his mind around what had happened to him in the street. He'd searched every inch of his body and there wasn't a mark on him. Not even a scrape. Nothing.

How is this possible?

Catching his breath, he stepped out of the shower and stood with both hands gripping the pedestal sink.

Noah looked up, meeting his own gaze in the mirror. Steam coated the surface, but he could still make out his own eyes. Those eyes should be milky blue by now. Dead. But somehow, he'd survived. No, not just survived. He hadn't even been hurt.

But he'd been bitten. He was sure of it. He'd felt it.

Noah's mind raced. It was just too much to handle. The virus. The death. The uncertainty. He had no idea how long any of them would survive or where they could go. For all he knew, the five of them could be the last people alive in the entire city of Washington D.C. Everything he had ever relied on in his life was gone.

So why was fate sparing him? Why was he still alive?

Thinking about it was almost enough to force him into insanity. He needed to get his shit together. There were four other people out there relying on him now. For whatever reason, they'd all found each other. They'd all survived.

Noah pressed his lips into a thin line and glanced down at his bag. He needed to understand what had happened to him, but he was scared. In some deep part of his mind, he was pretty sure he already knew what had happened, but he needed to see it for himself. He needed to know for certain.

He grabbed the duffel and unzipped the side pocket. He'd stashed a Swiss Army Knife in there right before they'd left his house. It had belonged to his grandfather. He'd grabbed it off his dad's dresser before they left, sure it would come in handy at some point. Now he was glad he had it.

He pulled the main blade out and ran his fingertip along the edge. Still sharp after all these years.

Noah held his left arm out over the sink, fist clenched. He took a couple deep breaths then pressed the blade against his forearm. He imagined his flesh splitting open and running red like a fountain of blood. But in reality, the knife merely skated over the surface of his skin. He felt the sharp pain of the blade, but saw no blood.

He lifted the knife and swallowed. This wasn't possible. Was the blade too dull?

He tried again, bracing himself for pain. This time, he really dug into his flesh, pressing down so hard that even a dull blade should have cut him. It should have mangled him. But instead, his skin stayed unmarked.

He opened the medicine cabinet and looked through Crash's things. He found a box of unused shaving blades and tore it open, holding the sharpest edge against his skin.

Noah cut again. And again. He tried his palm. His bicep. His stomach, legs, even his face. But no matter how hard he tried to cut into his skin, the blade never once pierced through. He dropped the razor blade into the sink and stared up at himself again, bringing his hands to his face and rubbing the confusion from his eyes. He wasn't sure how or why, but he had no doubt in his mind now that on top of his super-human strength and ability to help others heal faster, he'd also somehow developed a hardened skin that couldn't even be penetrated by a knife.

Or a set of teeth from a hungry rotter.

Noah shook his head as the truth of it began to really sink in. Tears stung his eyes and he smiled slightly, running a hand through his hair.

Holy shit. As the rest of the world lay dying, he had become invincible.

"What is all this?"

Karmen picked herself up off the couch and walked over to Crash's computer setup. She'd never seen so many monitors and blinking lights. She had some friends who were gamer geeks, but no one she knew had a crazy setup like this. What was this guy's deal? Did he live here alone?

Crash leaned back in his chair and smiled up at her, his fingers laced behind his head. "This is my pride and joy," he said. "This is how I've been gathering all the information on the spread of the virus."

"I still don't understand," Karmen said. She grabbed her backpack off the floor and tossed it onto the couch. It was covered by two brown blankets and she shuddered to think what the upholstery looked like underneath. Did people really live like this? "How are you the only one in the city with power if you don't have a generator? And do you mind if I charge my phone?"

Crash swiveled in his chair and locked eyes with her, smiling. "I know this is going to sound crazy, but I don't actually know how it works," he said. "The city lost power, but mine stays on."

"Why?" Parrish asked.

Karmen rummaged through her pack, looking for her cell phone and charger. She knew the phone lines weren't really working these days, but all her music was on that phone. She might as well enjoy the power while they had it, no matter how they'd come by it.

Crash shrugged. "Because I tell it to?"

Karmen stopped, her arms erupting in goose-bumps. "Because you tell it to? What the hell do you mean by that? You're communicating with the electricity?"

Any other day, she might have rolled her eyes and thought he had a few screws loose, but the world was freaking upside down. Dead humans walking around biting people. Parrish's glowing sword. Noah's ability to lift those desks back in the office building as if they weighed nothing. Her voice somehow reaching inside the mind of those things and telling them what to do. None of it made sense.

"Maybe," he said. "I can't explain it, but I have some sort of connection with all things electrical. The same way I was able to talk to you through that walkie-talkie back at the rescue site."

"You're telling me that you're somehow powering this entire apartment with your, what? Your will?" Her voice came out more bitter and biting than she'd intended. She hated that tone of voice, even if it was her own. She hated the way she sounded, like she was better than everyone. But she couldn't control it.

"Yeah, that's exactly what I'm saying," Crash said. She expected him to be harsh in response to her questions, but instead he seemed amused. "After all you've seen, is it really so hard to believe?"

"What about these?" Noah asked, gesturing to the computers. He'd just come out of the shower and was drying his hair with a towel. Fortunately, he hadn't bothered to put his shirt back on. "Can you still get on the internet?"

"Yep," Crash said, turning to the computers and jiggling his mouse to wake them up. Six screens lit up, filled with everything from maps to pictures to some kind of running code Karmen couldn't understand. She felt like she'd walked into a scene from The Matrix. "I know it sounds crazy, but I've been able to hack into any security system in the world the past few days. Any information we need, I can get."

Karmen was going to ask him what he knew about the army and any safe zones, but Parrish cut her off.

"What do you know about New York?" she said.

Karmen's stomach twisted. It was sweet that Parrish was still thinking about her little sister in New York, but come on. They'd barely survived the trip to D.C. There's no way they were making it to New York City, even if Zoe was still alive by some miracle.

Crash frowned. "Why?"

"My sister's there," Parrish said.

Crash sighed. "It's a nightmare in New York," he said, sorrow in his tone. "I'm sorry, but the roads and bridges in and out of Manhattan are blocked by miles of cars. Just like here, a lot of people thought they could get out in time to save their families, but by the time they started to flee the area, the National Guard had already set up a quarantine of the city.

No one could get in or out. Once the infected rose from the dead, the people still alive in the city were—"

"Zoe's alive," Parrish interrupted. "I talked to her."

"That was days ago," Karmen said.

Parrish spun toward her, anger in her eyes. "She's alive." She turned back to Crash. "She was staying with our dad at the Four Seasons. I talked to her on the hotel's land-line before our cell service stopped working a few days back. I told her to gather as much food and water as she could and barricade herself in the room. I told her I'd come get her."

Noah moved to put a hand on Parrish's shoulder and a look passed between them. Very touching.

Karmen didn't stay to hear the rest of the conversation. If Parrish still wanted to go to New York, she could go, but Karmen was staying put as long as she could. She wasn't about to go out on some suicide mission just to save someone who was probably already dead.

Plus, she still hadn't totally come to terms with the budding romance between Noah and Parrish. Sure, Karmen had dated some of his friends throughout the years, but that didn't mean she wasn't interested in him. She'd always felt a connection to him she couldn't explain, and she'd spent more than a little time daydreaming what it would be like to kiss him. But he'd always had mooney eyes for Parrish.

Of course it was just her luck that when the end of the world came, she was stuck with the two of them instead of Noah by himself. If they'd never teamed up with Parrish, he and Karmen might be safely snuggling at his house right now. It wasn't fair.

She wandered into the hallway to look around at the rest of the apartment. There was a tiny little bathroom on the right with nothing more than a toilet, a sink, and a shower. No bathtub, not that she'd dare take a bath in this dirty place.

A bedroom about half the size of hers back home had three sleeping bags spread on the floor. There was no other furniture in the room, but the walls were stacked with bottles of water. There had to be three hundred bottles in here. Damn, this kid wasn't kidding when he said he'd been preparing for them.

Karmen walked down to the end of the hall. This place was really small and dark. It might be enough room for the five of them for a few days, but how long were they planning to stay here? She wasn't sure she could survive months in such a small space. They'd end up killing each other within a week.

There was one more bedroom at the end of the hall, smaller than the other one, with a twin bed on the floor. There was a stack of books sitting on top of a grey milkcrate beside the bed. Was this Crash's bedroom?

Karmen glanced back toward the living room and when she saw no one was paying attention to her, she slipped into the room. She sat on the bed and picked up a couple of the books. Most of them were about coding and gaming, but her hand lingered on a tattered ear-marked copy of *The Catcher in the Rye*.

She inhaled and held the breath inside as she picked up the book. The cover was so worn, it practically fell apart in her hands. More than fifty pages had been marked and there were underlined passages all through the book.

Karmen held the book against her heart and looked around the room, seeing things differently now. She'd first read this book when she was fourteen, and the copy she'd picked up at the bookstore a few years ago looked about like this one, marked up and read a hundred times.

Was it possible she actually had something in common with Crash?

She didn't tell many people she was a reader. Most of her friends liked to talk about boys and TV shows and movies. Music. Never books. That was more the kind of thing she used to talk to Parrish about. But the truth was that Karmen loved to read more than anything.

Sometimes, when things got too hard to handle and the truth of her own life seemed too overwhelming to think about, she lost herself in books, imagining she could step inside and be the main character instead of herself for a while.

The Catcher in the Rye was one of the first books that made her think that maybe she wasn't as alone in this world as she thought. Maybe there were other hopeless people out there who felt like their lives were full of nothing but pretend people and constant lies.

She stared down at the book, wondering what passages meant the most to Crash. And why?

"What's up?"

Karmen jumped and dropped the book to the floor. She stood quickly and straightened her shoulders.

"Sorry, I was just..." She looked around and shrugged, not really sure how to explain what she was doing other than being nosy.

"No problem," Crash said. "Mi casa es su casa, or however that goes."

He crossed the room to her and came so close, it made her heartbeat race a little. He bent over and grabbed the book from the floor.

"Do you read?" he asked, holding the book toward her.

Karmen inhaled, part of her wanting to tell him that yes,

she loved to read. She wanted to ask him about *The Catcher in the Rye* and why he'd made so many marks inside.

But instead, she shrugged and pushed past him toward the door.

"Not really," she said. She started to leave the room, but something made her turn back. "Do you?"

Crash's eyes met hers and he smiled. He looked down at the tattered paperback in his hands and nodded. "I love to read," he said. "Sometimes it's just nice to lose yourself, you know?"

She nodded once, but felt the ice around her heart starting to melt. It scared the crap out of her.

She didn't even know this guy. She didn't need to go spilling her secrets. Not after a lifetime of hiding them so well.

"I gotta go," she said, turning around so fast she nearly knocked herself out on the edge of the doorframe. She stumbled into the hallway and made a beeline to the bathroom where she closed herself inside and waited for her hands to stop trembling.

EIGHT

THE WITCH

*S*o these are the guardians.

The young witch looked at the four kids in the room. They were just children, really. Hard to believe they had each lived more than a dozen lifetimes. It was obvious none of them remembered anything from their past, which was good. The Dark One would be pleased to know that they were unaware of the true origin of this so-called virus. As long as these children were still trying to figure out what was going on in their world, the Dark One was safe.

Her mistress's powers were growing. With each death and rebirth, the Dark One's power blossomed. With each day that went by, and each life that was taken by the virus, her mistress grew stronger. Strong enough to reanimate the dead in droves, making each one a slave and minion to her will.

Someday soon, she would be strong enough to break through the ice. Then, once they had drained every drop of life and power from this pathetic world, the two of them would return to their home world and finish what the Dark One had started centuries ago.

Complete and total domination of both sides of their world. Ice and fire.

The witch listened to the young humans talk of their newfound power.

She smiled. They knew nothing of power.

She cradled her burned hand in her lap. The Dark One had given her only a glimpse of the power she had locked inside. How was it possible these guardians had ever been strong enough to defeat her?

No, that was wrong. They hadn't been able to defeat her. They'd merely locked the Dark One in a cage of ice and buried her here in this wasteland of a world. They'd simply delayed the inevitable, giving the Dark One centuries to formulate a plan that would unleash her wrath on this poor place. What her mistress had accomplished with the power to grow a single rose was staggering and brilliant. A single flower had brought this world to its knees before her, and all this while she was still entombed in ice.

What would she accomplish once she was free?

A shudder of anticipation ran down the witch's spine.

It was her job to help free the Dark One, and if she proved valuable, it would be her at the Dark One's side when she became ruler in their homeland. What would the elders have to say when they saw their little servant girl at the right hand of the most powerful witch who'd ever lived?

The witch straightened and hid her smile. All her life she'd been treated as nothing. Never even worthy of a name.

She would show them all.

And these guardians were the only ones who could stand in her way.

All she had to do was mislead them. Trick them. Keep them from discovering the truth. All she had to do was give her mistress more time.

Getting into their group had been easy enough. She'd only had to search Crash's mind to find out what he knew about the fifth. Crash was the dreamer—the one who would always be the first to see his fellow guardians and seek them out as he slept. She knew he would be dreaming of the fifth, but for some reason, the fifth had kept his face hidden from Crash. He'd only seen glimpses of the one who was supposed to make their group complete. Because of this, he'd had no idea what the fifth looked like. It could just as easily be her as anyone else.

Making him believe it was her was simple, but keeping them from the truth would be much more difficult. Now that four of them were together, their powers would begin to increase. Their dreams would become more frequent and more detailed.

That was how the reincarnation spell worked—the guardians chose to stay here in this world to protect their people from the Dark One. With each human life, they gravitated toward one another, staying close so that if the magical seal on this world were ever broken, they would be able to find each other and work together to make sure the Dark One stayed frozen and powerless.

But their memories wouldn't fully return until all five of them were together.

As long as she could keep them from the fifth, she would be okay. They might see images from their past or get glimpses of their true purpose, but by the time they figured it out, it would be too late for them.

She smiled again and sank deeper into the couch, watching them as they talked about the little girl in New York.

The one with the sword—Parrish—seemed intent on getting to a place called New York City to save her little sister. A very sweet notion, really. The witch had never had anyone who loved her as much as this girl seemed to love her sister. No one since Marilon.

She closed her eyes and pictured the small child's face. Marilon had not been her real sister. The witch had no real sisters. She had no family at all except for the elders of the Council, and none of them would claim her even if they could. But Marilon had been her little angel, so pure and beautiful and small.

Warm tears welled up behind her closed lids and she shrugged them off, taking a deep breath. It would do her no good to think of the little one from so long ago. Marilon was long gone and there was no reason to think of her. Not now. Not ever.

After Marilon's death, the witch had vowed to never love anyone again. She would never let anyone into her heart. She'd learned the hard way that loving someone was nothing but a sign of weakness.

But as she listened to them talk about New York City and the sister lost inside, the witch knew that where there was weakness, there was opportunity.

If the Dark One's minions could get to this little one before Parrish, the sister might be of some use to them.

She needed to talk to the Dark One and give her the good news.

NINE

PARRISH

"Any luck finding my sister?"

Parrish finally had a quiet minute to talk to Crash, and she was dying to know if he'd made any progress getting in touch with Zoe. Earlier when she'd mentioned New York to him, he'd refused to show her any videos of the area. He didn't want to upset her, but had promised he would look for a way to connect with Zoe's cell phone if he could.

They'd only been at Crash's for a few hours, so she didn't want to bug him, but she had to know if her sister was still alive.

"I was able to locate a signal from her phone, but when I tried to ring through, nothing happened," he said. "I think it's just too far away. I can't seem to connect to it. But from GPS, it looks like her phone is still at the Four Seasons, though, just like you said."

Parrish let out a sigh of relief. That meant Zoe had listened to her and barricaded herself inside her room instead of trying to make it to a so-called safe zone. According to Crash, none of the safe-zones he'd researched had survived. Too many people pushing to get in and not enough security measures in place to tell if someone was infected or not. Especially since symptoms of the virus didn't always show up right away. All it took was one infected person to make it inside a safe-zone and the entire population was knocked out.

But if Zoe was still in her suite at the hotel, there was still a chance she was alive.

"What about calling her room? 2358," Parrish said. The numbers she'd written on her arm had long since faded, but she still remembered them.

She crossed the room to stand behind Crash. There was so much information up on his giant computer screens, she couldn't even make sense of it all.

Crash gave her a sad half-smile before turning back to his monitors. "Give me the information. I'll try everything I can."

Parrish bit her lower lip. She hated to think of her sister surrounded by zombies in a hotel in New York City. If their dad was already sick when she'd last talked to Zoe, Parrish knew it was foolish to hope he'd gotten better. She didn't want to think about that. She just wanted to believe her sister was still okay.

She needed to believe it.

"Keep trying, please," she told him. "Whatever it takes."

Crash nodded, but she could tell from the way he looked at her that he didn't hold out much hope of survival. "Not wasting power might be a good place to start," he said, shooting a look at Karmen who was just coming out of the bathroom after drying her hair.

Parrish wanted to strangle her. Who brought a hair dryer with them in their backpack during the zombie apocalypse?

"Did you honestly think it was necessary to blow dry your hair?" Crash asked, an amused look on his face.

"Yes," Karmen said, brushing imaginary dirt off the couch before sitting down. "So?"

"So, you do realize that we're running off some kind of mystical power source that seems to be connected to my mind, right? I have no idea how long I'll be able to keep this up, and honestly, since we've been running the lights and stuff nonstop, I'm starting to get a headache. We have to try to conserve power. A hair dryer is one of the worst things you could use."

"Okay, mister I've-got-a-thousand-computers-running," Karmen shot back.

"These computers are our only link to the outside world," Crash said, his voice louder and much less amused. "Hardly as important as making sure your hair looks good for all the boys you're going to meet, I know, but if you could please restrain yourself, I'd appreciate it."

"Fine," Karmen said.

"Fine."

Parrish kept her mouth shut. She didn't want to get in the middle of their argument. Besides, she couldn't stop thinking about her sister. She had to find a way to get to her, but New York might as well have been on the other side of the world. They had barely survived the trip to Crash's house, and he only lived twenty miles away. Dark hopelessness washed over her.

"As far as I'm concerned, your computers are worthless if

they can't even tell us exactly what happened back there in that office building earlier tonight," Karmen said.

"What do you mean?" Crash asked.

"Um, I don't know," she said. "Scary monster zombies with glowing red eyes and long, pointy fangs? I figure someone with such an impressive link to the outside world would have some info on things like that."

"I'd really like to talk about that more, too," Noah said, entering the room. "We kind of got interrupted earlier when we started talking about it. Maybe we could bring everyone in here and try to make sense of it before we all crash for the night."

Parrish's heart skipped a beat as she watched him cross the room. The only thing he'd bothered to put on after his shower earlier was a pair of plaid flannel pajama pants. His body was tan and muscular, and as he came to stand beside Parrish, she could feel the heat of his skin through her shirt. She had to force herself to look away.

"I've been searching for more information on those monsters since we got home," Crash said. "I can't find a single instance of anyone talking about any kind of mutation or super-zombie, so I put the word out about your experience back there in the street. Hopefully something will turn up."

"Wait, there are others?" Parrish asked.

"Sure," Crash said. "Power's not out everywhere. If a plane hadn't taken a nosedive into the largest power station in the area, we might still have power here in the city."

Parrish sucked in a breath. So they weren't the only ones alive. As much as she hated to admit it, she'd been worried that maybe the whole world was gone.

"The internet's still up for a lot of people out there like me who decided to hole up in their houses or apartments and survive on their own, but people are dropping off the forums everyday," he said. "None of us know if it's because they lost their connection or if they, well, you know."

"But no one out there seems to have seen any of these super-zombies?" Karmen asked.

"You saw them appear on the infrared right before they attacked us, right?" Noah asked.

"Yeah," Crash said, nodding. "Like less than five minutes before they came after you, they were just suddenly there."

"Where did they come from?" the new girl asked from the kitchen. She'd barely said more than two words since they'd gotten to Crash's.

"Not a clue," Crash said, clicking on various websites and videos as he talked.

"So why did they show up on infrared if they were just zombies?" Parrish asked. "The regular zombies don't show up, you said."

"I was wondering the same thing," Crash admitted. "At first, I thought maybe they were still alive. Like maybe they were suffering from a really bad fever or something. But when I saw them through the satellite feed, I knew they weren't alive. They barely looked human at all."

Parrish closed her eyes and tried to recreate the scene in her mind. They had been standing out on the street when Crash first warned them about the strange figures on his infrared. "Wait, where were they when you first saw them on the satellite feed? Where did they first appear?"

"They were on the roof of the building across from the accountant's office. Why?"

"So, they were five stories up, all the way on top of the roof of the building, and they came directly for us?" Parrish asked.

"I don't see why it makes any difference where they were," Karmen said, pulling a bottle of pink nail polish out of her bag. "The important thing is figuring out what they are so that we can avoid them in the future."

Parrish stifled a smart response.

"No, I get what you're saying," Noah said, placing his hand on her shoulder. Parrish tried to ignore the butterflies she felt at his touch. "They came after us fast. Like they knew we were there."

"Maybe they smelled us," Karmen said. Parrish couldn't believe she was painting her nails like it was any normal Friday night in front of the TV. That girl was an anomaly.

"I think it was more than that," Parrish said. "I've been thinking about it a lot. It felt different somehow. Like they were coming for us, specifically. Like assassins or something."

As soon as the words left her lips, she felt stupid for even suggesting it. Zombie assassins? How ridiculous. But she couldn't deny the feeling that what had happened was more than just an unlucky coincidence.

Crash opened his mouth to respond, but apparently thought better of it, turning back to his monitors.

"What?" she asked, pressing him.

"Nothing." He shook his head and ran a hand through his messy black hair. "I need to do some more research, that's all."

Parrish wanted to know what he was thinking, but it was getting late and everyone was starting to show their exhaustion.

"Maybe we should get some rest," she said. They were all

exhausted. "It's been a long day. Tomorrow when everyone's up, we can talk about all this and try to make a plan."

"Good idea," Noah said. "Maybe we'll be able to look at it all with fresh eyes once we've had some rest. We've still got so much to talk about."

Crash nodded and rose from his chair. "I'll show you guys where you can sleep," he said. "I don't have beds for everyone, but I laid out some sleeping bags for the girls in the spare bedroom. I hope that'll be okay. Any of you ladies are welcome to take my bed if you want."

"No thanks," Karmen said, making a face.

"I didn't mean with me in it, Barbie," Crash said, raising an eyebrow. "Although that could be arranged."

"Do not call me Barbie," Karmen said, walking past him toward the spare room.

Parrish couldn't help but laugh, and the sound carried down the hallway.

She stopped herself, realizing just how strange laughter sounded at a time like this when the world was filled with so much horror and death. Would there ever again be a time when she could laugh without death looking over her shoulder?

Would anything ever be normal again?

She headed toward the small bedroom, but turned back and ran down the hallway.

"Parrish?" Noah called after her.

She grabbed her sword from where she'd stashed it near the recliner and made her way back toward the others. "Just in case," she said.

Noah nodded and smiled. "Probably a good idea."

"Where are you going to sleep?" she asked, her cheeks

growing warm. There were no parents to keep them apart if they wanted to be together, but it still felt awkward to think about doing whatever they wanted to do. Besides, she wasn't even sure he'd want to sleep by her side. It was probably a ridiculous thing to think about, and she suddenly felt stupid for asking.

Noah's eyes searched hers and her stomach erupted in a thousand butterflies.

"I was thinking I'd take the couch," he said. "If that's cool with Crash. It's closest to the door, anyway, just in case someone needs to keep watch."

"Nah, man, you can take my room for a while," Crash said, clapping a hand on Noah's shoulder as he passed by. "I'm going to stay up for a bit and do some research online. I'll wake you up if I need to switch. We can take turns keeping an eye on the place while the girls sleep."

Karmen and the new girl had already settled down inside the spare room. Crash disappeared into the living room again. That left Parrish alone with Noah in the hallway, neither of them making a move to go to bed.

She wanted him to ask her to join him in Crash's room, but that would be weird right? Awkward for everyone in the apartment. But damn, she wanted to be close to him. Not for sex or anything like that, but just to know he was there. To feel the solidness of his body.

Was he feeling the same thing? This incredible pull, like the ocean's current? She'd always felt drawn to him, but ever since the world ended, it had intensified. Maybe that was just normal when there were only a handful of people left in your world.

"I wanted to tell you I'm sorry about earlier," she said,

breaking up the tense silence between them. "I never should have hit that car horn. That was so stupid. I thought we could handle it, but there were more of them than I realized. I don't know what I would have done if you'd—"

Noah lifted a finger to her lips and she stopped talking, her heart racing at his touch.

"I'm fine," he said softly, taking a small step toward her.

He was so close, and all she could think was that it wasn't close enough.

"Get some rest," he said.

He leaned in, cupping his hands around her chin. He placed a whisper of a kiss on her forehead, his lips lingering for several seconds before he pulled away.

Before she could regain her voice or calm her heart, he had turned away and disappeared into Crash's bedroom. Parrish stood in the hallway a little while longer, staring at his closed door and wondering again if they would ever be free enough to be happy.

TEN

CRASH

Hours after the others had fallen asleep, Crash sat in front of the computer with his headphones on, replaying a video he'd recorded from just before the super-zombies attacked. He had a quick record button on his keyboard, and he'd gotten in the habit of capturing video images of things he saw with the help of the government satellites. He'd spent hours watching surveillance cameras in cities all over the world, hoping to find one place that wasn't crawling with infected.

When he'd finally come to terms with the fact that nowhere on earth had been left untouched, he'd started recording the rotters just to watch their behavior. He'd never seen anything like the ones that attacked his new friends downtown, though.

When he first saw the figures on his infrared, there had been six of them. Five red-hot figures, and one normal, human-looking figure. As he replayed the satellite camera footage, he focused in on the human figure. He'd almost forgotten about the human until Parrish had said something about the attack feeling deliberate. Assassins, she'd called them.

But that didn't make sense. He'd watched these rotters long enough to know they had no mind of their own. All they cared about was infecting and eating anyone who was still alive. Why weren't they attacking the other human on the rooftop? And why would a group of them deliberately go after a group of humans down on the street?

They wouldn't. Not unless someone was controlling them. Telling them what to do. Now, as he watched the human figure standing in front of the super-zombies, he realized Parrish had been right.

The attack hadn't been random at all. This wasn't just some new stage of whatever disease had ruined the world. The five super-zombies were standing in a line, like they were taking orders from the human. It was almost military in feel. Whoever it was standing there had been explaining their mission. Not once did they attempt to attack that human.

The whole scene gave Crash the creeps. The idea of super-zombies was bad enough, but the thought of a human giving them orders was even worse. Who would send a group of zombie assassins after them? And why?

Chills ran down his spine, and he sat back in his chair, staring at the video on his screen.

The zombies had special powers, but so did they.

Part of him wanted to believe it was all a coincidence. A terrible virus had caused all this, unlocking hidden abilities. It was evolution, not fate.

But he knew better.

The dreams had started long before the virus had taken over the world. He couldn't ignore that.

When Crash had first started having those dreams, he'd searched the web looking for information about omens and prophetic dreams, but all he'd found were new-age type sites talking about destiny or clairvoyance. He knew what he'd been experiencing was different, but he couldn't put his finger on it. He'd honestly started to wonder if he was losing his damn mind.

But when the virus broke out and everyone got sick, it all started to make sense. He wasn't crazy. He was connected to this thing somehow. Not the cause of it, exactly, but his destiny was tangled up with this virus. The virus wasn't some catalyst for human evolution. It was a key, unlocking powers that had been sleeping inside him for years. Lifetimes, maybe.

When he'd started hacking into satellites and protected websites without even breaking a sweat, he knew he'd been right. The way he could control the power, the internet, even simple alarm systems, was no coincidence. When the world began to die, something inside him switched on.

The question was why? Why him? What was so special about the five of them?

He had a feeling if he could figure that out, he'd know exactly why those super-zombies had come after them.

Crash had no idea where to look for the answers.

Short of going onto what was left of the forums he visited and asking if anyone else had started manifesting some amazing powers like being able to control electricity and dreaming about the future, he was at a total loss.

Besides, he was pretty sure he already knew the answer to whether anyone else had powers like he did.

There was no one in the world like the five of them, and even though they hadn't had a chance to talk about it yet, he was certain that each of the others had started manifesting powers just like he had.

He'd hoped getting the five of them together would trigger something. Memories, maybe. Or at least some path to the answers he was seeking.

So far, nothing like that had happened.

He leaned back in his chair again and stared at the reinforced door he'd had installed a month ago. Ten sets of deadbolts and a steel door had made him feel safe until now. No normal zombie was getting through that door.

But what about super-zombies? What about a human with the power to control them?

He thought about the three sleeping girls in the next room. He'd brought them here, thinking they'd be safe for a little while. Maybe months considering how much food and water he had stored away.

Now he wasn't so sure.

Somewhere in this city, there was a human with a vendetta against them. Even if they were lucky enough to have escaped the area without being followed, that person had found them once. He didn't think it would be all that hard to find them again. Not if they had a way of tracking their abilities. Hell, in terms of power usage, his basement apartment might as well be lit up like a fracking Christmas tree.

Crash closed his eyes and rubbed his forehead.

He needed sleep, but so did the others.

He turned back to his computer and started typing. He'd wake Noah up in a few hours to take the next watch, but for now, he was going to pull up every single surveillance camera in D.C. if that's what it took. Somehow, he was going to find the person who'd sent those zombies after them.

He just hoped he found them before the next wave of zombie assassins came knocking at his door.

ELEVEN

THE WITCH

The infected rat crawled up the zombie's leg. The rotting man leaned down, taking the animal in its decaying hands and petting it as if it were a tiny kitten.

"Good girl," the corpse said. The witch cringed as the rat began chewing on an exposed sore on the zombie's hand.

She had waited until the others were all asleep before she left her room and made her way up to the abandoned apartments upstairs. Crash hadn't seemed to want to go to sleep, so she'd had to use her powers to force him into a deep sleep. She knew she didn't have much time before the spell she'd cast on him wore off, but she needed to tell the Dark One what she'd done and what she'd learned so far.

"Mistress," she said, bowing before the corpse. "I did as you asked and infected five dead humans with enormous amounts of the virus, but—"

"You failed." The zombie turned its head to look at her. One of its eyes was missing. "You failed when there were only three guardians. When their powers were still weak. Now, there are four. I can feel their connection to each other growing. They're getting stronger, and it's only just the beginning. They cannot ever reach the fifth or their memories and the full force of their powers will return to them."

"I tricked them into believing I'm the fifth," the witch said, bowing her head. "They won't be looking for anyone else, now."

"Foolish child, you are a slow learner," the Dark One said. "Are you really sure you're worthy of my attention? Of my presence?"

The witch sucked in a breath and bowed her head. The Dark One had been so nice to her at first, praising her and telling her she was special. What had she done to deserve this change in her mistress? Had she disappointed her that badly?

Her chest tightened. "Yes, Mistress," she said. "I'm sorry."

"The five guardians will always be drawn to each other. As long as they are not together, they will always be looking for the one who completes their group," she said. "And the fifth will be looking for them, too."

The witch looked up, finally understanding. Her trick wouldn't keep them apart for long. The spell that bound them to this world would keep drawing them back together.

"What do you want me to do?"

"Mislead them," she said, her voice resonating in the head of the male zombie. "Get them to doubt one another. Put them in danger every opportunity you get. And whatever you do, don't let them get to the island."

"Yes, Mistress."

"Every day, I see through new sets of eyes," the Dark One

said. "Millions answer to me now, their life now flowing through my veins."

"Your powers are growing," the witch said.

"I do not need you to tell me about my powers," the zombie said. "I need you to help me escape this prison of ice."

The witch recoiled at the tone in her mistress's voice. Even though the body her mistress used was weak and rotting, her voice was strong and terrifying.

"I will, Mistress. Just tell me what to do. I'll do anything to serve you," she said. Hot tears stung the corners of her eyes. She just wanted to please the Dark One. She wanted to be important to someone. Valuable.

"If the guardians awaken before I am free, they'll restore the magical shield they placed on this world centuries ago, and I'll be trapped here forever," the Dark One said.

"I won't let that happen," she said. "The stone. I have the fatalis stone. The island will mean nothing without the stone. And I can use it to see if the last guardian is nearby. The fifth isn't here in the city with the others, but if you want me to, I can track him just like I tracked the others."

"No, stay with the group for now," the Dark One said. "But keep an eye on the stone. The fifth's symbol, what is it?"

The witch thought of the five symbols etched into the five sides of the stone. An infinity sign for Parrish. A cross for the healer, Noah. Crash's symbol was a lightning bolt. And the other girl, Karmen, was a rose with thorns.

"The fifth symbol on the stone is a spiral," she said.

"The symbol of the wind," the Dark One said. "The fifth is a male. Yurick was his name in the old days. It's his spell that keeps the guardians together, their souls reincarnating at the end of each life. He won't be far, and it's likely that wherever he is, he remembers more than the rest of them. He'll be harder to find because of that. He'll know we're looking for him."

"But he's also the most vulnerable."

"Yes," the Dark One said. "I'll have my minions begin the search for him. He won't be far from where you are, even if he's not there in the same city."

"There's someone else," the witch said, realizing she'd almost forgotten her big news. "A girl. Parrish's sister."

The male zombie opened it's one eye wider, its mouth spreading open in a hideous smile. "A sister?" she asked. "Where? Is she alive?"

"She might be," the witch said. "She's in a city called New York, but Parrish believes she's still alive. She seems to care for her very much."

"This is good news," the Dark One said. "I will find her. She may be useful to us."

The witch swelled with pride. She'd finally managed to do something right. Maybe she would be rewarded.

But the Dark One seemed to sense her joy and turned on her. The zombie's eyes glowed a deep amber as it stood and crossed to her.

The witch swallowed and forced herself to stand tall, even though she wanted to back away.

"In the coming days or weeks, it will be too dangerous for us to speak this way again," the Dark One said. "If one of the guardians sees you talking to a rotting corpse, they'll know you are not who you say you are. And we can't have that."

"No," the witch said. "But how will we communicate?"

The zombie smiled again, and this time, it was standing close enough for the witch to smell its putrid breath. She closed her mouth and stopped breathing for a moment, struggling to stand still.

The corpse bent down to lower the rat onto the floor, and then stood, its bony hands circling the witch's head.

The moment the rotting skin touched her own, white-hot pain flashed through her skull. She tried to pull away, but couldn't move. Her vision went black and her entire body burned with fever.

She wanted to cry out, but was scared the others downstairs might hear. She clamped her mouth closed, biting her own lips and holding her breath to stay quiet through the pain.

She was transported back to the Dark One's icy prison below ground. The witch dropped to her knees on the hard floor. When she lifted her eyes to the block of ice that held her mistress, the woman's glowing red eyes were open, watching.

"Stand, child," the voice inside her head commanded.

The witch struggled to get back on her feet, her legs trembling in fear. The burn that covered her left hand ached. She didn't want to be here.

"Come to me," the voice said.

The witch took a deep breath and forced her feet forward. She had never known a worse pain than the one that had been inflicted on her the last time she'd been brought to this place, but what choice did she have but to obey?

She moved closer until she stood as close to her frozen mistress as she possibly could. Her breath escaped in a white fog.

"Place your hand against the ice," the Dark One's voice said. Her lips didn't move, but the voice was everywhere.

The witch's lips trembled. "Why do you punish me?" she asked.

"I do not punish you, dear child," the voice said. "I honor you. Pain is often a pathway to great power. If you are not willing to prove your loyalty, how do I know I can trust you with so much responsibility?"

The witch closed her eyes and took several deep breaths. She wanted to prove that she was loyal. Trustworthy. She wanted to show the Dark One that she was strong.

She clenched her teeth and opened her eyes, lifting her hand slowly toward the ice. Her mind protested, anticipating the pain, but her will pushed her hand forward, her desire to be a part of something greater than herself embracing whatever pain she had to endure to get there.

She pressed her hand against the ice. Lightning shot through her body, the burn starting at the palm of her hand and traveling rapidly through her arm and into her chest. She screamed, her knees giving out as the sensation spread through her, a white-hot fire that boiled her blood.

She struggled to pull her hand away and finally, the Dark One released her.

The witch's body fell to the ground and she pulled her knees toward her chest, her breaths short and her body twitching.

"What have you done to me?" she asked.

"It's what I have given you that's important," the Dark One said. "I have given you a small piece of my regained magic. I have entered your soul and your mind. I have poured myself into your body so that you can become my ambassador in the world. A part of my eyes and ears."

The witch didn't understand. All she knew was pain and terror.

"From now on, I will speak to you directly through your

mind," she said. "And you can speak to me the same way. If you need me, simply place your ruined hand on your temple. I will sense you and come to you. I will see what you see, and know what you know."

The witch tried to understand and listen and obey, but her body was still shaking on the floor of the cave. She closed her eyes, wanting to lose herself to sleep. Wanting the pain to end.

"Open your eyes," the voice said.

The witch forced her eyes open and looked around. She was back in the apartment building, the male zombie's hands still around her head.

She backed away and his hands fell to his side, his eyes lifeless and milky blue once more.

The Dark One was gone, but the sound of her voice still resonated in the witch's head. She lifted her hand and saw that the skin on her entire left arm was now covered in scars, as if the burn marks had spread from her hand to her shoulder.

And somewhere deep inside her soul, she felt the Dark One's hold on her grow stronger.

Stumbling, the witch made her way down the stairs and into the basement apartment. She locked the door behind her and crept back to her room, glad when she finally was able to slip into a deep sleep where she dreamed of ice and fire.

TWELVE

KARMEN

I *need coffee.*

Karmen was awake but groggy as she stepped over Parrish's sleeping body and made her way to the tiny little kitchen. This apartment was so gross. She didn't understand how anyone could live like this. And where were his parents? Was he really old enough to have his own place?

The kitchen itself was more like what Karmen would have called a kitchenette. There was a small toaster oven and a hot plate. No stove. No full-sized fridge. There wasn't much storage, either, but when she looked inside the cabinets, they were mostly bare. Except for dust. It didn't even look like he ever used them.

Now, the microwave, on the other hand, looked like it was used several times a day. The outside had a string of something that looked sort of like cheese caked on the door. Karmen had never actually seen a microwave that used a dial for the timer. She was used to the large digital stainless steel microwave back in her house.

Just the thought of her own house made her feel sick to her stomach. She hadn't wanted to leave it in the first place, but she didn't want to be alone either. In the beginning, she really thought it wouldn't be long before the government got things under control. She'd imagined them making sweeps of each neighborhood, securing the streets and restoring people to their homes.

Now, though, she wondered if there was even any government left. After what they'd seen at the rescue center, she wasn't so sure. What if there was no one coming to save them?

She closed her eyes and took a deep breath. She couldn't think like that. She just needed to sit down and have a nice cup of coffee to clear her head.

There was no sign of a coffee maker anywhere on the counter, so Karmen switched to looking through the cabinets. No luck there either. What kind of person didn't even have a coffee pot in their house? She was dying for a sugar-free vanilla latte with skim milk, but to be honest, she would have settled for a plain jane cup of coffee with milk at this point.

"Whoa, Barbie, what's going on in here?"

Karmen whirled around to find Crash standing in the doorway, rubbing his eyes and yawning. She wasn't going to let him get to her today.

"Good morning," she said sweetly, determined to keep from arguing. "I was just looking for the coffee maker."

"Well, you can stop slamming doors in here and tearing the place apart, 'cause I don't have one. Mine broke from overuse, and I haven't had a chance to replace it."

"What? How can you not have a coffee pot? Everyone has a coffee pot, even if they only pull it out when guests come over." She heard her shrill argumentative tone, but seriously? This guy was annoying.

"I guess you should call the etiquette police, then. Have them come arrest me for not being the best host. Forget that I saved your pretty little ass yesterday," he said with a laugh.

Did nothing faze him? Every time she got around this guy, she ended up heated and flushed, and he ended up laughing. It wasn't fair.

"Look, Nakamura, or whatever your name is, all I want is some caffeine. It's not my fault you're some kind of barbarian who doesn't care about common decency."

Crash walked forward, his black eyes holding her gaze. Karmen took a step backward, but he kept coming toward her. Her butt hit the counter behind her and she leaned back. Crash stood so close to her, it sent her heart racing like a pack of wild horses. What was he going to do to her? She imagined him pulling a butcher knife from a nearby drawer and splitting her open with it.

Instead, he yanked open the door of the cabinet at her hip and, without dropping his gaze, pulled out a silver can. "Here," he said, opening it with one hand. The soda let out a hiss as the carbonation released. "Red Bull. It's better than coffee."

Crash shoved the can in her hand. It was warm. She slammed the can down on the counter behind her as she watched Crash walk away. Fuming, she focused on that ball of red light she had recently discovered inside her. The energy of it was becoming familiar. Even though she wasn't exactly sure where this new ability had come from, she was slowly learning what she could do with it.

She felt the light pulse through her, narrowed her eyes on

the back of Crash's messy bed-head, and thought: *You cannot move. Your feet are frozen to the floor.*

Crash stopped in his tracks, his body lunging forward. His hands whipped around to steady his body and he tried to move his feet, but they were stuck like glue to the bad linoleum.

"What's wrong?" she asked. "Legs stop working?"

He turned his head to the side and she could see the confusion and fear on his face. He wasn't laughing now, was he?

"What did you do to me?" His voice was quiet, all amusement now replaced by fear.

"I have no idea what you're talking about." She kept her voice innocent and giggly, feeling high on the power of her new ability. Maybe next time he'd think twice before he called her Barbie.

"I can't move my feet," he said, his voice getting higher and more frantic. "What did you do?"

"What's going on in here?"

Of course, Parrish would be the one to ruin her fun. Karmen let go of her focus and smiled as Crash stumbled forward.

"Nothing." She grabbed the warm energy drink and took a long sip. "Crash and I were just getting to know each other."

THIRTEEN
PARRISH

In the dark basement apartment it was nearly impossible to tell what time it was. Parrish had woken up feeling groggy and disoriented. She'd slept in a large sleeping bag on the floor next to Karmen and the new girl, and even though she was grateful for the safety of this apartment, the sleeping arrangements left something to be desired.

She'd found herself staring at the new girl as she slept. Strange that she couldn't remember her own name. It didn't seem that she'd taken any trauma to the head or anything. Then again, maybe watching the world they'd all known completely disappear had sent her into some kind of shock. It wouldn't be unheard of.

She'd barely said two words since they'd rescued her from the closet where she'd been hiding. Was she really the one who would complete their group of five?

She had to be. Parrish had a dream about a man who had told her there would be five. It hadn't made any sense to her at the time and she'd been too worried about her mom to even think about it back then.

Back then.

Parrish almost laughed at herself. Had it really only been a couple of weeks since that horrible night? How had the whole world gone to hell so fast?

She shook her head and focused on the computer screens as Crash booted them up.

They'd been sheltered from so much of it in their small neighborhood, but it had been evident once they got to the city that the world had been violently ripped apart.

Other than Crash and the new girl, they hadn't seen a single human being since they'd left Noah's house. Not a living one, anyway. How many were left? And how many were now walking the streets, hungry for the taste of flesh?

She wanted to talk to Crash, but he seemed so busy as he got everything set up for the day that she didn't want to interrupt him. Still, if anyone had answers about how this virus began or how many were dead, it would be Crash. His ability to control machines, computers, and electricity was almost unbelievable. If she hadn't seen it with her own eyes, she wouldn't have thought it was possible.

Did they all have powers now? It was something they'd avoided talking about up to now, wanting to just get some rest and try to put the horrors of the day behind them. Today, though, they had no choice but to talk about what was happening to all of them. Were they the only ones? And why?

Parrish had way more questions than answers, and she was anxious to start asking some of them.

Crash looked up from the monitors briefly, worry etched

across his features. "How did you sleep?" he asked. "Sorry I don't have beds or anything more comfortable."

She stood behind him, trying to figure out what information he had just pulled up on his computer screens. "It was fine," she said. "Any place that's safe from the rotters is comfortable at this point. I have a feeling we're going to have to get used to discomfort for a while."

Crash raised an eyebrow and laughed. "Good point."

"What was going on between you and Karmen this morning?" she asked. "I got the distinct feeling I'd just walked in on a seriously awkward moment."

He shrugged, but the side of his mouth twitched nervously. "Nothing," he said, forcing a smile. "I don't think she likes me too much."

"Join the club," she muttered. "Karmen only likes people with no spending limits on their credit cards."

"She's in for a rude awakening, then," he said. "I'm pretty sure the world's about to start dealing in a completely different kind of currency. Those water bottles I have stacked up in there are probably worth their weight in gold at this point."

"Speaking of water, do you have anything to drink?" she asked.

He nodded and pushed away from the edge of his desk, his chair rolling across the concrete floor toward a tall mini-fridge. He pulled out a bottle of water and tossed it to her.

She caught it and downed about half of it before she came up for air. "Thanks," she said. God that water felt good against her dry throat. "How long was I asleep?"

"About four hours," Noah said.

She turned as he walked into the room. His hair was a little messy and his eyes were droopy, but her heart still beat faster at the sight of him.

"Is that all?" she asked. "I can't help but wonder if we'll ever truly have a good night's sleep again. I had the strangest dream, but I can't quite remember it."

"Me, too," Noah said, studying her. He shook his head. "It's like the images are on the tip of my brain or something."

"Weird," Crash said, spinning around in his chair. "You know, I wasn't even planning on getting any sleep until I was able to wake one of you guys up to keep watch, but I must have been exhausted because I passed out right here at my desk. I'd been downing Red Bulls all night, but I guess my body just gave out. I don't remember exactly what I was dreaming, but I remember it almost felt real, like it was really happening."

Parrish raised an eyebrow. "Weird coincidence."

Crash gave her a funny look and spun back around. "I think we have to start looking at everything in a different way now," he said. "There are no coincidences anymore. Not between the five of us."

"What do you mean by that?"

"Just that it was no coincidence I started dreaming of you guys months ago," he said. "No coincidence that we were all living so close to each other. That we all—or I assume all—have started experiencing strange new abilities."

Parrish shifted uncomfortably. Hadn't she just been thinking the same thing? They really needed to get the entire group together to discuss it, but the new girl had still been sleeping and Parrish didn't want to wake her up. Who knew where Karmen had run off to. She was probably putting on makeup in the bathroom.

"Here, sit down," Crash said, patting the seat of a rusted metal folding chair at his side.

"Thanks," Parrish said, sitting down and staring up at the screens. "What is all this?"

Crash picked up a pencil and tapped it against the top of the desk. "This is the mess we're up against," he said. He pointed to the monitor on the far left. "This is a map of the United States."

"What's the red mean?" The map was covered in red. Parrish already knew what it meant, but she still hoped she was wrong. She needed to hear him say it.

"That's the spread of the disease and the death toll," he said.

Parrish closed her eyes, her stomach turning over. "How many?"

"It's hard to tell exactly at this point," Crash said. "A lot of places have lost power and many of the health departments have completely stopped reporting numbers. Most government offices have shut down. This is my best guess based on the numbers that are still coming in and the rate of the spread of this thing before the lights went out."

"How many?" she said again.

Crash cleared his throat. "When the disease hit, there were approximately 320 million people living in the United States, give or take," he said. "By my best guess, only about 75 million are still alive. Maybe less."

Parrish brought her hand to her mouth and inhaled sharply. Tears stung the corners of her eyes.

"That can't be right," Noah said. He put a hand on her shoulder and squeezed. "You're saying less than a quarter of the population has survived this thing?"

No one spoke for a moment, and Parrish let the numbers sink into her mind. A pandemic with those kinds of numbers would be completely devastating even if that were the only issue, but death was really just the beginning. If the dead outnumbered the living, how many of them were out there now, walking around?

"What about the rotters?" she asked, her voice trembling. "Is everyone who died turning into one of those things?"

Crash shook his head and leaned back in his chair, hooking his hands behind his neck. "That's a much tougher question to answer," he said. "There are a lot of intervening factors. For one, the health departments in most cities started burning bodies when the death toll rose to uncontrollable rates. That was a good move. But not every hospital did that. That also doesn't account for the people who died in their houses and cars after the hospitals closed. From what I can tell, most of those people have risen from the dead and are walking around out there, but there's not a lot of data online about numbers, for obvious reasons."

"Why are they trying to eat us?" she asked. "I don't understand it. I mean, I've seen zombie movies just like everyone else, but I never thought it could really happen. That's what they want, right? To eat us?"

Crash shook his head. "Before yesterday, I would have said yes, but now? I think there's more to it than that."

So many questions ran through Parrish's mind, she could barely get a hold on them. She was terrified to ask him anything else. Hell, she wasn't even sure she really wanted to know the truth.

"You're talking about those super-zombies?" Noah asked. "The ones who came after us, specifically?"

Crash nodded. He sighed and after a moment, pulled up a new window on the center screen. "I wasn't sure whether to show this to you guys or not, but I think you have a right to know."

"A right to know what?" Karmen asked.

"Come take a look at this," he said. "Do you know if that other girl is awake yet? She needs to see this, too."

"Do you want me to go check?" Karmen asked.

Crash nodded and the three of them waited while Karmen ducked into the other room. Parrish's entire body trembled. What the heck was he about to show them?

When Karmen and the girl walked into the room, Crash turned back to his computer.

"Sorry to start the day with bad news, but I think we all need to realize what we're up against here," he said. He clicked play on a small video and enlarged it to fill the screen.

"What exactly are we looking at?" Noah asked, leaning between Crash and Parrish to get a better look.

"This is an infrared video of the rooftop of the building just across the street from where you guys were hiding yesterday afternoon," he said. "It's not a super clear image, but look here."

Crash pointed to a human figure standing on the roof. It was hard to tell on infrared, but it looked like a woman.

"Who is that?" Karmen asked.

"I don't know," he said. "But watch. She goes down the line of five zombies and touches them with her hand or something we can't see. Watch what happens."

A single figure was visible on the infrared at first, but suddenly, another figure lit up in front of the first, its heat signature blazing hot. The first figure, a human, stepped to the side and lifted their hand. A moment later another blazing hot figure appeared on the screen. This happened five times total until there was one normal human standing in front of five red figures. The super-zombies?

Parrish cried out and leaned forward on the desk. "Play that again," she said.

He moved the cursor back to the beginning of the footage and played it back again. Parrish could hardly believe what she was seeing.

"What does that look like to you?" Crash asked.

"It looks like someone created those things," Noah said, taking the words right out of her mouth. "Someone created them with some kind of magic and sent them to kill us."

"Maybe your theory about zombie assassins wasn't so silly after all," Karmen whispered to Parrish.

"I would have rather been wrong," she said.

"You and me both."

Parrish's stomach turned as she watched the video again and again, trying to make sense of what was going on. The reality of their situation seemed to keep getting worse. People rising from the dead couldn't be bad enough? Now there was someone hunting them down and creating nearly invincible super-zombies to kill them?

She closed her eyes and felt the room spinning around her.

As she slid off her chair and lost consciousness, the last thing she remembered was Noah's strong arms catching her before her body hit the floor.

FOURTEEN
THE BOY

The young boy woke from his dream with the strangest feeling deep in his belly.

He'd been waiting for the others for so long, knowing they were out there somewhere searching for him. He wasn't even sure how he knew. He just did. Ever since the disease that turned his mother had caught hold and spread through the city, the boy had started dreaming of the old man with the kind eyes. The man told him he was not alone. He was the fifth, and someday, they would find him. When they were all together, everything would be better.

Last night just after sunset, though, he'd felt something shift. Almost as if they had forgotten him. But why? Had he done something wrong? Should he leave his home and try to find them on his own?

He'd spent the rest of the evening curled up in his spot in the dark closet, holding his tattered blanket tight against his body. When the sun came up, he left the closet and went to the window of the small apartment he'd once shared with his mother. How would he survive here all alone?

He took in a deep breath and shook his head. They would come for him. He had to believe.

He didn't know who they were, yet he felt as if he'd known them forever. Lifetimes.

The sun was just coming up in the distance, its light shedding pretty tones of pink and purple across the sky. As long as he looked up, he could almost pretend that everything was okay. Normal. He could pretend his mother was in the kitchen cooking bacon and eggs for breakfast. He breathed in. If he could hope hard enough, maybe he would be able to smell the food cooking. Maybe he would be able to hear her humming as she worked.

But then his eyes drifted downward toward the street below and the game was over.

Rotting corpses shambled toward the cool shadows of the tall buildings.

He knew from the news reports on TV that people believed this was just some sickness. Like that time he had the flu and had to stay home from school for a week, only worse. A virus that got out of hand.

But the boy knew better.

He could see things other people couldn't see.

He knew the world had not gotten sick from the flu. This was no normal virus, and even if there were scientists still alive out there working on a cure, the boy knew they would never find one. She caused this. The Dark One.

He trembled thinking of the evil woman trapped in the ice. On the bad nights, she was the one who found him in his dreams, turning them to nightmares no child should ever know.

She can't get to me, he told himself. She was buried deep inside the ground where no one was ever supposed to find her. There was no way for her to escape.

Yet, somehow, she had grown strong enough to cause this. She had made the people sick.

He stared down at the biters and trembled. The Dark One had stolen their lives, sucking it from them like milk from a straw. She'd filled herself up with the force of their life and grown stronger with each person that died.

She was the one controlling them now. He could feel her dark power coursing through the dead. She could see through their eyes when she wanted to.

And she was looking for him.

He closed the blinds and pulled the thick curtain over the window. He didn't like living in darkness, but he knew that above all other things, he had to make sure The Dark One didn't find him before the others came.

FIFTEEN
NOAH

Noah pressed a cold washcloth to Parrish's forehead. She'd been out for more than twenty minutes, but her breathing had finally steadied and she was resting.

A drop of cold water slid down the side of her face and into her hair. Parrish opened her eyes and sat up. Any peace she had seemed to find during her sleep was gone, her eyes wide and her head shaking violently from side to side.

Noah gripped her arms and shook her. "Parrish, calm down," he said. "We're safe."

She took in a huge gulp of air and looked into his eyes. "What happened?"

"You fainted." He relaxed his grip, but kept his hands on her skin. It was strange how protective he felt of her these days. He'd always been attracted to her, but now that they were fighting for their lives, he found he was more worried about her than anyone else. What was it that pulled him to her?

Parrish shook her head and raised a hand to her forehead. The washcloth had slid down to her lap when she sat up and she grabbed it now, twisting it between her fingers. "It's too much," she said. "The sickness. The rotters. Now, someone's trying to kill us? Someone's sending those things after us? We'll never be safe again, Noah. What are we going to do? Why is this happening to us?"

"I don't know, but we're going to figure this out together." He looked around at the group gathered in the living room of Crash's basement apartment. "The five of us. There has to be some reason we found each other, right? Some reason we all have these powers we can't explain. Crash said he's been scouring the forums and can't find another instance of someone reporting supernatural powers or incredible strength or anything like that. It's just us."

"Do you think the virus did this to us?" Parrish asked.

"Not directly," Crash said. He stood up from his desk and walked over to stand next to them by the couch. "Sorry to interrupt your conversation, but I think there's more to it than that."

"You don't think the virus somehow mutated us?" she asked.

"No." He looked around the room. "I think the virus awakened something that was already inside of us."

Karmen took her headphones out of her ears and leaned forward. "That doesn't make any sense. Are you saying you think we were carriers or something?"

Crash shook his head. "I know it sounds insane, but I think we were waiting for this to happen. I think we were born with these abilities, but that they didn't activate until the virus showed up and the world needed our help to put an end to it."

Parrish swung her legs around to sit up fully on the couch, and Noah took her hand in his. Maybe the things he'd been feeling for her were not just normal teenage hormones. Maybe there really was something connecting them. Something deeper than any of them could have imagined. There was a part of him that knew Crash was telling the truth. "Maybe we all need to talk about what powers we think we have," he said. "Crash, you've had dreams about the future and you can do incredible things with machines and power. Anything else?"

"Should there be more?" he said with a laugh. "Cause I got nothin'."

Noah shook his head and smiled. "No, I think that's plenty. I just want to get it out in the open. Talk this through and see if we can try to figure out a pattern."

He turned to Parrish, going around the circle.

"Parrish has enhanced abilities with her sword," he started. "Before this started, she'd never even picked one up."

"And she can ninja kick," Karmen added.

Parrish laughed. "I guess that's what you could call it," she said. She brought her sword into her lap. "Something you said, Crash, makes a lot of sense to me. About us always having these abilities and connections. I know it's strange, but when I was a little girl, my parents took me to Japan because my mom had a gig with the Tokyo Opera. We saw this sword in an antique shop and I don't know, I just had to have it. I couldn't explain it. It was like I just knew it was mine. My mom said no way, but my dad seemed to understand that it was important to me. I think he also felt guilty about pulling me out of school all the time like that. So they bought it for me. When we got home, they put it up on the wall as a display, and I never touched it until the day after my mom died. The first time I saw a rotter, this sword saved my life. I knew how to use it and how to move my body in ways I shouldn't know."

"And there's more," Noah said, hoping she would forgive him for sharing something she'd told him in secret. "Tell them about the ice."

Parrish took a deep breath in and looked around the room. "Okay, since we're suspending disbelief and all, I got really upset after my mom's death and I started to cry."

"Crying is not a superpower," Karmen muttered.

"No, but having my tears turn to ice is kind of weird."

Karmen's eyes went wide and she looked from Parrish to Noah, as if to ask if it were true.

"I had a similar experience with ice," he said. He realized Crash and the other girl knew nothing about what had happened back in their neighborhood. "My dad had turned into one of those rotters and he came after Karmen. I didn't know what else to do, so I picked up my bat to swing at him. My entire hand and the handle on the bat all frosted over with ice."

"Whoa, that's intense," Crash said, running a hand through his messy black hair. "You had to kill your own father? Shit, man, I'm sorry."

"Yeah, it's not going down on my top ten favorite moments in life," he said, trying not to think about the horror of that day. "But what's done is done. We've all had to do hard things since this happened."

"You healed my leg," Karmen said softly.

He turned to her and swallowed back fear. She was right. "When I touched the wound on her leg, my whole hand went cold and tingly. It didn't totally heal her, but it definitely did something that made it heal faster and hurt less."

"That's why you weren't hurt when the rotters bit you," Crash said, his eyes wide. "You're some kind of healer."

He didn't tell them about the way he'd tried to cut himself in the bathroom. For now, he simply nodded. It was almost more than he could handle to think about these new abilities. There had been so much happening, the truth of what they were all suddenly capable of hadn't totally sunk in yet. Talking about it made it more real, somehow.

"And you're stronger," Karmen added, glancing over at him.

"You have incredible accuracy, too," Parrish said. "Even when we were running, you never once missed your target. Even with two guns."

He hadn't really put it together in his head before now, but she was right. He thought of that day he'd been shooting hoops before his dad died. It was like he couldn't miss.

"Karmen?" He turned to look at her, and she shifted in her seat. He wasn't sure what her ability was, but he'd seen her put a couple of those super-zombies into some kind of trance back in that office building.

"I don't know. Nothing special that I've noticed," she said with a shrug. She avoided looking at anyone, and picked at her nail polish.

"Bull," Parrish said, leaning forward. "You've got something going on. I saw you with those things that attacked us. What did you do to them?"

But Karmen didn't answer. It was like she was in denial of her own abilities.

Finally, Crash spoke up.

"She can get inside people's heads or something," he said. He stared at her, not letting up. "Right? Like mind control."

Karmen pressed her face against her knees, refusing to say anything.

"I felt it," Crash said. "Early this morning in the kitchen. She was messing around with me. I couldn't move my feet, like I'd lost control of my own body."

To Noah's surprise, when she lifted her head, her eyes were filled with tears. "I didn't ask for any of this," she said. "I just want things to go back to normal."

"That's what we all want," he said softly. "Do you think any of us wanted to lose our families and watch the world go to hell?"

Karmen raised a trembling hand to her face and shook her head.

"None of us asked for this, but we're changing. For whatever reason, we've been given these...gifts. If we're going to have any chance at understanding why, we need to be able to talk about it."

He was shocked when Parrish stood and crossed over to Karmen. She sat down next to her and put her arms around Karmen's shoulders.

"It's going to be okay," she said. "It's scary as hell, but we're going to get through this. We've made it this far, haven't we?"

Karmen sniffed and nodded.

"See? Whatever it is you've done or you've noticed, you can tell us. Whether you like it or not, we're in this together." She looked around at the group. "All of us."

Karmen swiped at her cheeks and sniffed again. "I guess Crash is right," she said. "I don't know how it works but if I really concentrate, I can send commands to people. Like with your dad." She looked up at Noah. "When he came after me, in my mind I just told him to stop. I told him to leave me alone.

I didn't even say it out loud, but he did it. Well, at first he did it. Until I got scared and screamed."

"Is that it?" Noah asked, not wanting to imagine what his father might have done to her if he hadn't killed him. "Have you noticed anything else?"

So far, all of them had discovered at least two or three new abilities.

She shook her head. "No, nothing else," she said. "Just the mind thing."

Noah nodded and looked around the room. He realized they'd reached the last person in the group. The new girl stood near the kitchen, her shoulder leaning against the wall and her arms crossed in front of her. She'd been so quiet, he'd almost forgotten she was there.

"What about you?" he asked.

She shook her head. "I'm not sure," she said. "Nothing that I can remember."

Chills broke out along Noah's arm. He got the distinct feeling she was lying. But why? What was she hiding?

"Are you sure there's nothing?" he asked. "Not even one tiny thing out of the ordinary?"

The girl stared at him, her dark eyes locked on his. "I'm not sure," she said. "I'm still shaken up from earlier. I can't remember."

"What does all this mean?" Parrish asked before he could press the girl further. "Let's say we did have these powers inside us all along, like Crash said. Why? And why are they just surfacing now?"

"I don't know," Crash said. "I had hoped that once the five of us were together it would all make sense, but it feels like something is still missing. Like we don't have all the pieces of the puzzle."

"So where do we go from here?" Noah asked. "What can we do?"

But when he looked around at the others, he only saw his own fear and questions reflected in their eyes.

SIXTEEN

PARRISH

"Any news on my sister?" she asked Crash. It had been three days since they'd arrived at his apartment, and this was the first time she'd had a chance to ask him about it. "I'm sorry to keep bugging you about it, but I have to know if she's okay."

"I'm sorry, Parrish," he said, shaking his head. "I tried."

Her stomach twisted, and a knot formed in her throat. "What are you saying?"

He spun toward his computer and brought up a new command prompt. He typed furiously for a moment and a bunch of new windows opened. "I've been trying to call her cell phone, but there just aren't any signals getting through to New York. Everything's completely jammed up there," he said.

"Did you try calling her room?" Parrish said. She moved to stand behind Crash, her fingers digging into the back of his leather chair. "I mean, maybe that part of New York wasn't hit as bad as some of the others."

Crash's sad eyes met hers for a moment before he turned back to his monitors. "It's bad everywhere, Par."

Tears rushed to her eyes, and she took a deep breath. Everything was going to be okay. She'd told Zoe to gather food and water and barricade herself in the room, and according to Crash, her cell was still there in the hotel. She was still alive, safe in her suite at the Four Seasons.

"What can you tell me about New York City, specifically?" she asked, her mouth suddenly dry again. Her heart pounded against her chest as she stared at a map of the United States Crash still had up on the top left monitor. New York was a brilliant mass of red.

"The biggest cities had it the worst," he said. "The more dense the population of an area, the faster the disease itself spread, and the faster the hospitals filled up. Also, with a city like New York, there was no place to burn the bodies. It wasn't like they could stack them up in the middle of Times Square and light a bonfire."

"So it's overrun?" she asked. She heard what he was saying, but she didn't want to think about what it all meant. She wanted him to just tell her the truth.

He didn't answer at first. Instead, his fingers moved fast over the keyboard. A window popped up on the large center screen. Several windows with videos popped up and he moved them around so that there were four open boxes organized in two rows on the screen.

"This is New York City," he said.

Parrish's eyes opened wide as she stared at the videos. The streets were growing darker, so some of the images were difficult to see now that it was almost night again, but she could see masses of bodies moving through the destroyed streets.

She turned her attention to the video on the top right of the screen. A fire had broken out nearby, illuminating the area around the camera. Hundreds of rotters made their way down the street, climbing over and around a huge pile up of abandoned and wrecked cars.

The walking dead wore clothes as if they were just normal people. Lab coats. Suits. Dresses. Pajamas. Uniforms. Jeans and t-shirts. But almost nothing else about them looked normal. They barely even looked human anymore.

Their bodies were decaying rapidly, their skin bruised and cut open. Many of them had blood dripping from their mouths and Parrish turned away, disgusted and afraid.

This can't be happening. Is this what the whole world looks like now?

She forced her eyes back to the scene. She wouldn't be able to help Zoe by being weak and scared right now. If her sister had any hope of surviving, Parrish was going to have to be strong. Strong enough to kill every single one of those rotters if she had to.

She clenched her jaw and took several deep breaths, forcing her stomach to calm down.

"What exactly are we looking at here?" she asked. "What part of the city?"

Crash studied her. "Why?"

"I want to know how close this is to my sister," she said. "Can you bring up any of the security cameras in or near the Four Seasons?"

Crash turned to the computer and typed in some directions, working fast. He opened a new window and clicked to make it full screen.

"This is the lobby of the Four Seasons," he said. "It's

getting dark in New York, so I doubt we're going to be able to
see very much."

The screen was almost completely black. Crash was right.
At this time of night, it was already too dark inside the building
to get a good look.

"Dammit," she said, pounding her fist on the back of his
chair. "I just want to know if she's okay. What if she's up there
all by herself? She's waiting for me."

"Hold on," Crash said.

Parrish waited for him to start tapping on his keyboard
again, but he didn't touch it. Instead, he sat back in his chair
and closed his eyes. His hands sat peacefully in his lap, and his
chest moved up and down as he took in several deep breaths.

She was watching him so intensely, she hadn't noticed
what happened on the screen until he opened his eyes and his
jaw dropped.

"Holy shit," he said. "I had no idea I could do that."

Parrish followed his gaze and froze. He'd actually managed
to turn on the lights in the lobby. The bright light illuminated
everything they hadn't been able to see in the darkness.

She fell into the metal chair at Crash's side, her hand rising
to her mouth and tears spilling down her cheeks.

The lobby of the hotel was a complete disaster. Bodies
littered the floor, many of them bloodied and half-eaten.

In the corner, a zombie had its head buried inside some
poor guy's stomach.

"That's her hotel?" Parrish asked in a whisper. "Are you
absolutely sure?"

Crash nodded. "This is what the security camera near
the door is showing right now," he said. "The power is definitely out in the city, but somehow I was able to turn on the

lights here in the lobby. I don't even know how, to be honest."

Parrish scanned the lobby, looking for any sign of hope that people in their rooms had survived. Were the elevators and stairwells barricaded? She couldn't tell.

"Parrish—" Noah had joined them now and was standing behind her, obviously staring at the carnage in the hotel.

"I know," she said through gritted teeth. "It looks bad, but this doesn't prove anything. The whole city is a mess, but that doesn't mean there aren't still people alive in their homes or their hotel rooms, right? When I talked to her, I told her to try to lock and barricade the doors and to get as much food and water as she could gather up. I told her not to answer the door for anyone. She could still be alive."

Crash ran a trembling hand across his forehead. "Theoretically, you're right," he said. "There is a slim chance your sister is still alive in her hotel room if she's been quiet and she was able to push something against the doors. How old is she? You said her name was Zoe, right?"

"She's ten," Parrish said, trying not to imagine what her baby sister had been going through.

"Was she alone in the room?"

She shook her head. "Our dad was there with her," she said, knowing what he was thinking. "When I talked to her last, she said he was sick. She said he'd locked himself in one of the bedrooms."

Crash made a face, and Parrish looked away. She didn't need anyone to tell her how bad this looked. She was crazy for even hoping her sister was alive, but what else could she do? She couldn't give up on her.

"I can't even imagine what she's going through," Parrish

said, her voice trembling. "Even barricaded in the room by herself, there's only so much a person can stand before they go totally insane. Your own father slamming and clawing against the door to come eat you for days on end? Yeah, that would seriously mess a person up after a while, right? And Zoe's just a little girl. Oh, God, maybe she's better off dead."

Tears streamed down her face and her hands shook violently.

"Don't say that," Noah said, placing a hand on her shoulder.

"Let's say she's still alive and has enough food to last for a couple weeks or so," Crash said. "What could we possibly do about it? You saw the video feed of the streets in the city. The whole place is crawling with rotters. Too many to kill. How would we get to her even if she is alive? We'd probably all die trying."

Parrish lowered her eyes. "I can't just abandon her," she said. "I told her I'd come for her. That might be all that's keeping her alive right now."

"Is there any way to find out for sure?" Noah asked. "Are there cameras inside the hotel rooms? If there was some way to know for sure Zoe was still alive, that might help. I mean, it's crazy, but if she's alive and Parrish wants to go after her, I'm going with her."

Parrish reached up to squeeze his hand. The fact that he was still with her after seeing the state of the city shocked her.

Crash raised his eyebrows and looked up at Noah. "You'd risk your life to go into that city?"

"I'm with Parrish," Noah said, squeezing her hand back. "No matter what. If she wants to go, I'll go. I just think it would be nice to at least know we're going in there with a strong hope of finding her alive."

Crash nodded. "I can understand that," he said.

Parrish's heart raced. "Try her cell phone again," she pleaded. "If you can tap into the lights in the freaking lobby even when the power is out in the entire city, maybe you can reach her even when service is down. Please, I need you to at least try."

Crash closed a few of the video windows he'd opened earlier and pulled up a new one. "What floor is she on?"

She gave him all the information she could remember, hardly able to catch her breath.

"This is the only camera on that hallway," he said when a new image popped up on the screen. "I only turned on one of the emergency lights in the hall. I don't want extra light to draw the rotters to her floor and make them think someone's home for dinner, but it looks like you can still see a little bit in the hallway here."

"This is close to her room?" Parrish asked, leaning forward, trying to make out exactly what she was seeing in the semi-darkness.

"Should be," Crash said. "I can't see very clearly, but it doesn't look like there's much activity up in this part of the hotel. Any chance she's on a secured floor? You know, like one of the ones that you have to have a special access code to get up to?"

"It's possible," Parrish said. "She's in a suite."

Crash whistled. "At the Four Seasons? That must have cost a pretty penny," he said. "What were they doing in New York?"

"My sister is a prodigy," Parrish said. "She plays the violin.

Zoe was scheduled to play a concert with the New York Phil-harmonic. They put her and my dad up in the suite when they got there and my mom was supposed to join them a few days later."

She didn't explain what had happened to her mom, and he didn't ask.

Noah moved around to her other side, and Crash scooted his chair over so they could all get a better view of that middle screen.

"Can you zoom in on her room?" Noah asked. "Or get any kind of better view to see if her door is closed?"

Crash shook his head. "There are no cameras inside the guest rooms," he said. "And this is the only security camera on this floor that I can tell. There's some movement. There."

He pointed to a flicker of movement at the edge of the screen. A single rotter stumbled into view, and Parrish brought her hand to her mouth.

"That's not bad, though," he said. "I only see the one. That's much better than what we saw down in the lobby."

He paused, and Parrish held her breath. "What?"

"Wait," he said, running a hand through his hair. "Where's your cell phone?"

Parrish pulled her cell out of her pocket. She'd been stupid and hadn't set it to charge at Noah's before the power went out. None of them had been expecting it to go out so soon. They'd thought they would have weeks of power, if not months.

She should have charged it when she got here, but she'd already tried calling Zoe so many times, and all it did was give her some automated emergency message over and over again.

She handed the phone to Crash.

"It's dead," she said. "I didn't think I'd have much use for it anymore."

The second Crash put his hand on the phone, it came to life. Parrish gasped and leaned forward. She tapped her toes against the legs of her chair.

If this worked, she would be the most grateful person in the world.

Just to hear Zoe's voice and know she was okay would give her hope. Purpose.

"Do you think this will help you reach her somehow?"

"I don't know," Crash said. "None of these machines and electronics should be working right now. It defies all logic, but for some reason, whatever's awakened inside me has given me access to networks that shouldn't be running anymore. I had trouble reaching Zoe from my own computer and cell earlier, but I just had the thought that maybe a phone that's already been connected to hers in the past might make it easier somehow."

Parrish held her breath.

Please, please, let this work.

The screen on her cell phone ran through her list of contacts even without Crash touching it. How was he doing that? She looked up and saw that he was studying the phone with intense focus.

The seconds seemed to tick by like hours as she waited. She held tight to Noah's hand.

The speaker on her phone clicked on and an outgoing ring came through the speaker.

Parrish cried out, and brought a trembling hand to her mouth.

Please, please, please.

Karmen and the other girl had come to join them, and the entire group now huddled around Crash, listening to the ring as it echoed through the small room.

She counted as it rang. *Four. Five. Six.* What if she didn't pick up?

Seven. Eight. Nine.

Noah squeezed her hand, and when their eyes met, the fear and sadness she saw there made her heart tighten inside her chest. Tears stung her eyes with each new ring of Zoe's phone.

She wasn't answering.

Why the hell wasn't she picking up the phone?

Parrish pulled her bottom lip into her mouth and bit down hard. She wanted to scream at her sister. Tell her to pick up the stupid phone, already. But every second that passed, every ring of that phone, was like the toll of a death knell.

Fifteen. Sixteen. Seventeen.

Too many. If Zoe was alive in that hotel room, she would have picked up the phone by now.

Her hand slid from Noah's and her body went numb. She could hardly breathe.

Eighteen. Nineteen. Twenty.

Crash let out a breath and slumped over in his chair, the phone falling from his hand and onto the concrete floor. Parrish screamed as the screen shattered and pieces scattered beneath the computer desk. She fell to her knees, scrambling to pick them all up, but it was no use. The phone was ruined.

It was over.

Noah pushed Crash's chair back and placed his hand on the guy's forehead, but when she looked up at him from her spot under the desk, he was staring at her, tears in his deep brown eyes.

"I'm so sorry, Parrish," he said.

She shook her head and sobbed, tears falling down her cheeks as she clutched the ruined phone against her chest. A few seconds later, the power went out.

PART TWO
THE DREAMS

SEVENTEEN

ZOE

S omething startled her from her dream and she sat up, her eyes wide open in fear.

She'd pulled all the extra blankets from the closet and made a little nest for herself in the corner of the room farthest from the doors behind a chair. It felt good to hide in the soft blankets where she couldn't hear her dad moving around in the next room.

But something had woken her up.

She huddled inside her cocoon and listened. It sounded like something was ringing. Was that her phone?

It couldn't be. Her phone had been dead for days now.

With shaking hands, she pulled the cotton ball out of her left ear and listened again. Her heart raced. What if someone was out there? What if help had finally come?

Another ring sounded across the room, and she jumped up from her spot on the floor. She tried to run around the side of the chair, but her feet tangled in the mess of blankets and she fell. Her knee banged against the metal frame and blood trickled from the scrape, but she didn't stop to look at it. She heard the phone ring again as she pulled her feet from the blankets and finally made it to the other side of the room.

She stopped and listened again, trying to ignore the way her father was scratching and bumping against the door of his room. The ringing had probably stirred him up, and she knew from experience that it would be hours before he calmed again and went back to pacing the floor like he usually did.

She didn't care. If someone was reaching out to her, maybe that meant she'd be safe. Maybe they were coming for her, and she'd be rescued from the hotel soon.

Zoe couldn't remember where she'd put her phone, though. Once it had run out of power, it was useless to her without a place to charge it. She'd put it somewhere, not even thinking.

But her heart skipped a beat. If her phone was out of power, how was it ringing? Was she losing her mind?

The phone rang again, and she sprinted through the darkness toward the couch. A slight glow emanated from that part of the room. It had to be her phone.

She banged her leg on the side table and a lamp crashed to the floor. She stepped on some of the glass trying to climb on top of the arm of the couch and winced as it pierced the bottom of her foot.

Dangit, she was tearing herself up trying to answer the phone in time. She didn't even understand how it could possibly be ringing, but she didn't care. All she cared about was answering it before whoever was on the other end of that call gave up on her.

Zoe flopped onto the cushions and stretched her hand

across to the other side. She could see it now, the phone's light muffled by the pillow she must have placed on top of it earlier.

As her hand closed over the plastic case, the light went out and the phone stopped ringing.

"No," she cried, shaking it up and down. She pressed the power button and waited, praying she would see some kind of light coming from the screen.

Nothing happened. It was just as dead and out of power as it had been for the past few days.

Zoe shook her head violently. What was going on?

She could have sworn she'd heard it ringing. She saw the light. Someone had tried to call her.

She turned the phone over in her hand, not understanding. Had she imagined it?

Her breath came in uneven gasps as she tried to make sense of it. She'd been asleep. She'd heard the phone and gotten to it as fast as she could. She'd seen the light. She was sure of it. There was no other explanation. Her phone had been ringing.

She pressed the power button again, this time holding it for several seconds. She waited, praying for the light to come on and the phone to restart. It was so dark in the room now that she could barely see her own hands clutching the case, but the darkness was all she needed to see to know she was losing her mind.

Her phone was dead. No one was calling her. It was impossible. Even if Parrish had tried to reach her, the call wouldn't have gotten through. There was no battery left.

Zoe leaned back against the soft cushions of the couch, her body shivering. In the next room, her father groaned and rammed against the door of his bedroom, trying to get out.

She'd made too much noise, and now he was trying to get to her.

The same thing had happened when she'd been stupid enough to play her violin the other night. Loud sounds agitated him, and she knew all he wanted to do was get through that door and tear her apart, the way she'd watched so many of those things kill in the streets.

Someone else banged on the main door to the suite, and Zoe screamed.

She clutched the phone tightly in her small hands and pushed her back as deep into the couch as she could.

Who was that?

She listened, hoping against reason that her sister's voice would come through the door, saying they were here. They were safe. Instead, she heard the familiar scratching sounds of a zombie trying to get in. There was another one out there in the hall, and she'd drawn it toward her with all her banging around.

Hot tears spilled from Zoe's eyes as she listened to the two zombies trying to claw their way through the doors. No one was coming for her. No one was normal anymore. The whole world was dead, just like her father, and after weeks of being alone, she was losing her mind.

She clutched the phone tighter in her hands, wishing she was strong enough to crush it to pieces. No one had called. This was just her mind playing some cruel trick. Somewhere in her subconscious she must have wanted this to happen so badly that she'd imagined it was real.

Or maybe she was still dreaming, locked in some neverending nightmare.

Her mind had created hope when there was no hope left.

Anger surged through her. It wasn't fair. She was supposed to be in Europe right now having the experience of a lifetime. She should have been safe in Paris with her mom and dad at her side, and Parrish safely back home with their aunt. None of this should have ever happened.

Zoe wished the virus had taken her, too. Why leave her alive to watch all this death and horror? At least her father had gone quickly.

She was going to die slowly. She had enough food and water to last a while, but it wouldn't last forever. If her father didn't manage to break through his door and kill her, she would die of starvation. One way or another, she would join the rest of them.

It wasn't fair.

It had been hard enough to handle just being alone and listening to the groans of those things in the streets. But this? She stared down at her phone. This was the worst of it all.

She couldn't even trust her own eyes and ears anymore.

Zoe pushed herself off the couch and fell to the floor. Screaming, she banged the phone against the floor over and over as hard as she could until it came to pieces in her hand. She smashed the pieces with her hand until she felt the warm trickle of blood on her palm.

Sobbing, she leaned back against the couch and placed her wounded hand against her shirt.

No one was ever coming for her.

Zoe Sorrows was going to die alone.

Noah held his fingertips to Crash's neck and felt for his heartbeat. It was weak, but there.

"Can someone find a flashlight, please," he said. "I need some light."

Behind him, someone tripped over something and cursed. Karmen. A few seconds later, she turned on a light and shone it toward him.

"Thanks," he said. He glanced down at Parrish. She was still sitting on the floor beneath the desk, rocking back and forth, tears streaming down her face. He wanted to comfort her, but he also needed to make sure Crash was okay.

"What's wrong with him?" Karmen asked. She moved beside him and shone the light toward Crash.

"I don't know. I guess the strain of trying to keep all this going was too much for him," he said. "He's probably going to need to rest for a while. I'm going to move him to the couch so we can keep an eye on him."

"Do you need help?" the other girl said. They still didn't

know her name, so in his head, Noah had just been calling her the girl. He didn't know what else to call her.

"Would you mind clearing those backpacks off the couch?" he asked. "Karmen, just shine the light on the floor from here to the couch so I don't trip over anything."

Noah put one arm under Crash's legs and lifted him from the chair. He was thankful for his extra strength, because even though Crash wasn't a huge guy, he still had to weigh at least a hundred and seventy pounds. Noah lifted him like it was nothing, and carried him to the couch.

The girl grabbed a blanket and spread it across Crash's legs and chest.

"What do we do now?" Karmen asked. "We won't have any power until he wakes up."

"We don't really need power," Noah said. "Not right now. We just need to sit tight and make sure everyone is okay."

"This place feels weird in the dark," Karmen said. "I don't like it. And listen. Do you hear that?"

"Hear what?" he asked.

Karmen pointed toward the ceiling. "Someone's walking around upstairs. One of them."

Noah grew still and listened. She was right. Now that the power was off and the loud computer fans weren't running, he could hear the sound of footsteps shuffling against the floor above them.

"We're safe down here," he said.

"For how long?" Karmen asked. "You heard what he said earlier. There's some kind of witch or assassin looking for us right now. What if they find us down here? What happens then? We're like sitting ducks in this place."

"All you ever think about is yourself," Parrish said, finally crawling out from under the desk.

Karmen swung the light toward her and Parrish held up a hand to shield her eyes.

"I do not," Karmen said.

"Yes, you do," Parrish shouted back. "Ever since that first night we got attacked, all you've ever talked about or cared about is what's going to happen to you. You don't even seem to care that your parents never came home. Did you even stop to think that maybe they're still alive out in California? Just because they couldn't catch a flight home doesn't mean they're dead. Does that even matter to you? Or is getting to a safe place where you can feel like you're being watched out for the only thing that matters anymore?"

Noah stood and walked over to her, but she held up her hand to keep him away.

"Stop," she said. "I know what you're going to say, but I don't want to hear it. I'm tired of walking on eggshells around here, trying not to upset anyone. Life sucks, okay? We are in danger and you know what? There's nothing we can do about it. There's nowhere else to go that's going to be safe. The safe zones the government set up are all destroyed. There's no one left to help us. We're probably all going to die, just like your dad. Just like all our parents. Just like my sister."

Tears streamed down her face, and Noah just wanted to pull her into his arms. She was angry. She had every right to be, but lashing out at Karmen and the rest of them wasn't going to do any good.

He stepped toward her again, but she shook her head.

"I can't do this right now," she said.

She grabbed her backpack off the chair and rummaged

through it until she found her flashlight. She switched it on and walked toward the front door.

"Wait a second," he said. "Where are you going?"

"To the roof," she said. "I have to get out of here."

"Parrish, wait," he said, but she had already unlocked all the deadbolts and yanked the heavy door open. Before he could stop her, she was gone.

Noah sighed and looked over at the other two girls. He felt responsible for all of them, but everything was going to fall apart if they started arguing now.

He went to his own bag and got his flashlight, too.

Karmen put a hand on his arm. "Don't go after her," she said. "She's just upset about Zoe. Give her some time to cool off. She'll come back in a little while feeling better, I promise."

"I can't just let her roam around out there by herself. She didn't even take her weapon."

"Crash secured all those doors, remember?" she said. "The rotters can't get into the stairwell unless they suddenly learned to open locks."

Noah sighed and looked over at Crash. He was sleeping soundly and there was no telling how long he might be out. He hated to leave the girls down here by themselves, but there was just no way he was letting Parrish go up to the roof alone.

"I have to go," he said. "Lock the door behind me and don't open it for anything or anyone except us."

"Noah—" Karmen started, but he was out the door before he could hear her finish whatever it was she was going to say.

He shut the door behind him and waited until he heard the sound of the locks clicking into place before he rushed up the stairs after Parrish. He took them two at a time, his flashlight beam jumping up and down as he moved.

He paused at the top of the fifth flight of stairs and leaned over the metal railing, trying to catch sight of Parrish's light in the dark stairwell. She was at least six floors ahead of him and moving fast.

Noah had only been up to the roof once, the day after they arrived. Crash had shown them the path as an emergency escape route, just in case the apartment got overrun.

He'd somehow managed to get ahold of the building manager's keys and had locked all the main doors to the stairwell after most of the survivors had fled the building. He'd told them he'd had to kill a few rotters to clear the place out, but that as long as those doors held up, the stairwell should be free and clear.

So far, so good. Noah was thankful for Crash's plan, because otherwise they'd likely have a swarm of those things down on the basement floor trying to get into the apartment. Noah wasn't sure how they knew where the living were, but there was no doubt they seemed to smell or sense someone who was still alive.

They see us as food.

The zombies were predators now, all their humanity stripped from them when they died. All they cared about was spreading infection and eating the flesh of anyone who had survived the virus.

As he passed another floor, he wondered how many of the dead were still walking around in this building? They'd heard at least one in the apartment above them, but it was possible that some of these apartments held several of them each. Entire families, maybe.

He shuddered and sped up his pace, grabbing the railing to help hoist himself up.

He was winded by the time he reached the last floor and pushed out onto the roof. Cool wind slapped him in the face and made the door slam loudly behind him.

Parrish stood at the very edge of the roof, looking out over the city. She didn't even turn when the door slammed.

Noah took a second to catch his breath and walked over to stand beside her.

"Hey," he said softly.

She glanced at him. "I thought I told you I didn't want to talk to you right now."

"Who said anything about talking? I just came up here to get some exercise," he said. He lifted his arms above his head and stretched. "Nothing like a frantic jog up ten flights of stairs to get the blood flowing."

She shook her head and wiped some of the tears from her cheek, but he could have sworn he saw the start of a small smile on her lips.

"I guess Karmen's probably pretty mad at me right now," she said.

"Karmen's fine," he said. "She's probably more upset about the fact that she can't watch TV with the power out."

Parrish rolled her eyes and laughed, but the moment the happy sound left her lips, her face crumpled again and the tears were back.

She bent over, her hands covering her face as her shoulders began to shake.

Noah's heart tightened, and he put his arm around her as she cried.

Parrish had cried around him before, but he'd never heard her sob like this. Like there was no hope left in the world. She sank down to her knees on the tarred roof, and he went with her, pulling her close to his chest and stroking her hair.

She leaned into him, her face pressed into his shirt and her shoulders shaking. He wasn't sure how long they stayed that way, but it didn't matter. He would stay up on that roof all night if she needed him to.

He didn't say anything or ask if she was going to be okay. He knew it would never be okay again. They might someday find safety or answers to the questions about why this had all started or why they had been given these special abilities, but nothing would ever erase the pain of these first weeks when they'd lost everything and everyone they loved.

When her sobs had quieted and the flow of her tears had stopped, she pulled away and looked up at him.

"Thank you for coming up here with me," she said. Her voice was raspy and weak. "I thought I wanted to be alone, but I didn't realize how much I needed someone right now."

"Parrish, I'd do anything for you," he said. And he meant it. It wasn't just because they were two of the only people left in their group of friends or maybe even this part of the world. There was more to it than that. "I know we've always hung out with different crowds at school and kind of gone our own way, but I've always felt drawn to you. I never understood it until now."

She wiped her face on the sleeve of her t-shirt and looked at him questioningly. "What do you mean?"

"I think we were always destined for this," he said. He motioned to the darkness around them. "As messed up as it sounds, and as much as I wish this wasn't our fate, it somehow feels like it was always meant to be this way. The two of us together at the end of the world. Does that sound crazy?"

She sniffed and smiled, her eyes almost purple in this dim light. "It should, but you're right. It doesn't," she said. "I've always felt drawn to you, too. I never have told anyone this, but sometimes, it was like I knew when you were close to me. I'd be sitting in the cafeteria eating lunch and even though I couldn't see you, I would know you'd just walked into the room."

Chills ran down Noah's spine. "The same thing happened to me a lot, too," he said. "And it only got stronger over this past summer before school started. I'd sometimes go outside to play basketball just because I knew you were outside. I didn't even have to look out my window to be sure. I just knew."

Her eyes met his. "So that's why you were outside shooting hoops all summer," she said with a smile.

He shrugged, the blush of embarrassment hot on his cheeks. He couldn't believe he'd really just admitted that, but it was the truth. Any time she was near, he wanted to be closer to her. Always. Even before this all started.

"Why do you think we're so connected?" she asked softly. "It's more than just liking someone, isn't it?"

He nodded. "I think it is. I think I've always known there was something more between us, but I couldn't explain it," he said. "I still can't. Not really. But I think it's somehow related to the rest of this. To the virus and the rotters. Crash says it's the five of us who were always meant to come together, and that we have some kind of purpose as a group, but there's something different between the two of us, Parrish. I—"

He stopped himself before he said what he'd been thinking.

I love you.

The words had been on the tip of his tongue, and in his

heart, he knew they were true. Even after years of growing up across the street from each other, he'd barely spoken to her before this mess broke out. He barely knew her.

Still, he did love her. He had always loved her. It just took the end of the world to make him realize it.

"I'm so sorry about Zoe," he said, instead. He was afraid to tell her what he'd been feeling. She'd been through so much today. He didn't need to complicate it with his own feelings right now.

"I just can't believe she's gone," Parrish said, her voice catching. "I was so sure she'd answer that phone, you know? We just talked to her a few days ago and she was fine. I can't even think about what must have happened to her. I promised her I'd come for her."

They were sitting across from each other on the roof, their legs folded beneath them criss-cross style like they were kids. He reached over and took her hand in his.

"You did everything you possibly could," he said. "You saw those videos Crash showed us. Even if we hadn't gotten attacked by those super zombies in the city the other night, we never would have made it through the streets of New York alive. There are just too many of those things now."

She lowered her head and swiped at her eyes again. "My brain says you're right, but damn it, my heart says I should have tried harder," she said. "She's just a little girl, and she died all alone and scared."

"It's not your fault," he said. He wished he could find the words to comfort her, but how could any words make up for such a loss?

"I was mean to her," Parrish said, surprising him.

"No you weren't," he said. "You were willing to go all the way up there and risk everything to get to her."

"I don't mean now," she said. "I mean before all this. I resented her because she was the talented one."

Parrish looked at the buildings surrounding them, and Noah followed her gaze. The moon was bright tonight and without the lights of the city to block them out, the sky was full of stars. Below them on the streets, they could hear the hungry rotters moaning and moving around. Noah sat in silence, sensing that Parrish wanted to say more and giving her the time she needed to say it.

"It was hard trying to live up to my parents' expectations for me when I was little," she said. "More than anything else, they wanted to have a child who was as talented as they were, and I just couldn't do it. But Zoe?"

She shook her head.

"I'll never forget one day my mom was playing piano in the living room and little Zoe went to sit beside her like she often did. She was probably about three years old at the time. Mom finished the song and Zoe put her tiny little hands on the keys and picked out the melody, just like that. She'd never had a music lesson in her life and she didn't miss a note. It was like some kind of light turned on in my parents that day. They'd finally gotten the music prodigy of their dreams, and I was nothing but a disappointment. They put her in suzuki classes immediately so she could learn to play the violin. After that, I was invisible. I was only nine years old, but I felt the shift of their focus like the earth slipping on its plates. They lived for her, and I hated her for it."

"Parrish, don't do this to yourself," he said.

She pulled her hand away from his and looked up. "I need

to talk about it," she said. "I have to find a way to forgive myself for never letting her know just how much I loved her."

"She knew," he said. "You were the only person who treated her like she was a normal kid. Everyone else put the weight of the world on her shoulders, Parrish, but you were the only one who played with her and teased her and treated her like any little sister would be treated. Maybe you couldn't see it, but I could tell how much she looked up to you. She knew how much you cared about her."

"Did you know she was sick when she was younger?" she asked.

Noah nodded. "I remember something about it a few years back, but I never knew the details. What happened?"

"She was six when she passed out for the first time. It was during a violin rehearsal and they'd been going for hours," she said. "They treated those little kids like soldiers in boot camp or something, pushing them to the limit for every concert, and when it happened, everyone just wrote it off as fatigue at first. She was tired, that was all. But over the next few weeks, it got worse. By the time my parents took her to the doctor, the leukemia had gotten so bad she almost died."

Noah raised his hand to his mouth. "I had no idea," he said. "No one told me."

"My parents wanted to keep it to themselves," she said. "They were afraid to talk about it to anyone, like discussing it would make it real. It was the scariest time of my whole life, Noah. Seeing her there in that hospital bed with all those tubes connected to her. Most days she could barely keep her eyes open."

"How long was she sick?"

"I don't remember. Months, I guess. Maybe a year. She got

so pale and thin," she said. "The doctors told my parents her best hope was to get a bone marrow transplant and after testing, we found out I was the best donor."

He didn't know what to say. He'd never heard anyone talk about Zoe having cancer as a child. He remembered that she was sick and hadn't been around for a while, but he hadn't known how bad it was. And he'd had no idea Parrish had done so much to save her sister already.

"I remember being so scared," she said. "Not just for Zoe, but for me, too. It was so painful, and I resented that even though I was going through something difficult too, all my parents could talk about was whether Zoe would ever be well enough to play the violin again. I know that sounds harsh. I know they loved us both, but they were obsessed with this dream of having a child prodigy."

"The transplant worked?"

She nodded. "She got better after that," she said. "It wasn't long after that she came home from the hospital and life started to go back to normal again. Violin lessons started back up as soon as she was strong enough to play, and the rest is history. I guess I always felt like it was my responsibility to keep her safe after that. When this all started and we figured out that we were both immune to this virus, I thought maybe since I'd helped save her once, I could save her again. I can't believe she's really gone."

Parrish collapsed into tears, and he threw his arms around her. He kissed her forehead and when she pulled away, their lips were so close he could smell the cherry scent of her lipgloss. He leaned forward, but before his lips touched hers, an explosion rocked the night.

NINETEEN

THE BOY

The boy crawled from his hiding place in the closet and felt across the floor for his flashlight. He had several stashed in different places in the apartment, but kept a small one near the closet door. He had chosen this one for its very dim light.

With the blinds and curtains closed, he didn't think it would be visible from the streets below, and he wanted to make sure he didn't draw any extra attention to himself.

He'd been dreaming of the old man again. Tobias. They had become friends in his dreams, talking about the past as if they had known each other for lifetimes. And maybe they had.

The boy liked it when the man spoke to him. The best part was that the boy could speak back. He'd struggled his entire life with a speech delay and his mother hadn't had enough money to send him to the kind of specialists his teachers had suggested. Instead, she'd taught him other ways to communicate through gestures and writing things down on a piece of paper.

He still wasn't great with spelling, but he knew most of the words he'd needed in order to tell adults what he wanted them to understand.

Still, he liked that he could talk in his dreams. He liked to hear the sound of his own voice and be free to say everything that was on his mind.

If it were up to him, he'd have lived in those dreams. But something had interrupted his conversation with the old man, and when he'd woken, the symbol had been burned into his mind like a brand.

The boy opened the door and kept the dim light on the floor, careful not to shine it toward the windows or the door where it might be seen by someone outside.

He needed to get to his notebook.

He crawled from the bedroom closet all the way to the living room on his hands and knees, moving so slowly he barely made a sound. Now that he knew something evil was looking for him, he had been very careful not to be noticed.

The notebook was just a small one that he used to carry around in his back pocket for when he wanted to write a message to his mom or his teacher. Last year when he'd started second grade, his mom had surprised him with an entire box of them.

Ever since the virus had taken his mother, he'd used the notebooks to draw the things he saw in his dreams. Anything that might be important later was put onto the page. Memories, conversations. He wasn't great at drawing, but he'd gotten better with practice. And he had a lot of time on his hands these days.

When he found it on top of the kitchen table, he pulled it down with him to the floor and lay on his belly under the table.

He propped the little light up against the leg of a chair and flipped through the first few pages. He'd started a new notebook just a few days earlier since the first one was already full, so there were only five pages filled in so far. Each page had a single symbol drawn on it. One for each of the five he knew he was supposed to be with now that the Dark One had awakened.

His own symbol was first. A spiral. He'd started drawing this symbol about three weeks before the first reports of the virus. His mother had scolded him for wasting the paper, but he'd kept on drawing that spiral circle, knowing that there had to be some meaning behind it.

He understood now that they were an early sign of what was to come. The power that had awakened inside him was special and important somehow. A spiral, like the wind. Speed. Swiftness of thought.

He flipped the page.

He'd drawn a lightning bolt next. This was the symbol of the one who held the power to control machines and electricity. His ability was fire-based and powerful.

On the next page, he'd drawn a cross for the healer. His power was ice-based and ancient. The boy felt a calm fall over him whenever he looked at the cross. The soul behind the symbol was kind and strong. A protector who cared deeply about those he watched over.

Fourth, he had drawn a flower. A rose with a thorny stem, it's petals engulfed in flame. She had the ability to see inside people's minds and control them.

But it was the fifth symbol that had interrupted his dream that night. He flipped to the next page and ran his pencil over the infinity symbol, tracing it back and forth across its looped ends.

He closed his eyes, but his pencil continued to move along the lines of the symbol.

This one was special. Their leader. She held a power none of them could ever match. She was a rare witch, even amongst those in the world they'd originally come from. He could sense that she hadn't even uncovered the second half of her power yet, but it would come soon.

In his dream, he'd seen her symbol covered in blood and had felt her presence close by. Was she here in the city with him? His body trembled as he thought of her.

Just yesterday, he'd felt that she was far away, but now, he sensed her close. And she was injured.

He opened his eyes and stared at the symbol, his heart racing with fear.

She was his leader and she needed help. She was bleeding and scared, and she was alone.

Tomorrow, when the sun had risen and the rotters had gone back to their hiding places in the cool shade of the buildings, he would have to go and find a map of the city. He'd need supplies to take with him on his journey.

It was a risk, but he had no choice.

When the sun came up, he would start making his plan of how to reach her.

TWENTY

THE WITCH

It was a pity that in order to earn the trust of these four humans, she was going to have to try to kill them.

But after watching them for the past few days, she realized the best way to gain the trust of people like this was to save their lives. Once they had put their lives in her hands, she would be able to control them. They would listen to her and include her in their decision-making. They would trust her lies without thinking twice.

As much as the young witch hated rodents, they were all she had been able to sneak in through the barriers Crash had set up throughout the building.

She'd crept out of the apartment in the early morning when the others were still sleeping to look for some kind of weakness in the building's defenses.

She knew there were more than a hundred rotters above them in the smaller apartments on the higher floors, but Crash had been clever in choosing his home. There was no direct access from those upper apartments to this one down below except for a small service elevator and a single narrow stairway. He had cut all power from the elevator, of course. And the entrances to the stairway had been completely sealed off on most of the floors, the doors welded shut. To break it down, she would have had to use too much of her energy. Plus, there would have been no explaining how all the rotters had gotten through the doors all at the same time without some kind of foul play.

She considered opening the door to the garage, but it would be too easy for them to tell that it had been tampered with.

No, she needed this to look like an accident. Or an attack from the outside. Above all things, the others could never suspect that she was behind any of the attacks or unrest amongst the group. Once they suspected her, she was useless to the Dark One.

Instead, she'd summoned the rats.

Hundreds of them. They ran through the sewers beneath the streets in packs, their nimble bodies able to squeeze through even the smallest of openings.

The witch created just such an opening at the far corner of the garage behind a row of abandoned cars. It was dark and out of the way. No one would ever see the rats gathering there.

Many animals were immune to the Dark One's magic and the virus had not taken hold in them. Dogs, cats, horses, most domestic animals. But there were others who had been infected easily. Monkeys. Bats.

Rats.

The witch leaned down and reached her hand toward the large rat with the red eyes. It skittered up her arm and up onto her shoulder, rubbing its furry body against her cheek tenderly.

Pride seeped into her bones. The Dark One approved of her choice.

"Soon," she told the rat. "As soon as the sun sets."

She crouched and let the rodent run back to the others who were gathering in the garage.

Tonight, things were going to get interesting.

TWENTY-ONE

KARMEN

S he was cold. She opened her eyes and sat up. What was that sound? Something had woken her, but it was distant and booming. She struggled to orient herself, but it was so dark in here. Were the others still asleep?

She listened, but heard no breathing or movement in the room with her. Where had they gone?

She shivered.

She didn't like this feeling of being alone in the dark. She missed light and the subtle humming sound of electricity.

Crash must have still been out of it. How long would he be sleeping? And what would they do if he never woke up?

She heard the door to the apartment open, followed by the low rumble of voices down the hall. Parrish and Noah must have been on the roof for most of the night. She needed to go see what had happened, but she couldn't maneuver in the darkness. She had a flashlight in her backpack. She just had to find it.

She climbed out of her sleeping bag and crawled across the

floor to where she thought she remembered leaving it last night before she went to bed.

She moved slowly, putting her hand down carefully as she crawled. She was convinced she would put her hand down and feel someone's dead leg or something.

Finally, though, her hand landed on something.

Not a leg. Thank God.

Her tennis shoes. Or someone's anyway.

She felt around the shoes and found a backpack. She unzipped it, moving by feel alone, getting her first real dose of what it would be like to be blind. She'd never been in such pure darkness in her life.

She'd pulled almost everything out of the bag before she realized it wasn't even her bag she was rummaging through. Crap.

What even was this?

A blanket? A dress? She felt her way around some long piece of fabric. It was strange and heavy, unlike any material she'd ever touched. Silky in some ways, but not quite as soft and smooth as silk. It was more like a silky chain, but that made absolutely no sense.

She decided she would make a terrible blind person. She couldn't even trust her hands to tell her what she was holding.

She shoved the fabric back inside the bag and moved along the floor until she found another backpack.

She unzipped it and sighed in relief, pulling her flashlight from the bag and switching it on, so grateful for the light.

Karmen shone the light on the fabric she'd been touching inside the other bag and her eyes widened. Wow. It was gorgeous. The material glittered in the light, as if diamonds had been woven into its fabric.

She looked around for a place to prop the flashlight up so she could get a better look.

Whatever it was, it was long. She stood and held it up so the fabric draped across the floor. Was it a cloak? Who wore cloaks anymore? It looked like a costume from some fancy play or masquerade ball.

She looked down at the bag she'd pulled it from, glancing guiltily toward the abandoned sleeping bags.

She hadn't meant to go rifling through the new girl's bag, but damn. This was one serious piece of clothing.

Karmen couldn't help but wonder why in the world anyone who knew they could only carry one single bag full of possessions with them into the apocalypse would choose something so bulky and extravagant.

She shook her head and carefully stuffed the cloak back into the girl's bag, zipping it closed as best she could.

This chick was weird. She didn't really seem to fit into their group.

But even so, Crash had somehow known she was there. He said he'd dreamed of her and that somehow, she was meant to be a part of their group. He seemed to believe the five of them had some kind of mystical purpose in the world now that everything had gone nightmare-mode.

Whatever.

Karmen wasn't sure what to believe anymore.

Maybe they were all losing their minds. Or maybe they were all already dead and this was hell.

There was no use sitting around here trying to figure it out. Everyone else was obviously already awake and moving around, and she wanted to know what had caused that loud noise.

She rummaged through her own bag real quick and grabbed her makeup case and her hairbrush then picked up the flashlight and headed out to find the others.

She hated that there would be no warm water, because she'd been dying for a hot shower.

As soon as she opened the door, she could hear Parrish and Noah talking in the living room. She passed the open door to the bathroom and looked longingly at the shower. She'd take a cold one if she had to, but she hoped it wouldn't come to that.

Despite the way he'd been teasing her, she prayed he was going to be okay.

Noah and Parrish had set up a battery-powered camping lantern on a TV tray beside the couch. The apartment was very sparse. A definite bachelor pad if she'd ever seen one.

She kept meaning to ask Crash about his family, but hadn't had the chance yet. She didn't see him at first, but as she moved into the room, she noticed that he was still asleep on the couch. Parrish and Noah were sitting together on the floor. They both looked up as she walked in.

"Hey," she said. "What time is it? Did you guys hear that noise?"

Without a single window here below ground, she was constantly disoriented.

"About four-thirty," Noah said. "There was some kind of explosion on the other side of the city."

"Oh my God, what caused it?"

"We're not sure," Parrish said. "But from the looks of it, most of that side of town is now on fire."

"Is that going to be dangerous for us here?" she asked.

"Maybe," Parrish said. "We'll be able to tell more when

Crash wakes up. We need to keep an eye on it, though. Just in case."

"Did you get some rest?" Noah asked.

Karmen shrugged. "I guess," she said. "It's a sleeping bag on the floor. Not exactly an ideal situation."

"Better than sleeping on the street," Parrish said, a forced smile on her face and sarcasm dripping from her tone.

Karmen narrowed her eyes at her. "I didn't say I wasn't grateful to be here," she said. "I just don't like sleeping on a hard concrete floor."

She looked around the room.

"Where's the new girl?"

Parrish frowned. "She's not asleep in the bedroom?"

"No. When I got up she was already gone."

She didn't mention that she'd opened the girl's bag and rummaged through her stuff. Or that the girl apparently thought they were on their way to a Renaissance Fair.

"Weird," Noah said, his eyebrows scrunched together. "Maybe she's in the bathroom."

"The door was open," Karmen said, hooking her thumb back toward the hallway. "I didn't see her in there."

Parrish stood. "Where else could she be? It's not like there are a lot of places to hide in here."

Noah and Parrish pushed past her toward the bedroom and Karmen rolled her eyes. She'd just told them the girl wasn't in there. They never took anything she had to say seriously.

She followed them out into the hallway, shining her flashlight into the bathroom. Empty.

"She's not here," Noah said.

"Duh," she said. "I already told you that."

"Maybe she went in the other bedroom since Crash was out here?" Noah asked.

Karmen pushed past them and opened the door to Crash's bedroom.

The room was empty.

"Where else could she be?" Parrish asked, a touch of panic to her voice. "You don't think she went outside, do you?"

"Maybe she went out for eggs and pancakes."

Parrish turned around and gave her an ugly look. "Don't make jokes," she said. "This is serious."

"Oh, I think you're plenty serious for all of us," Karmen said. She both loved and hated that she could get under Parrish's skin so fast. She knew she should be taking it easy on her since she'd just found out her sister was zombie food, but Karmen hated the fact that Parrish had spent the night alone with Noah while she had spent it on the cold concrete floor, alone.

"Stop it," Noah said. He moved toward Karmen and motioned for her to head back to the living room.

The three of them froze as the locks on the main door clicked open simultaneously. The door to the apartment opened and the girl walked through, her head down as she carefully backed into the room and closed the door behind her.

She turned as if she was going to sneak back toward the bedroom, but stopped short and looked at them.

"What the hell?" Karmen said, holding a hand to her heart. "You just scared the crap out of us. Where did you go?"

"I'm sorry," the girl said. "I went to check the doors and the entrances to the building. Crash usually does it in the mornings, but he's still asleep. I thought someone should still do it. Did I mess up?"

Beside her, Noah sighed and shook his head. "No, that was probably a good idea," he said. "Just next time let us know before you leave. We were worried sick."

"I didn't think you guys would be awake yet," she said. "I'm sorry. I came back when I heard that loud noise. What happened?"

"How did you open those locks so easily from the outside?" Karmen asked. What she really wanted to ask was why the heck do you have a Shakespearean cloak in your backpack like a traveling minstrel, but she held her tongue. "You don't have the keys."

The girl shrugged. "I don't know. I placed my hand on the door and they opened."

"You controlled them with your mind?" she asked.

"I guess," the girl said. "I don't know how it works."

"All that matters is you're safe," Parrish said. "Let's all grab something to eat and drink. We need to talk about that explosion."

All they ever did anymore was talk. Karmen was sick of talking. She was sick of being trapped in this apartment. And she didn't like the new girl's explanation of where she'd been. Something about it stank like week-old bullshit. Just recently, she'd claimed she had no powers that she was aware of, but now she was confident enough to leave the basement without the keys? How did she know she'd be able to lock or unlock the doors so easily?

"There was an explosion?" the girl's eyes widened.

"Can our conversation wait until I've at least had a shower?" she asked. "I need a minute to wake up before we get into it. Besides, we've done nothing but talk for days. Can't we at least hang out here for a while and enjoy the fact that we're safe? Maybe play some cards or something fun?"

"You can't take a hot shower without any power," Parrish said.

Karmen glanced at the guy sleeping on the couch. He was kind of cute when he wasn't running his mouth.

"Has anyone tried to wake him up?"

"You're not waking him up just so you can have hot water," Parrish said, her hand on her hip like she owned this place and everyone in it.

"I wasn't suggesting we wake him up," Karmen said. "God, you always suspect the worst from me. I'm not a total asshole, you know."

"Could have fooled me," Parrish mumbled.

Karmen wanted to scream. Why did she have to be so difficult? It was going to be an awfully long apocalypse if the two of them had to stay cooped up in this apartment for the rest of their lives.

"Why don't we just eat some breakfast?" Noah asked. "Crash has some stuff in the fridge that's still cold. Karmen, can I get you anything?"

"Any diet Coke or something with caffeine?" Karmen asked, perking up. What she really wanted was a huge cup of coffee, but there was no hope of that any time soon.

Noah crouched down by the mini-fridge and opened it up. "Let's see, there's Red Bull, Dr. Pepper and Mountain Dew. And there's water."

He looked up at her expectantly, and she wrinkled her nose. Was this guy some kind of sugar and caffeine addict or what? She wished he had at least one diet drink in there, but she knew she was being difficult. She probably ought to get used to settling for whatever was available.

"I'll take a Dr. Pepper," she said.

Noah handed it to her and she popped it open and took a sip. It was still ice cold from the fridge and the bubbles tingled against her throat.

Screw diet drinks. Sugar was delicious. She'd gotten so used to dieting all the time, trying to stay thin so her dad wouldn't yell at her. He liked her thin, he said.

She shuddered as she thought of the way he'd wink and tell her how pretty she was before he touched her arm in that way—

No, she wouldn't think about that right now. That was over. For good. She would never have to see that man again.

She took another sip of her Dr. Pepper and sat down on the rug near the couch. She took several deep breaths and slowly, her shoulders began to relax.

Her father was dead now and she would never again have to hear him call her his pretty little girl.

TWENTY-TWO

CRASH

Crash opened his eyes, a camping lantern the only source of light in the room. The group sat around the light, playing a game of cards. He smiled and sat up, rubbing a hand over his face.

"How long was I out?" he asked. His brain was in a fog.

Everyone gasped and stood, coming to stand or sit beside him. Noah grabbed a bottle of cold water from the mini-fridge and handed it to him.

"About sixteen hours," Noah said. "How are you feeling?"

The cold water was so nice on his dry throat. He felt like he'd been run over by a truck.

He'd been running the power and computers for weeks without any real side effects. Sure, he sometimes got tired and had to down a few energy drinks to keep going. Sometimes in the early days of the virus, he'd slept for twelve or thirteen hours at a stretch after staying up all night working, but he'd never passed out like that before.

"As bad as I look, I'm guessing," he said. "Sorry about the power. Is everything okay?"

He looked at Parrish, remembering everything that happened last night. Damn. He had really hoped they'd find out the girl was still alive. They needed some good news these days.

"I'm sorry about your sister," he said.

She nodded. "Thanks," she said. "And thank you for doing what you did. I know it took a lot out of you to stretch your powers so far. At least now I know the truth."

"I wish it had been a better truth," he said.

"Me too."

Silence filled the room at the mention of the little girl who had lost her life in New York. He didn't know her, but no child should have to die like that. The world was seriously messed up.

"So are we going to talk about that explosion now?" Karmen asked.

His mouth dropped open. "What's going on?"

He tried to stand, but the room spun and his stomach lurched.

"Whoa, buddy, take it easy," Noah said. "You might want to just chill on the couch for a little while. Can I get you something to eat?"

Crash took a deep breath and blinked several times to clear his vision. "Wow, I guess that call took more out of me than I expected," he said. "Yeah, if you could grab some crackers out of the cabinet, that would be great. They're in the kitchen on the far left."

Noah returned in a minute with a sleeve of plain saltine

crackers. Crash's mom used to make him eat these when he was sick, and they always made him feel better. Man, he really missed his mom.

She had passed away several years ago, leaving him alone in the world at the age of fifteen.

The state put him in foster care, but it wasn't too long before he ran away. He took some of the money his mom had stashed in the bottom of her dresser and paid for a fake ID that said he was eighteen. He dropped out of high school and disappeared before anyone could come looking for him.

He hadn't had much back then, but he'd eventually rented this crappy apartment, bought a used computer, and hooked up with a couple other gamers online. When you were desperate, there were ways to make a decent living gaming if you knew the right tricks. He'd grown really good at creating characters on popular MMORPG's like World of Warcraft and Everquest II. He'd grind them up to max level and then sell the accounts on ebay for good cash.

He'd gotten by, investing any extra money he had in new computers and monitors. When the dreams had started, he'd switched to spending his money on building a supply of bottled water and food.

He ate his crackers and downed another bottle of water, feeling better already.

"So tell me about this explosion," he said. "What happened?"

Noah moved to stand beside Parrish. "Early this morning when we were on the roof, we saw some kind of explosion to the west, possibly near the White House."

"What was it?" Crash asked. Crap, an explosion was not

good. With no active fire department, a fire could spread through the entire city.

"We couldn't tell," Noah said. "It could have been anything. Probably a smaller fire reached something explosive like a gas station? I don't know. But it was big."

"That's not good," Crash said.

"What does it mean?" the girl asked. "If it's on the other side of town, we should be safe here, right?"

"It depends," he said. He set his water bottle on the floor and walked to the computer, taking each step with care. His head didn't spin when he stood this time, so that was progress. He sat down in his computer chair and took a deep breath. He didn't want to push himself too hard, but they needed to see what was going on out there.

He concentrated on connecting with the computer's power. He could feel it there right on the edge of his awareness, but the connection was fuzzy. The CPU kicked on with a whir and a sharp pain pierced his temple. The computer shut down again and he brought a hand to his forehead.

"Hey, man, don't push yourself," Noah said. "We can check it out later after you've had more rest."

"What could happen?" Karmen said. "Could it spread here to us? How long would that take?"

"I'm sorry, guys," he said. "I wanted to pull up some surveillance cameras, but I just can't do it right now."

"It's okay," Parrish said. She brought his water and crackers to him and patted his arm. "We can always go back up to the roof to see if it's moving this way."

"If the wind is just right, it could spread through the city pretty fast, I would think," Crash said. "And what's worse, it could push all the undead toward us in herds."

"Herds?" Karmen asked. She was sitting on the couch, and she pulled her legs up toward her chest. She was wearing a pair of shorts that showed off her legs, and Crash had to force his eyes away.

That girl was too hot for her own good.

"Huge groups," he said. "Maybe thousands in a group."

"Oh my God," she said. "Could they break through the gate in the parking garage, you think?"

"If a group that large was able to tell we were alive in here somehow, that's totally possible. With large enough numbers, they could destroy an entire block."

"What are we going to do?" Noah asked.

"I think Parrish's suggestion about going to the roof is a good one," he said. "We need to know if the fire is pushing them our way. I have a feeling we'll be facing either fire or thousands of rotters by the end of the week."

"That's not good," Parrish said. "Noah and I will go up and take a look in a few minutes. Do you have a printed map of the city? Maybe we could try to mark the areas that look bad."

"I can go with you," he said, but when he tried to stand, the spinning was back. How long was he going to be out of it? He needed to get back on his computers. "Or not. I guess I need more rest before I can be of any help."

"Go back to your bedroom and get some more sleep," Noah said. "We'll wake you up in a few hours if it looks bad. We'll figure this out."

Crash nodded and glanced around the room. They had only been here as a group for a few days and they were already facing the possibility of having to get the hell out of dodge. Where would they go?

Without his computers, he couldn't even come up with a good escape plan.

"I'll be in the back room then, if you need me," he said.

As he made his way down the hall to his room, he couldn't shake the feeling that his entire plan of keeping everyone safe and together in his apartment was about to go to hell.

TWENTY-THREE
KARMEN

Sleeping in the complete and utter darkness was harder than Karmen would have thought. There were no sounds at all. No fans running. No hum of electronics in the background. The air was warm and thick without air conditioning and every time she took a breath, she felt her lungs clog with the humidity of it.

The group had spent most of their day playing cards and hanging out by the light of the lantern in the living room. Crash had eventually left his room and joined them for a few games, but he still wasn't feeling up to turning the power back on. Even without the electricity, there was comfort in being awake and around the others, but there was a vulnerability now that the light was off and everyone was asleep.

She'd never really given much thought to the noises of her old house, but now, in the silent darkness of a foreign place, she missed every single sound. She missed the bathroom fan. Her brother's music thumping through the wall even though he was supposed to be asleep hours ago.

She missed the sound of Zoe's violin next door well after the small child should have gone to bed.

She even missed the sound of her mother's snoring.

What she didn't miss was the sound of her father's footsteps in the space just outside her door. Or the way the knob used to creak when he turned it, trying to be quiet so no one else in the house would know.

How many nights of her childhood had Karmen spent huddled up in bed, praying not to hear that sound?

She closed her eyes and listened to the thundering of her heart.

He's never coming back. He's dead now.

He was gone. Replaced instead by another threat. An unpredictable one. At least with her father, she knew he wasn't going to kill her. She knew that no matter what, she could live through it and that someday, she would escape and have her own life.

In this new world, she didn't know what to expect. She didn't know if she'd be alive tomorrow, much less ten minutes from now. Now, instead of the turning of the doorknob, she found herself listening for the shuffling of feet or the groan of the undead.

It was quiet enough here in the dark that she could almost convince herself she could hear them. They were coming for her now, their footsteps shuffling across the floor just outside the door to the bedroom.

Karmen gripped the edge of her sleeping bag and drew it up tight under her chin. She squeezed her eyes shut and reminded herself to breathe.

It's just your imagination, dummy.

But there it was again.

Not a shuffling of feet exactly, but something else. Her eyes flew open and she stopped breathing completely.

What the hell was that?

She wanted to sit up, but she was paralyzed with fear. There was definitely something outside the door. She could hear it moving around, sliding against the walls.

She was afraid if she forced herself to breathe, it would come out as a scream. They would all wake up and call her crazy. Everyone else was either asleep in the two bedrooms or in the living room. They had all retired early tonight.

Parrish and Noah had gone up to check the roof several times throughout the day and the news was not good. They said the rotters were most definitely starting to come their way. The fire had spread across a good portion of the city, the flames and smoke rising into the air for miles. They needed their rest tonight so they could figure out where the heck they were going to go tomorrow or the day after.

If she woke everyone up for some trick of her imagination, they would never let her hear the end of it.

She convinced her shoulders to relax and opened her throat to let in a tiny whisper of air. Everything would be okay. There was nothing out there.

The door to the bedroom squeaked open and she turned her head and sat up.

"Parrish?" she whispered.

No answer. Karmen swallowed thick air and panic.

"Crash? Is that you?"

Again, nothing. But the door was open. She could feel it.

And then she heard them.

Tiny feet skittering across the floor. The chattering of teeth and an awful, high-pitched squeaking that was definitely not human.

She tried to yell, but nothing came out at first. Not until she felt the first of the rats climb onto her sleeping bag, clawing their way up toward her.

That's when she finally found her voice and screamed.

TWENTY-FOUR
PARRISH

The match burned down to her fingertips before she was able to wrap her mind around what her eyes were seeing.

She'd heard Karmen scream and had tried to find her flashlight, but all her fingers landed on was a book of matches she'd used earlier to light a candle.

The apartment was flooded with rats. Hundreds of them. The main door was closed, but they seemed to be coming from somewhere in the kitchen.

What the hell was going on?

But there was no time for questions. The wave of rodents was almost to her, and she couldn't take the risk that they were carrying the virus. Hell, even uninfected rats in a pack of hundreds could eat the flesh off a person in minutes.

Parrish dropped the match to the ground and reached for the sword propped against the wall beside her. The room plunged into darkness, and she only had her ears to guide her.

She slashed and heard the screech of rats and the thud of their small bodies as they were lifted by her sword and dropped again to the floor.

"Noah," she screamed. "Help."

She had no idea what part of the apartment he was in. The back room, she thought probably. He'd said goodnight more than half an hour ago. She hoped he wasn't asleep.

She hoped the rats weren't in his room.

How had they even gotten in here?

Parrish slashed again, turning her body around in a circle to get more leverage on her blade.

Her sword began to glow with an icy blue frost. Her eyes drank in the light, grateful she could at least see the critters rushing toward her. But God, there were so many of them.

She frantically looked toward Crash. He was asleep on the couch and even though she shouted his name, he wasn't waking up. She had to do whatever she could to protect him.

Karmen screamed again, and Parrish's stomach tightened into knots.

Where the hell were Noah and the girl? If the others didn't start helping her fight these things, she had no idea what they were going to do. There were too many of them.

Parrish kicked and spun, slicing rats to pieces. Their blood sputtered up into her face and across her clothes. Her stomach lurched at the gore of it, but she had no choice.

This new world was about survival no matter what.

And keeping the ones you loved alive.

Parrish forced her stomach to settle. She tightened her fist around the hilt of her sword and kept swinging through the darkness.

Finally, a light shone down the hall, and Noah called out to her.

"Are you okay?" he asked. "Where did these things come from?"

He pushed through the mass of rodents, beating them down with his bat.

"I don't know, but I think they're infected," she said. She sliced through another group of them, but they just kept coming. "Where are the others?"

Crash stirred, and then, wide-eyed, jumped onto the cushions of the couch. He closed his eyes and power kicked on for a moment before clicking off again. He cursed and shook his head.

"Dear God," Parrish whispered. The lights had only been on for a second, but it had been enough to see what was really inside the apartment with them.

It had to be thousands. Thousands of rats.

"What are we going to do?" she shouted. "We can't possibly kill them all."

She and Noah made their way to the couch and climbed on top with Crash. Even with all three of them fighting, they were barely keeping their little space on the couch clear of the rodents.

From the hallway, an eerie red glow lit up the darkness. Parrish strained her neck to get a closer look, but she couldn't tell what was making that light.

Please, do not be some kind of super-rat like those zombies the other night.

She shuddered. That was the stuff nightmares were made of, and she'd had her share of nightmares lately.

As the red glow spread across the room, though, she

noticed the rats fall into some kind of daze. They stopped moving, their eyes locked on the red light.

The girl stepped forward, walking slowly and deliberately through the mess of rats. Her palms were covered in red flames, and she held them in front of her as she walked.

Parrish held her sword still, ready to attack if the rats started coming toward her again.

They were entranced by the fire, somehow, their beady little eyes glued to it.

"What in the—" Crash started, but Parrish grabbed his arm and shook her head.

She had a feeling the girl was concentrating very hard, and the last thing they needed was for her to drop her focus right now.

The girl made her way to the center of the group of rats, and then slowly lowered to a crouch. Parrish couldn't believe she was getting so close to them. What was she planning to do?

None of the rats moved. They were mesmerized, completely under her control as she turned her hand palm-up and brought it toward her chin. She blew a puff of breath across the top of the fire and the flames rolled forward in a wave.

The rats screamed as the fire enveloped them, their furry bodies bursting with a bright red light that spread through the entire group of them in an instant. Parrish raised her hand to her eyes, squinting against the light.

When she looked again, every single rat in the place was dead. Their bodies were burned and still, but the fire had not caught anywhere else.

"How did you do that?" Parrish asked, letting her sword drop to her side. She'd never seen anything like it.

"I don't know," the girl said, shaking her head. Her hands trembled at her sides. "I didn't know I could do that."

Parrish collapsed onto the couch, wincing at the stench of the burned bodies. They were safe and they were alive, but damn, they were definitely going to need a new place to stay.

TWENTY-FIVE

THE BOY

rat skittered across the floor in front of him. Its eyes were milky and clouded, and there were sores along its back.

The boy stood up, grabbing the map he'd laid out to study.

He ran to his bedroom and shut the door. He probably should have killed it. It was obviously infected, but for now, he just wanted to shut it out.

The second he took his hand from the door, a vision seized him so strongly that it brought him to his knees on the carpet.

He leaned forward, his eyes closing as an image forced its way into his mind.

A girl with a blue sword. She was fighting rats, too. Hundreds of them. Her eyes glowed almost purple in the light of her sword, and he recognized her in that moment.

He'd never seen her before in his life, but he knew her. He knew those eyes. That sword.

She was his leader. The girl with the infinity sign as her symbol. And she was in trouble.

He struggled to hold on to the vision, but as quickly as it had taken hold, it released him. The boy collapsed onto the floor, his chest rising and falling with each labored breath.

Pain shot through his temples and when he tried to open his eyes, his vision blurred. He closed them again, wincing against the pain.

I'm coming for you, I promise.

He wasn't sure how he'd be able to help her when she was so obviously skilled with a sword, but when he connected to her power here in the city, he got the strong sense that she was alone and afraid. If only he could reach her, maybe he could help her remember who she really was.

Maybe they could help each other.

But there was something odd about his connection to her. She was at once both close and far away, almost as if he were thinking of two different people. How could she be here in the city, but still far away?

He didn't have an explanation. Maybe when he reached her, there would be answers to all his questions.

When the pain in his head had gone away, he spread the map of the city on the carpet and went back to his task of planning. He must have left his red pen in the other room, which was a shame, because now he was too scared to go back out there and face that rat.

If it was infected, maybe that meant the Dark One could see him through its eyes. Was that possible? Had she gained so much power she could control humans and animals alike, seeing through their eyes whenever and wherever she wanted?

The boy knew it would be a mistake to underestimate the Dark One's powers. She was an ancient kind of evil, cunning and meticulous. And she'd had a very long time to think through her plan, trapped down there in her prison of ice.

She was not free, but she had eyes everywhere now.

The boy stood and grabbed one of his mother's shirts from the closet. He forced it under the door, sealing all the cracks so that no light shone through.

Just in case, he thought, and went back to his planning.

TWENTY-SIX

CRASH

The gate that had stood between them and the outside world lifted, bringing with it the first rays of sunshine Crash had seen in days.

He squinted, looking out at the block he'd lived on for the past four years.

The street outside the apartment was still littered with the corpses of the dead they'd killed on their way inside. They were starting to stink, not that anything could compare to the way the inside of his apartment smelled right now.

He'd never been more disgusted in his life. There was no way they could stay in that hell-hole now. After only a few days together in safety, they were being forced to leave, but he figured it was just as well. Between the fire and the hordes of zombies headed their way, it was better to get out as early as possible and try to find a new place to hide out until they had a better plan.

Parrish and Noah loaded more of the supplies into the back, but space was limited. Crash had hoped they'd be able to carry more, but with five people and all their gear, they were going to have to get creative about loading the rest of the supplies.

He should have rigged a way to strap them to the top of the vehicle. Why hadn't he thought of that?

There was no telling what things would be like outside the city. From the videos he'd watched, most places had gotten looted pretty hard, everyone scrambling to get water and food before the entire world went to hell. Supplies would be limited out there, so they were lucky to have the food, water, and ammunition he'd managed to get his hands on before the virus made an appearance.

Still, it wouldn't last forever. They'd have to be careful not to use it up too fast. Or have it stolen by some kind of raiding party on the road. People out there would be desperate and scared, and that could mean some pretty ugly encounters with survivors.

Not to mention the undead.

Luckily, the streets here in the Trinidad section of D.C. were quiet this morning. The fire from the explosion the other night had forced hordes of rotters out of their hiding places, so he'd been afraid they were going to see a lot of them today, but so far, so good. If they got going in the next half hour, they might be able to get out of town without too much trouble.

"That's the last of it," Noah said, coming to stand behind him at the gate. He jogged into the street and picked up the shotgun he'd dropped there a few days earlier. "It doesn't look too bad out here, does it?"

"I've seen a few stragglers on the cross streets," Crash said, "but it's surprisingly quiet."

"What about the roads out of town?" Parrish asked. "On

the way into the city, there were some ugly pile ups and traffic jams that made it impossible to stick with my mom's car. We had to abandon it a lot sooner that I'd hoped."

"I've got a few possible routes mapped out," Crash said. "I'm bringing my best two laptops and my GPS, too, so that should help us if we get into any trouble with finding a way out. We can't afford to lose the Humvee and get stranded on foot."

"Do you need anything else from inside?" Noah asked. "I think we're all about ready to go."

"I'll do a final check and get the girls," he said. "You guys go ahead and get inside. We'll meet you out here in a few minutes."

Crash walked down the stairs to his apartment for the last time, his stomach tense and his heart heavy. This had been his home since shortly after his mom died and left him on his own. He'd created a life for himself here, and an identity separate from anyone and anything else he'd ever known. It wasn't going to be easy to leave it all behind.

"You ladies about ready?" he asked when he walked into the apartment. The stench of dead rats made the idea of leaving a lot more enticing. Holy crap, it smelled in there. He was surprised Karmen had spent more than five minutes there after what had happened.

"Are there a lot of rotters on the streets?" Karmen asked.

She seemed different this morning. Vulnerable and maybe even, dare he think it, nice.

"Only a few here and there," he said. "Grab your bag and go straight to the Humvee. You'll be safe, I promise."

"Where are we going to go?" she asked. "Do you think

there's any hope of a government safe zone still active out there?"

Crash shook his head. "It's unlikely, I'm sorry to say. I think we're going to be on our own."

Karmen's eyes filled with tears, but she looked away quickly. Probably trying to hide it from him. Heaven forbid the ice queen actually had some soft spots.

He touched her arm and when she looked up at him, he thought she looked fragile and terrified. "Hey," he said softly. "It's going to be okay. We're together now, and I promise, I'm not going to let anything happen to you."

He expected some ugly retort or for her to snatch her arm away, but instead, she swiped at her eyes and smiled.

"Thank you," she said. "I know I've been really hard on you since I got here, but I do appreciate everything you've done for us. I'm sorry you have to leave your home."

Crash didn't even know how to respond to that. Karmen being nice and saying thank you? Maybe it really was the end of days.

"I got your back, Blondie." He flashed her a smile and winked.

She let out a huge sigh and pulled her arm away. "Nice," she said. "Better than Barbie, I guess. I'll see you in the truck. You coming?"

Karmen turned to the girl and she looked up, nodding. She'd been staring down at the rats, almost as if she was shocked or sad she'd killed them all the way she had. If it hadn't been for her, though, Crash wasn't sure how they would have survived it.

He still wasn't sure what to think about the attack. Were

the rats just infected and searching for survivors in packs? Or had they been sent, just like the super-zombies?

He didn't know, and he wasn't about to stay behind to find out. If they got out on the road and kept moving, they'd be a lot harder to track. He hoped, anyway.

Anything had to be better than staying in one place where they were sitting ducks for anyone who wanted to harm them.

The two girls left the apartment, and Crash walked over to his desk and stared up at his monitors. He'd spent so much time and money putting this system together. It sucked that he had to leave it behind like this, but they were just things, right? He doubted people had been looting computer equipment, so maybe once they found a new place to settle down, he'd be able to go out and scavenge for another great system somewhere.

For now, he unhooked his two best laptops from the mess of cords under his desk and slipped them into a leather messenger bag. He didn't even bother bringing the chargers. He didn't need them anymore.

Stepping over the bodies of the dead rats, he made his way back to his bedroom. There wasn't much he wanted to take with him. He'd packed a couple changes of clothes, but other than his computers and the food and water he'd stored up, there wasn't a lot more he cared about.

He grabbed the tattered copy of *Catcher in the Rye* and a photograph of his mom from his nightstand and slipped them into his bag with the computers.

Crash walked back down the hallway to the door, and with a final glance at the place he'd called home, he gave a quick salute and walked away.

Getting out of Washington D.C. proved to be a lot easier than getting in had been. For one, they had a military-grade vehicle that could off-road way better than her mom's van. Second, there were several routes out of the city, and Crash had done his homework. He'd used video surveillance and reports he could find online to determine the best path, taking them north up the Anacostia Freeway. There was only one brief section of I-95 where he had to take them off the road and ride on the bumpy shoulder for a few hours.

Cars were lined up for miles in an endless traffic jam out of the city. Parrish saw glimpses of half-eaten faces inside cars. Some rotters were still trapped inside, beating against the windows but strapped in with seat belts that would hold them for possibly years before they gave out.

She didn't see any survivors.

Parrish wasn't sure what she was expecting, really, but she

was surprised there was no one else on the road. There had to be survivors somewhere.

Had they all just locked themselves away in their houses for now?

Crash had told her that the earlier days—the days when she and the others had been safely tucked into their quiet suburban neighborhood—had been rough. Panic had taken its toll and people had started looting grocery stores, Walmarts, gun stores and the like. A lot of the survivors who ventured out during those times had either been bitten or murdered.

Others had decided to wait this thing out as long as they could. They'd gathered whatever supplies they could get their hands on easily and, like she and Noah and Karmen had done at first, they'd boarded up their windows and locked themselves away from the rest of the world. Praying for a cure.

But there was no cure. And all the good men who were working on one were dead. Including Noah's father.

Parrish shuddered and leaned her head back against the seat as the Humvee bounced along the shoulder at the edge of the traffic jam. She'd been geared up to fight their way out of the city, but as they broke through the line of traffic and settled back on the main highway, D.C. fading in the rearview, she dozed off and started to dream.

The dream was familiar—almost more of a memory, really.

Deep blue water stretched out in front of her for miles, the boat under her feet rocking gently back and forth in the waves. In the distance, a small island came into view, filling her heart with hope for the first time in what felt like forever.

———

"Is that Baltimore?"

Karmen's voice woke Parrish and she opened her eyes. The dream had felt so real, it was difficult to come out of it and be plunged back into the nightmare of reality.

"What's going on?" Parrish asked.

Karmen had scooted toward the front and put her head between the seats. She pointed just ahead and Parrish saw what she'd been looking at.

Smoke billowed up in the distance like a wall of darkness beyond the trees.

"What is that? Another fire?"

"Holy crap," Crash said. "Baltimore must be burning, too."

"The whole city?"

"It looks like it," he said. "If I had to guess, D.C. will probably look like this before too long."

As they drove, smoke seeped into the Humvee from the outside. Parrish lifted the top of her shirt to cover her mouth and nose.

"What the hell happened here?" she asked.

Crash shook his head and threw the vehicle into park as the outer limits of the city came into view. He stared ahead, his jaw slack.

The city was on fire, alright. Even from a distance, she could see the flames devouring everything in sight. Tall buildings had toppled to the ground. Homes were completely destroyed and turned to ash. It was scorched earth.

"It's been burning for a while," she said.

"Days, at least. Maybe longer," Crash said.

"How many people do you think lived there?" Noah asked, leaning forward.

"Over 600,000, I think," Crash said, the number bringing tears to Parrish's eyes. "I don't think there's any way to tell exactly what happened, but whatever it was, there wasn't anyone still alive here who was able to put it out once the fire got started."

"I hope some of the survivors got out," she said. She thought again of New York. How many big cities would be lost completely to fire or other disasters over the next few months? With no fire departments to keep it contained, all it would take was one building going up in flames to take down an entire city.

She thought of all the survivors in the big cities, holed up in their homes or apartments. They'd made it through the virus just to be burned to death in their own houses? She couldn't even imagine it.

Maybe it was for the best that Zoe was gone.

As Crash started rolling again, she took it all in as best she could through the thick smoke that hung in the air for miles.

Everyone in the Humvee covered their mouths as Crash navigated around the burning town. They were all quiet, watching the destruction but unable to fully comprehend its meaning.

Until Crash slammed on breaks.

"What?" Parrish asked, staring at him. Why had he stopped?

She followed his gaze and peered through the dense smoke, her eyes growing wider as the outline of rotters appeared.

Hundreds of them, fleeing the city.

"Turn around," Parrish yelled. "Get us out of here."

Karmen leaned forward to look out the front windows and screamed. There was a line of rotters ahead of them, making their way through the smoke.

"Already on it," Crash shouted, putting the vehicle in reverse and pushing down on the gas so hard it thrust her forward.

Something thudded against the back of the Humvee and Karmen screamed as her head banged against the metal side of the vehicle.

She spun around in her seat. Rotting hands clawed at the small window in the back of the Humvee. She scooted down the bench to get a closer look and gasped.

"We're surrounded," she said. "They must have just come out of the woods behind us. They must have heard the sound of the engine."

"Shit," Crash mumbled. "Everybody hold on."

Karmen grabbed the canvas loop above her head and

pressed her feet hard into the floorboard as he turned the wheel and gunned it. Crash took them off the highway and into the grass on the shoulder. It was tough to see exactly what they were up against because of the smoke, but the line of rotters covering the road extended out toward the woods and there didn't seem to be any way around them.

Crash stepped on the gas and plowed into the bodies. Some of them were still on fire. Some of them were barely more than skeletons. Rotters flew up on the hood of the Humvee as Crash moved through them. The vehicle bumped and jerked as they ran over the bodies of the undead. Others clawed at the sides of the windows and doors as they passed.

Karmen kept her eyes open against her will. She needed to see what was going on in case they got stuck and had to fight, but she wanted to just shut it out. These were images she really didn't want invading her dreams later.

Crash jerked the wheel of the vehicle, barely missing the back end of a semi's trailer that had turned over and was blocking most of the road and the shoulder. He traveled beside it, continuing to plow down the bodies of the dead. He had to go across the median and up onto the other side of the highway to get around the truck, but as soon as they made it back onto the road, he slammed on the brakes. There was no way through.

Cars spread out across all four lanes and into the median. There were wrecked cars piled up on the far shoulder all the way to the treeline. In the smoke, it was hard to see any way out of this, but they had to do something. The rotters were banging on the outside of the Humvee now that they were stopped, and Karmen could hear their hungry groans. If they didn't move soon, they would be overwhelmed by them.

There was no telling how many rotters were out there. It could be thousands for all they knew.

"What do we do?" Parrish asked.

Crash gripped the steering wheel so tightly his knuckles were white. "I don't know," he said. "We could try going back the way we came and finding a way around, but if we get stuck somewhere in the middle of that horde, we're screwed."

"Well, we can't go this way," Karmen said. "And the longer we sit here, the more likely we are to get stuck."

"Do you think you could use your mind control to clear a path?" Crash asked, turning around in his seat to meet her eyes.

"You could do it," Parrish said. "If Crash drives slowly and you switch to sitting up front, maybe you could connect with the ones in front of us and get them to move out of the way."

Tears spilled down Karmen's cheeks and she shook her head. "I can't do it. There are too many of them," she said. "I'm too scared."

Parrish grabbed Karmen's face and forced her eyes upward. "You have to or we're going to get trapped here," she said. "You can do this."

Parrish unhooked her seat belt and climbed into the back. She pushed Karmen forward.

"Get up there," she said. "You have to move."

Crash turned the Humvee around, slamming into a group of rotters behind them. "It's now or never," he said.

"Okay," Karmen said. She wiped her tears from her face and climbed into the front seat, buckling herself in. God, she really didn't want to do this. What if she got them all killed? What if she couldn't do it?

She leaned forward, concentrating on the group of zombies

just in front of the truck. Any time she'd used her powers in the past, she'd only been focusing on one person at a time, not a whole group.

She didn't even know how her powers worked. How was she supposed to do this when she didn't even understand exactly what she was doing?

"You ready?" Crash asked. He looked over at her and reached out to take her hand.

His skin was clammy and cold, but just knowing she wasn't alone in this gave her the strength to push ahead. She had to at least try.

Karmen squeezed his hand and nodded. "Let's go," she said.

Crash winked and put his hands back on the steering wheel. "I'll take it slow," he said. "Do your thing."

Behind her, she could hear Parrish pull her sword from her bag. They were ready in case Karmen couldn't pull through, but it was up to her right now to save the group.

If they had to go outside and fight through this large horde, they were as good as dead.

Karmen clasped her hands together and took a deep breath. She stared at the group of rotters directly in front of the truck. They reached up onto the hood with their decaying fingers, leaving small trails of dark blood along the green paint.

Karmen locked eyes with one and in her mind told the old man to move. She imagined him stepping to the side, pushing the others of his kind backward, away from the Humvee.

Two seconds later, he did it. The old man who'd been clawing at the truck closed his hungry mouth and stepped backward.

One down, a bajillion to go.

Karmen breathed in and out, ignoring the smell of smoke that filled her nose. She could do this. She had to.

She focused on the next small group in front of the Humvee, but her heart was racing so fast she could barely breathe. She tried to command them to move, but nothing happened. The truck rocked back and forth as the horde grew closer and began beating on the sides of the vehicle.

"I can't," she screamed. "It's not working."

"You have to try," Noah said. "Please, you can do this."

She tried again, but couldn't focus. She attempted a deep breath, but it was as if her lungs were closed for business.

She shook her head. "I can't," she whispered.

A warm hand gripped her arm, nearly burning her with its heat. She tried to pull away and jerked her head to the side to find the girl inches from her face.

"I can help," the girl said. She reached up and took Karmen's hand in her own, the heat of her skin painful to the touch.

"You're hurting me," Karmen said.

"Focus," the girl said harshly.

Karmen's stomach lurched and she pressed her lips together, trying not to throw up. There was something about this girl's touch that repulsed her. For the first time, Karmen noticed that the girl's hand was badly burned, her skin scarred and wrinkled. But it wasn't the appearance of her skin that had turned her stomach. It was something dark about her touch. Something sinister.

"Karmen, I know you're scared, but we need you to try to focus," Crash said. "If we don't get out of here now, we're all going to die."

Trembling, she closed her eyes and nodded her head.

"Focus on the heat," the girl said. "Let the fire fill you from within. I know it hurts, but it's who you are. Embrace it."

Bright red flames erupted behind Karmen's eyelids. She imagined herself stepping into them, letting them consume her body.

And suddenly, the power seized her. She opened her mouth and gasped, air filling her lungs as her veins pulsed with energy.

She opened her eyes and stared at the huge horde of rotters in front of them. She imagined a wide path opening up, rotters stepping to the side. She commanded them to obey her, reaching into their rotting minds and forcing them to listen.

She had never felt more powerful in her life, and it both excited her and scared the crap out of her.

A flame ignited on the road in front of the Humvee, shooting forward in a straight line down the asphalt. Rotters backed away, stumbling over each other to avoid the flames.

"Go," Karmen said.

Crash nodded and took a deep breath, a smile on his lips as he punched the gas.

The flames died as they drove through the middle of the horde. Everyone cheered, but Karmen couldn't celebrate. She pulled her arm and hand away from the girl, briefly meeting her eyes.

The girl smiled, but there was something in her eyes that chilled Karmen's soul. Something that left her feeling uneasy and sick to her stomach for hours.

On the other side of the smoke, they caught their first glimpse of survivors. A cluster of people, soot smeared across their faces, sat on the rails of a track that crossed the road at the edge of a small town. They looked tired and beaten down. Hopeless.

Crash pulled over toward them.

"What are you doing?" Karmen asked, rousing from her sleep. She'd been mostly out of it ever since she'd used her powers. "Why are you stopping? What if they're infected?"

"They're not infected," Parrish said. "They're just tired and dirty and probably hungry."

"I don't think we should stop," Karmen said, crossing her arms in front of her chest and turning away.

Parrish shook her head. Was there no end to that girl's selfishness?

She gave her a pass since Karmen had just saved their lives, but how she could turn away from the first survivors they'd seen in weeks was unreal.

Crash parked the Humvee a few yards shy of where the group was sitting. He opened his door and one of the adults in the group, a tall man who looked to be in his fifties, stood and walked toward them. Noah opened the back door for her and she jumped out.

Karmen and the girl stayed inside.

"Hey man, you guys doing okay?" Noah asked, shaking the man's hand.

He shrugged and squinted toward the direction of the smoke billowing up around Baltimore's city limits. "We spent the last twenty-four hours trying to get away from the fire, but we finally had to stop and rest. We lost our car back a ways and had to trudge through the woods to get to someplace we could breathe again."

He sounded tired, his voice almost flat. Maybe he was in shock.

"Do you guys need anything?" Parrish asked. She hadn't asked Crash if it was okay to start handing out his supplies, but she didn't think he'd mind. They had plenty to go around for a while, and these people had obviously been through some rough times.

The man's eyes widened. "Do you have water? Food? We have nothing left," he said. He gestured toward his small group. "Most of us haven't had anything to eat or drink in a couple of days other than some water we got out of the creek down the way and a few bags of chips and other junk food we had in our packs."

Parrish looked at the group of people on the tracks. Three of them were small children, no older than Zoe had been. Two others were women, probably in their twenties. There were five men of varying ages ranging from teens to middle age. She wondered if they were a family or just random people from Baltimore who'd managed to get out in time.

"We've got a few bottles of water and some food we can spare," Crash said.

"How did the fire get started?" Noah asked.

The man followed Crash toward the back of the Humvee. "We're not sure what started it, but it originated somewhere downtown," he said. "It could have been anything. Everything's just..."

His voice trailed off, but Parrish knew what he meant. It still just didn't seem like normal, real conversation to be talking about bodies getting up and walking after they were dead.

She went around to the back of the vehicle and grabbed a case of bottled water. She lifted it up and walked over to the rest of the group. She set it down on the ground and pulled her sword from her back then sliced through the plastic that held it all together.

When she grabbed a couple of bottles and looked up, she saw the fear and awe in the eyes of all the survivors. She almost laughed. Yeah, it would probably be weird to see someone pulling out a katana to open up a case of water. Everything had changed so quickly it felt like second nature to her now to use the sword.

She put it away quickly, though, and handed out the water. They were guzzled down so fast, it made her stomach hurt just thinking about how scared and thirsty they must have been.

Noah came over and started handing out packs of nuts and crackers.

"You guys doing okay?" he asked the smaller kids.

They nodded, but Parrish could see in their eyes that they were not okay. Something in her heart tugged at her to stay and take care of them. She would have given anything for the chance to take care of Zoe.

Tears stung her eyes and she looked away.

"Most of the walking dead burned up in the fire, I think," the older man was saying as he and Crash walked over carrying a few more boxes of supplies.

"I wouldn't count on it," Crash said. "We ran into a huge horde of them on the road a few miles back. The smoke and fire seemed to be pushing them away from the city. They could easily head this way. You guys need to find shelter."

"Where will you sleep?" Parrish asked.

One of the women stood. "There's a house just outside of town here that belonged to my mother. It's been empty for a while, but it's big enough for our group. We'll be alright. We'll be safe there."

Noah looked to Parrish and when their eyes met, she knew they were thinking the same thing.

No one was safe anywhere. Not anymore.

Maybe not ever again.

THIRTY

KARMEN

K armen sat in the back of the Humvee, her jaw tense and her legs crossed underneath her. The others were outside giving away half their water and food and she was stuck in the truck with the girl. She had a bad feeling about this girl, like she'd been keeping secrets from them.

A headache pounded in her skull, and all Karmen really wanted to do was close her eyes and sleep. Connecting with that huge group of rotters on the highway had taken a lot out of her. And it had honestly scared her to her core.

No human should have that kind of power. It made her feel dangerous, like she couldn't quite trust herself.

She leaned her head against the back of the seat and closed her eyes.

They had managed to get through that group of rotters by some miracle, but what happened if she couldn't do it again? What other horrors were they going to face on the road?

There was no way to know, but stopping to give away a

bunch of their limited supplies to people they didn't even know was not the answer.

It wasn't that Karmen was completely cold-hearted. She was happy to finally see some survivors, but Parrish and the others needed to get real about how the world was going to work from now on. It was every man for himself out there now. Karmen knew it even though they hadn't had a chance to see it first hand. She wasn't stupid. She knew the horrible things seemingly good people hid behind their perfect families and respectable jobs.

There was no reason to hide the ugliness now. No one would send the bad men to jail, so why not show their true nature? Why not take the things they always wanted?

No government. No consequences.

People would be different now. They weren't going to accept a couple of cases of water and say thank you from the bottom of their hearts.

No, people would see that you had supplies and they would do whatever they had to do to take all of it. They would see kindness as a weakness, and they would exploit and manipulate. It was human nature, and with no government to tell people otherwise, the whole world would go to shit.

Karmen scowled and glanced through the windshield. Noah, Parrish, and Crash were still out there talking to the group of soot-covered people. The older man pointed toward the road that led out of town. Maybe he was giving them directions to a safe place where they could stay. Karmen hoped they were wrapping things up so they could get the heck out of here soon. She did not want to be stranded somewhere on the road come nightfall.

"What's wrong?"

The girl's voice startled her, and Karmen tensed.

"Why do you care?"

The girl shrugged and looked toward the front windows. "I just wonder if these people are your friends or if you somehow got stuck with them and can't seem to get unstuck," she said. "At first, I thought you guys were all close friends from before, but you don't seem to particularly like them much. Especially the other girl. Parrish."

Karmen swallowed and shifted her legs on the seat. "What about her?"

The girl's eyes seemed to see right through her, and Karmen squirmed under the feel of her gaze.

"You guys were friends before this all happened?" she asked.

Karmen looked down at her fingers and picked at the pink nail polish she'd just put on the other day. It was already ruined from her messing with it, and she realized she'd left the bottle at Crash's. "We were frenemies, I guess."

The girl shook her head. "What's a frenemy?"

Karmen rolled her eyes. Seriously. What planet did this girl grow up on? She seemed to be about their same age, but she was clueless. They'd had to teach her every card game yesterday, as if she'd never played in her life. Then there was that weird cloak in her bag. What was her deal?

"Friends, but enemies," Karmen said.

"How can you be both at the same time?" the girl asked.

Karmen shrugged again and peeled another long section of paint off her nails. "I guess you really can't."

She looked up to see Parrish and Noah squatting together by the supplies, their eyes locked on each other. It twisted her stomach to see them so lovey dovey. They should just kiss already and get it over with.

She pressed her lips together and swallowed her feelings of regret. She'd liked him for such a long time, but it had been his best friend Aaron who had shown interest in dating her. Not Noah.

Never Noah.

Karmen had really only gone out with Aaron to try to make Noah jealous. She'd thought maybe if he had to see her with another guy every day, he would realize how much he liked her.

That plan backfired horribly. She should have known better, really. Noah wasn't the type to ever betray a friend. Once she agreed to go out with Aaron, she was pretty much guaranteeing that Noah would never go out with her. Even if he had liked her.

Which she was sure now he never had. Not in that way, at least.

Thinking back, it seemed that he must have always had a thing for Parrish.

Why had she never realized that before? And why on earth had he never acted on it? Even now that they were all together and were literally, like, the last people on earth, he still hadn't told her how he felt about her. At least not that Karmen could tell.

She peeled the last of the paint off her nails and sighed. She needed to get over it. She couldn't torture herself with this forever. Especially if she was going to be with this group for the rest of her life—however long that might be.

She couldn't even imagine being parted from them anymore. No matter what else happened, they were in this thing together, for better or for worse. And whatever was happening between Parrish and Noah, it was right somehow. Meant to be.

That didn't mean she had to like it, though.

"I was wrong," she said to the girl. She watched as Parrish touched Noah's arm and smiled. "I think you actually can be close to someone—maybe love them—even if you don't always like them."

THIRTY-ONE

THE WITCH

The witch watched as Karmen stared longingly at the others.

These people were so easy to read. They wore their emotions on their faces like badges of honor.

This girl, Karmen, obviously had a thing for Noah, even though he didn't return her affection. Still, there was a part of her that felt sorry for Karmen. When she'd touched her arm earlier, she'd seen visions of the horrible things the girl's father had done to her.

The witch understood that kind of pain. The pain that came from betrayal by the very ones who were supposed to protect you.

She hadn't expected to feel such a connection to Karmen. She'd judged her as a selfish girl with no concern for anyone around her, but the truth was that she kept everyone at a distance in order to protect herself.

The witch had done the same thing for most of her own life.

She was supposed to hate the guardians. To destroy them at all costs. But now that she knew more about Karmen's past, her feelings of pity confused her.

She wanted to tell Karmen to move on. No matter what she might feel for Noah, there was no hope of a romantic relationship with him.

Noah and Parrish had always been a couple, lifetime after lifetime. Whether they realized it or not, the witch knew the stories about the guardians. The leader and her lover. Their relationship and the sacrifices they'd made for each other were legendary.

Back home, the two sides didn't mix. The Iceborn lived on an island to the north, while the Fireborn lived on the southern island. The two races rarely spoke or mingled unless they had business in the Middlelands.

It was forbidden for an Iceborn and a Fireborn to fall in love and start a family. The danger of producing a hybrid child was simply too great.

Hybrids, capable of wielding both sides of the world's powers, were rare but extremely powerful. And extremely dangerous.

One power was often dominant, but the most disciplined and powerful hybrids had learned to control both sides, some even learning to combine them, creating an entirely new strain of magic.

After the Dark One was banished to the human world, the elders declared that the very existence of a hybrid was dangerous to everyone in their world. They created a law forbidding Iceborn and Fireborn to marry or have a child together. Any baby born a hybrid under the new law was sentenced to death, so for the most part, the people obeyed, afraid of a power too great for them to understand.

Legends say that before the war, most hybrids either went insane—killing everyone in sight and destroying entire villages with their rage—or they became too powerful for the Councils of Fire and Ice to control.

The Dark One had been the first, most powerful hybrid of all, threatening the Councils' rule. She'd been born back in a time when marriage between the two sides was still permitted. Before the world knew how dangerous it might be. When her parents discovered her gifts, they worked with her tirelessly, training her in both sides of her power day and night.

As she grew older and stronger, her abilities grew beyond her parents' wildest dreams. She wielded the very power of life and death. She could heal someone who had been pierced through the heart with a sword, bringing them back from the dead. And she could kill the most powerful sorcerer with nothing more than a flick of her wrist.

By the time she was an adult, there were whispers of her overthrowing the elders of both councils and becoming Queen of both kingdoms, uniting them for the first time under one ruler. The elders made the mistake of trying to lock her away, and their actions had started a war that lasted more than a hundred years, leaving both kingdoms in poverty and ruin for decades after.

It was the guardians that had ended the war, finally banishing the Dark One to this world and trapping her inside an icy prison beneath the earth. Their names were still celebrated centuries later, and they were regarded as heroes. The saviors of their people.

But not everyone agreed that the guardians were right.

The witch grew up hearing tales of the Dark One whispered in the shadows among some in the city who believed she was wrongly banished. As a young girl, the witch came to idolize the Dark One, wishing that someday her own name would be spoken in such reverent tones.

Of course, growing up, these tales of guardians and war seemed more like a fairytale. Legends had sprung up over the years, and no one really knew which stories were true and which were not.

But the Dark One was real.

And she wanted the witch to be her most trusted servant.

She should be happy, but she hadn't expected the Dark One to be so cruel. The witch cradled her burned arm against her body. Hadn't she done everything the Dark One had asked of her? Hadn't she been the one to break the magical seal that kept her mistress from casting magic? The entire virus and the Dark One's growing powers were because of her.

Why did she torture her this way every time they spoke?

The guardians, on the other hand, had been nothing but kind. They had risked their lives to save her, given her food and shelter, and included her in their group without question.

Was she really on the right side in all of this?

The witch straightened her shoulders and filled her lungs. No, she would not let her devotion waver. The Dark One was her path to glory, and she wouldn't mess that up. Not now. Not after everything she'd done.

The elders would be brought to their knees when the Dark One returned to exact her vengeance, and the young witch would be there at her side, showing them all that they should have never underestimated her.

In the end, her pain would be worth it, just to see the looks on the elders' faces when she brought them down.

The only thing standing in the way of her dreams now were the guardians. If she could keep them from each other long enough, the Dark One would go free and they could return to the homeland.

But how was she going to do it?

They were just children, really. Without their mentor and their memories, they were practically harmless. The witch knew her most important duty was to make sure they never reunited with the true fifth. She had to distract them from their mission and their dreams and find a way to tear them apart.

She had to figure out their weaknesses and find a way to destroy them. She couldn't let their kindness sway her.

Besides, one of them had been through her bag. She'd noticed her cloak was crumbled up, not neatly folded the way she usually did it. How kind could they be if they were going through her things without her permission?

At least they hadn't found the stone.

She would need to get rid of the cloak, of course. It was too suspicious and strange for this world, and it would bring up questions. At her first opportunity, she would have to slip into a clothing store and switch it out for normal human clothing. She already mourned the loss of her cloak. It was her most beloved possession, but she had more important matters to deal with now.

As she watched Karmen's face, seeing the agony of unrequited love, the witch knew exactly where she needed to start. Their powers were growing and as long as they worked together, they would not be so easily destroyed by hordes of rotters and fire and pestilence.

Their weakness was in their emotions. Their trust and vulnerability towards each other.

A few well-timed lies and any human could be manipulated to feel whatever you wanted them to feel. Jealousy. Fear. Heartache.

As the rest of the group climbed back into the Humvee, the witch looked from Noah to Parrish and back again. The relationship between those two was the strongest of any in the entire group. The closer they got to each other, the more likely they were to risk everything to keep the other safe. They would work together, and if there was one thing that was true about the ancient guardians, it was that the more they worked together, the more powerful they all became.

Parrish was their leader, but without Noah, she would be weak. If the witch could make them doubt each other now, before the full memory of their love emerged, the entire group might fall apart.

Karmen moved to the back of the Humvee and Noah took the seat up front with Crash. When he glanced back to ask if they were all ready to get back on the road, the witch caught his eye and smiled.

He paused in his words, as if he'd momentarily forgotten what he was trying to say. Then, slowly, he smiled back.

She held his gaze for a long moment, feeding him with their connection. Making him believe there was something important between them. Her powers of coercion and manipulation would be easy to use against someone so innocent and caring.

Beside her, Parrish tensed and cleared her throat. "Are we going?"

Noah blinked and shook his head, as if coming out of a daydream. "Yeah, let's head out," he said. "We need to find a safe place to buckle down for the night."

He nodded to Crash and the engine revved. The witch kept her eyes on Noah, watching as he waved to the survivors they'd helped.

As she knew he would, he dared one last glance back toward her, their eyes meeting for only a moment before she looked away, her cheeks flushed.

In an instant, the mood in the Humvee changed. Parrish's confusion and doubt hovered near her like a dark cloud.

The burns on the witch's arm tingled, and she pulled it tight against her body, warming herself with its decay.

THIRTY-TWO

NOAH

They were back on the road, but Noah was restless.

He kept glancing at the new girl, wondering if there was something she needed to say to him. They'd hardly spoken since she'd been brought into the group, but today when he got back in the truck, they'd shared something. He couldn't quite explain it.

He'd felt connected to her somehow. He'd actually imagined, for the briefest moment, what it would have been like to kiss her.

There was no doubt she was beautiful, but he didn't even know the first thing about her. Not even her name. Where had these feelings come from?

He couldn't shake it. Maybe when they stopped again, he'd offer the front seat to Parrish again so he'd have a chance to talk to the girl. Get to know her. But the thought of being attracted to someone else made him uncomfortable. Wasn't he finally getting somewhere with Parrish? He'd felt connected to her his whole life. He didn't need to complicate it by thinking there was something special about the girl they'd picked up in D.C. He was probably just feeling the effects of their group's connection. Nothing more.

He sighed and turned around.

He also couldn't get the survivors of the burned town out of his mind. They were the first people the group had seen in a very long time, which gave him some hope that there were people still out there fighting to stay alive through the worst of this thing. But at the same time, these were grown men and women barely hanging on by a thread.

It sent chills up his arms. What if mankind didn't survive this?

It was the first time the thought had really come across his mind. Before now, he'd known that the virus and everything that came with it had destroyed billions of lives. But still, he'd never once entertained the idea that humanity wouldn't eventually win this fight.

Now that they were out in the thick of it, actually seeing what was going on out here, he was more afraid than ever.

As if to punctuate that fear, a group of hungry undead appeared in the distance, all huddled together at the edge of the highway.

"What's going on up there?" he asked, pointing toward the group.

Crash squinted ahead. "Good call," he said. He slowed the Humvee down just a little bit as they approached.

They moved closer and Noah suddenly realized what had brought this group out here during the hottest hour of the day.

There were six of them all huddled around a single object. A body. Noah watched as one of the zombies—a girl who couldn't have been much older than him—reached into the stomach of the body on the ground. She tore something from its innards and shoved it into her mouth.

Noah looked away, feeling sick. "Jesus," he said.

They were eating someone like buzzards on roadkill. He was going to be sick just thinking about it.

It was one thing to see hints of it on video or to get the feeling that this was happening, but to actually see it with his own eyes was something else entirely.

"What is it?" Parrish asked from the back. She leaned forward to try to get a better look, but he shook his head and held his hand out.

"You don't want to see," he said. He turned to Crash. "Just keep moving."

Crash had been staring at the group, nearly bringing their vehicle to a stop so he could get a better look.

"That's the most disgusting thing I've ever seen in my life."

"Come on, man, seriously, let's get out of here."

Some of the zombies were starting to look up from the mangled corpse. They didn't need that kind of attention. No matter how safe they felt inside this Humvee right now, they didn't need to be taking any chances.

One of the zombies opened its mouth in a type of hiss and stood up, staring straight at Noah.

"I mean it, man, let's go."

Noah smacked Crash's arm, which seemed to bring the guy out of whatever trance he'd been in. Crash nodded and tore his eyes away from the group of undead.

The Humvee sped away, but Noah couldn't get the girl's bloody face out of his mind. And he couldn't stop wondering if the person she'd been eating was someone she used to know.

I t was nearly an hour later when they finally stopped to take a break. Karmen had been in the back complaining that she had to pee for the past forty minutes, and apparently, Crash had finally had enough.

Plus, this was the first place they'd come to that didn't look extremely dangerous. Most of the towns they'd passed had either been burning or crawling with rotters. This was the first place that didn't show signs of total destruction, so they decided to take their chances.

They'd navigated through a maze of abandoned cars, but other than that, there was no sign that anything bad had even happened here. It just looked like a quiet afternoon.

Crash pulled into the parking lot of a small gas station. "I'm going to check and see if there's any gas left in these pumps," he said. "I think I can run the truck without gas, but it's easier on me if I don't have to. Karmen, there's probably a bathroom inside, but be careful. Just because it looks quiet here doesn't mean it's safe."

Noah opened his door, stretched his legs, and grabbed his bat. "I'll go in and check it out," he said. "Wait here."

Karmen climbed out of the back of the truck. "You've got to be kidding me," she said, dancing around with her legs pressed together. "I'm going to pee my pants."

"Better than getting eaten by a rotter," Parrish said.

There was a definite smirk on her face, and Noah had to hide a smile of his own.

"I'm coming with you," Karmen said.

"You don't even have a weapon," he said.

Karmen sighed and rolled her eyes. "You've seen what I can do," she said. "I can handle myself."

"You really think you'll be able to concentrate in your current state?" Parrish asked her, stepping up to them with her sword in hand. "What are you planning to do? Pee on them to death?"

"Fine, clear them out if there's any in there, but do it fast," Karmen said. "I'm serious."

Noah opened the door and let Parrish step in ahead of him. She held her sword in front of her and walked inside.

The place had a row of windows along the top of the main room which gave them a lot of light, but it was small and cramped and Noah knew one of those things could be hiding anywhere.

They went separate ways as they tiptoed around the rows of candy and chips and soda. Noah took the left side while Parrish checked the right. Neither of them said a word, but lately he had started to feel as if he could just tell what her next move would be. They were definitely in sync with each other, and it was a very cool feeling.

Their eyes met over the top of a shelf full of chips and Parrish shook her head. There were none on her side that she could see. He gave a single shake of his head, telling her that he didn't see anything either.

"Are we good?" Karmen asked. She didn't even try to keep her voice down.

Noah brought a finger to his mouth and she rolled her eyes.

Well, let her roll her eyes all she wants. He was keeping her safe. Did she really not see that, even after all they'd been through?

Something bumped around toward the back of the building near the bathrooms, and Noah snapped his attention away from Karmen.

It sounded like a bucket being kicked over.

He moved forward very slowly, his bat up and ready, and he did his best to listen for more footsteps or movement. Someone was definitely back there.

The moment he walked around the corner where the bathrooms were, a middle-aged man growled and lashed out at him, teeth bared and bloody. The guy had to have weighed at least two hundred and fifty pounds and he threw all of that weight onto Noah, sending him hard to the floor.

Noah's bat fell and rolled under one of the shelving units. He cursed and lifted his arm in front of his face. The man bit down hard and Noah was about to punch the crap out of him when the glint of silver on Parrish's sword flashed in his eyes.

The man's head fell against Noah's and clunked to the floor.

"That was gross," he said.

"Sorry." Parrish held her hand out to him. "He was biting you. Are you okay?"

He took her hand and stood. He studied his wrist. No marks except the blood from the man's mouth. "I seem to be fine," he said. He still hadn't told them about his experiment with the razor blade in the bathroom. "I don't think they can hurt me."

"Don't get too comfortable with that thought," Parrish said. She pulled her hand away.

"What do you mean?"

"I'm just saying that they may not be able to bite through

your skin, but that doesn't mean they can't hurt you," she said. "There's no need to get reckless."

He nodded. She was right. The moment someone got cocky was when they put themselves into the most danger.

"Let's check the rest of this place before Karmen pees her pants."

"Would that really be such a bad thing?" she said, eyebrow raised.

He laughed and walked back to the restrooms. They were clear.

"Karmen, you can come back," he said.

"Thank God," she shouted, running past him and slamming the door behind her.

"I'm going to use the men's room real quick, too," he said. "Then I'll head out and check on the others. See you back out there."

Noah stepped into the men's room and closed the door. It was pitch dark in there and he hadn't thought to bring a flashlight or anything.

The hairs on his arm kept raising every time he thought of the possibility of someone standing behind him in the dark. It made it hard to pee.

Finally, though, he finished and headed back to where there was a lot more light.

He didn't want to admit to anyone else that he'd been afraid in the dark all alone, but it was true. It gave him a very strange feeling, like he was being watched.

When he came outside, the door to the women's room was closed and Karmen was ransacking the shelves of the store, tossing everything she could into plastic bags. Through the windows, he could see Crash pumping gas and looking at something on his cell phone as if nothing had changed in the world. His ability to power anything he wanted was incredible, and Noah smiled. At least they had gas.

But where was the new girl?

Noah walked outside and glanced inside the back of the Humvee, expecting her to be in there, but it was totally empty.

He turned completely around, hand lifted against the fading sun. There was no sign of her. Weird. And dangerous. She shouldn't be anywhere all by herself.

"Hey, did you see where the girl went?" he asked.

Crash turned around and shrugged. "No. Did she go inside with the other girls?"

"Not that I saw," he said. "I'm gonna walk around real quick and see if I can find her. I just want to make sure she's safe."

"Okay," Crash said. "I'll be here."

Noah nodded and looked around again, trying to guess which way she might have gone. There was a row of shops across the street. Maybe she went over there to look for some new clothes? He'd overheard the girls in the back talking about wanting new stuff to wear. But why would she risk going alone?

He tried to ignore the part of him that had been hoping for a moment alone with her. After the way she'd looked at him earlier, he hadn't been able to stop thinking about her. He couldn't explain it.

Out of habit, he looked both ways before jogging across the street to the row of shops, and movement in one of the windows caught his eye. Long black hair? He couldn't be sure.

He kept his bat up and ready on his shoulder as he pushed

into the clothing store. With his foot, he slid a trashcan in front of the door to keep it open. Just in case.

When he walked inside, he felt something strange. Off. But he couldn't quite put his finger on it. He didn't like this place and he definitely didn't want to stay very long.

"Are you here?" He kept his voice to a whisper and waited near the entrance, half-expecting a group of rotters to come shambling out of the darkness. He really hated that he didn't know her name. They were going to have to do something about that. He couldn't just keep calling her you or girl.

Inside the store, no one moved or made a sound.

He knew he hadn't imagined the movement. But what the hell was she doing in here?

Reluctantly, he moved away from the door and ventured further into the shop. It was all racks of women's clothing, so maybe he'd been right after all. It was a stupid time to go shopping, though. What was she thinking?

"Hello?" he said again, a little louder this time.

At first, he didn't hear anything and almost turned around to go back to the gas station. But then, a faint cry sounded on his right. He turned toward it and moved quickly, terrified she'd gotten hurt or bitten.

When he found her, she was sitting on the floor, her back pressed against the wall of the shop. There was a shopping bag full of clothes at her feet.

Noah crouched down beside her, frantic. "Are you okay? Are you bit?"

She looked up and tears flowed down her face. Something inside him softened.

He looked for any sign of blood or struggle, but there was nothing. What was she doing down here?

"Hey," he said. He suddenly felt the overwhelming urge to touch her face. He wanted to wipe the tears away from her eyes and kiss her cheek. He wanted to protect her above all things and tell her that everything was going to be okay.

He didn't understand it, but he was suddenly so drawn to her that he couldn't even take his eyes from hers to make sure there were no rotters around.

She reached out for his hand and closed her fingers around his. "Oh Noah," she said, her voice a mere whisper that sent shivers down his spine. "Will you sit with me?"

He couldn't do anything but what she asked. He set his bat on the floor and moved next to her against the wall. She entangled her fingers with his and put her head on his shoulder.

"I came over here just to pick up a few things," she said. "I wasn't thinking about being alone. I'd been alone for so long, it didn't seem like a big deal. The whole town seems quiet. I thought it would be safe."

"I'm so glad you're okay," he said. "I don't know what we would have done if you'd been hurt."

They'd never spoken so openly to each other and he wasn't even sure where this was coming from, but there was something about seeing those tears on her face that had changed him.

The more she pressed her body into his, the more right it felt to be close to her. How had he not seen just how beautiful she was before now?

She lifted her head from his shoulder and he reached out with his free hand to wipe the tears from her cheek.

"I'm so glad you're with me, Noah," she said. Her black eyes shone with tears. "I need you."

"We all need each other," he said. His heart tightened. He

shouldn't be in here alone with her like this. It felt wrong, but at the same time, he couldn't help himself.

His heart beat a little faster as she gripped his hand. He couldn't stop staring at her lips. He leaned toward her, unable to control himself or think about what it meant. He just wanted to be closer to her.

A rack of clothes a few feet away toppled over and Noah grabbed his bat and stood up, prepared for a group of rotters. Instead, Parrish stood there, staring at them. He called her name, but before he could get to her, she ran from the store, kicking the trash can on her way out.

THIRTY-THREE
PARRISH

When they got back on the road, Parrish sat up front with Crash. She refused to look back and see if Noah and the new girl were snuggled up together the way she'd found them in the clothing store.

Her heart was all the way in her toes. She didn't want to admit just how much she was growing attached to Noah. She'd always been attracted to him, but lately it had seemed like there was something more growing between them. The other night on the roof, he'd really been there for her. Maybe she had read way too much into it and he was just being her friend in a rough time.

Parrish crossed her arms in front of her chest and stared out the window.

It was a dangerous time to let herself get attached to anyone, anyway. No one knew if they were going to be alive two hours from now, much less long enough to have a real relationship. It was stupid.

She would be much better off concentrating on survival and not letting silly things like this bother her.

Good luck with that.

She was already bothered, and nothing was going to change that. What exactly was going on with them in that store? Was he about to kiss her?

She tried her best to shrug it off, but every time the girl laughed or she heard the low rumble of Noah's voice in the back of the truck, her shoulders tensed.

"Do you have any music we could listen to?" she asked Crash.

He glanced at her and smiled. "I thought you'd never ask."

He reached into a small pocket on the inside of his green army jacket. The jacket was hardly recognizable as its old self with the sleeves torn off, but it seemed to look right on Crash. He had a bit of military spirit about him, even if he did like to break the rules. It made him both complicated and awesome at the same time.

He pulled out a small USB flash-drive and handed it to her.

Parrish raised an eyebrow. "What's this?"

"Music," he said.

She held back a smile. "Duh. What kind of music? I don't want to pop this in and find Justin Bieber blaring through the speakers."

Crash rolled his eyes. "Just play it."

Parrish stuck the thumb drive into the USB slot in the stereo and waited. She was hoping for anything but Classical or teen pop. What played was neither. To her surprise, Crash had loaded the drive with everything from The Beatles to Eminem. She was pleased.

An old Metallica song came on, and she turned the music up as she and Crash sang along at the top of their lungs.

And for just a little while, she forgot about Noah, the fires in Baltimore and D.C., her sister dying alone in New York, and the end of the world as they'd known it.

THIRTY-FOUR

CRASH

T he sun was getting way too low in the sky. They needed to find a place to stay for the night or they were going to be in trouble.

He'd been studying the towns and out-of-the-way places they'd passed on the road, but nothing had seemed right. Too many rotters in the towns. Too many trees surrounding houses out in the middle of nowhere.

At this point, though, anything was better than spending the night in the truck.

He turned the radio down and got Parrish's attention.

"What's up?" she asked, straightening.

"What do you think about this farmhouse coming up?" he asked, pointing to an old blue house in the middle of a field. "It's starting to get dark."

She stared out the window and nodded. "It could be good," she said. "There might be people living there, though. We can always knock and see, but just keep in mind that people might be pretty fierce about protecting their property right now."

"I know," he said. "There's a car in the driveway."

He slowed the Humvee and turned into the gravel drive. Slowly, he brought them up to the house and shifted into park. "I'm going to check it out. I'll leave the truck running, though. Do you think you can drive it if we have to get away fast?"

"Probably," she said.

"Why don't you move to the driver's seat and turn us around? If anything goes south, I'll jump in the passenger side and we can roll."

He grabbed the pistol from the cup holder and stuffed it into the back of his jeans. If there was anyone inside, he didn't want to scare them by walking up with a machine gun strapped to his back. Still, he needed to be ready for anything.

"Be careful," Parrish said.

"What's going on?" Noah asked, leaning forward.

"I'm going in," he said. "Watch my back."

Crash got out of the vehicle and walked toward the front porch. Behind him, he heard the door shut and the tires crunch against gravel as Parrish turned the Humvee around.

He swallowed a huge lump of nerves in his throat and forced his feet to move. As he passed the windows on the first floor, he tried to see inside, looking for any sign of movement. The curtains were drawn, making it too hard to really see anything.

He made his way up the steps of the porch and took a deep breath before he knocked on the door.

His feet tapped on the creaky old wood as he waited. Something banged inside, and he reached back, putting his hand on his gun.

He knocked again and listened.

Another crash inside, like glass hitting the floor. He leaned in, putting his ear to the door. Footsteps shuffled against the floor and he knew. No one was alive in this place.

He glanced back at the others and motioned for them to come up to the house.

Noah climbed out of the back, his bat strapped against his back and his shotgun in hand.

"There's at least one rotter inside," he said. "And it knows I'm out here."

"Maybe we should make more noise. If there are a few of those things in there, we can draw them toward the door, so when we open it, we can just blast them all," Noah said, joining him on the porch.

"Good idea," Crash said. "I hope."

He took the pistol from the back of his jeans and banged the butt of the gun against the door as hard as he could. "Come and get it, assholes," he shouted.

Within seconds, they could hear the scratching of finger-nails against the door. He couldn't make a guess at how many were inside, but at least this way, there was only one direction they would have to shoot.

"You ready for this?" Crash asked.

Noah nodded, stepping back to the edge of the porch, his shotgun pointed toward the door.

Parrish and the other girls had climbed out of the Humvee, weapons ready.

"You guys need some help?" she asked.

"Just stay back," Crash yelled. "And be ready to run."

He really hoped this worked. The sun was going down fast, and they needed to get inside. The house was in the middle of a field, but the stretch of dark woods in either direction had him concerned. There was no way to know how many rotters might be hiding in the shadows, waiting for the cool night air to go looking for food.

"Let's get it over with," he mumbled.

He turned the knob on the door—surprised to find it unlocked—and with a quick nod from Noah, he pushed it open.

A rotter stumbled forward and Noah blasted him with his shotgun. The rotter's head exploded and he fell to the ground.

Crash stepped back to Noah's side and aimed at the next target—a woman with grey hair and wild milky blue eyes. One of her arms had been half-eaten. Crash ignored the turning of his stomach and aimed for the spot between her eyes.

One by one, they took out the entire group of five rotters. From the looks of it, they had been a family once. Grandma, grandpa, a middle-aged couple, and a teenaged boy.

Crash leaned over the side of the porch railing and emptied his stomach. This was now the average American family? It was sick and twisted.

"You okay?" Noah clapped a hand on his shoulder.

Crash wiped his mouth on the sleeve of his tshirt. "Nah, man. There's nothing okay about any of this," he said. "But here we are. Let's move these bodies out of the way and make sure the house is clear."

He motioned to the sky.

"We've got about fifteen minutes left of daylight," he said. "Parrish, can you and the girls grab what you can from the Humvee and pull it right up to the porch, as close as you can get it? Noah and I will check the rest of the house. Once we're all inside, we can start moving stuff in front of the doors and windows, just in case it's a rough night."

They quickly dragged the bodies to the other side of the

porch and dumped them over the side. It felt wrong, like they should be burying them. After all, they had been people at some point. They deserved better than this. But there was no time.

Crash settled for covering them with a blanket he found on a chair in the entryway of the house.

"How should we do this?" Crash asked once he and Noah were inside the house. It was a big place, at least four thousand square feet if he had to guess.

"As fast as possible," Noah said with a laugh. "Just take it one room at a time. We'll go together, just in case."

Crash nodded and led the way. He started in the big family room to the right of the doorway, inching his way through, his pistol cocked and ready. It was getting dark inside, but he wasn't sure if he should turn on the lights. It would make their job of clearing the place a lot easier, but it would also make them easier to spot if anyone was out looking for a meal.

He decided to open the dusty curtains instead, letting what was left of the sun's light into the living room.

"Clear," he said. "Kitchen?"

Noah nodded.

They made their way through the entire downstairs and didn't see any signs of more rotters. Crash motioned the girls inside.

"We haven't checked upstairs yet," he said. "Come on in and get set up here in the main room, try to push whatever you can in front of the windows, but leave the front door clear until we've checked upstairs."

"It smells in here," Karmen said, scrunching her nose as she walked into the living room.

"Get used to it, Barbie. The whole world is going to stink for a while," he said.

She sighed, but he caught the hint of a smile as she pushed past him.

He started up the stairs, but by the time they reached the upper landing, it was just too dark to see anything.

"Should I turn on the power?" he asked.

Noah grimaced. "I don't know," he said. "We probably don't want to light this house up like a Christmas tree."

"That's what I was thinking, but damn, it's too dark to see anything."

"We could just make sure all the doors are closed up here and call it good," Noah said.

Crash was tempted to say yes. That would definitely make it easier and faster, but he didn't want to take the risk of a rotter here in the house with them.

"Let's just check the rooms real quick," he said. "You got a flashlight?"

Noah shook his head. "No, but I can grab one."

Crash stepped into the first room on the left while Noah ran down the stairs. He nudged the door open with his gun and peered inside. A shiny pink material had been draped across the windows, but enough light shone in to show him that this had been a nursery. A crib was pushed against the far wall, decorated with stuffed bears and pink blankets.

They hadn't seen a little girl on the front porch, and when he looked closer, something under the blankets moved.

Crash closed his eyes, his stomach turning on him again. He stepped forward, not wanting to see this, but unable to stop himself. He needed to know.

He moved closer, lowering his gun.

Carefully, he leaned over the crib and moved the soft pink blanket to the side.

Tears stung his eyes and he turned away, dropping the blanket.

Footsteps on the stairs made him move quickly. He didn't want anyone else to have to see this. The horror of it was too much. He quickly put an end to the child's suffering and walked away, shutting the door behind him.

Parrish met him at the top of the stairs. "Noah said you needed this," she said. She peered past him. "What's wrong? Find anything in there?"

He shook his head and cleared his throat. "No, nothing," he said.

He took the flashlight and closed the door behind him, wishing he could shut the door on all the horrors of this new world.

Once the doors and windows were secured, Parrish grabbed a flashlight and looked through the cabinets for extra food and supplies.

They'd already stripped some of the blankets and sheets from the beds upstairs and set up a group sleeping area in the living room. Sleeping in a bed would be more comfortable, but in the end, they'd decided it was safer to be close to the front door and to stick together.

Crash didn't want to turn on all the lights in the house, but they'd convinced him to turn on a couple lamps in the living room. They'd set them on the floor and made sure the windows were all closed up tight. Hopefully none of the light would show from the outside.

The others were all hanging out on the floor in the main room, but Parrish wanted some time to herself. She'd grown up with a lot of time to herself, mostly hanging out in her room with her music and her journals. She didn't like always being surrounded by people. She was grateful not to be alone, but at the same time, she missed the privacy of her own bedroom.

She made her way through the cabinets, one by one, taking out any canned foods or things that would last a while. In the last cabinet, she found the family's candy stash. A big bag of miniature candy bars, some Junior Mints, and a bag of suckers. Score.

She unwrapped a Blow-Pop and stuck it in her mouth. Cherry, her favorite. She hadn't had a chance to brush her teeth since yesterday, so candy was probably a bad choice, but she didn't care. It was delicious.

She leaned against the counter and took a deep breath. Was this what the rest of her life was going to be like? Scouring cabinets in abandoned houses for food? Having to constantly watch her back? Never knowing exactly where they were going to stay when darkness fell?

Where were they headed, anyway?

Crash had said he might know a safe place they could go, but he hadn't given them any details. Other than that, they were just wanderers.

Seeing those survivors on the side of the road had at least given her hope that there were others out there, still fighting against the rotters. They weren't alone in this world, even though it sometimes felt like it.

They just needed to find more people. Start some kind of new town where they could fortify themselves and create a safe place. It had to be possible.

A shadow appeared in the doorway, and Parrish reached for her sword, her heart jumping into her throat.

"It's just me," Noah said.

She relaxed and let out a breath. "You scared me."

"What are you doing here in the dark?" he asked.

"Eating candy," she said with a laugh.

"Seriously?" he asked, walking toward her. "Care to share?"

"You're welcome to it," she said. "But the cherry Blow-Pops are mine."

He laughed and flipped on his flashlight. He dug into the bag of candy bars and pulled out a Butterfinger.

When he turned and leaned against the counter, his arm brushed hers and she moved away. She could feel him tense at her side.

"Hey, Parrish, look—"

"You don't have to explain anything to me," she said. Her heart tightened in her chest.

"I do, though," he said. "I went looking for her and she was crying in that store. I was just trying to comfort her."

It sounded like the kind of line guys used when they'd been cheating on their girlfriends. But she wasn't his girlfriend. He didn't owe her anything.

"It's fine," she said. This conversation was ruining her cherry-sucker-happiness.

"It doesn't feel fine," he said. "It feels like you're upset with me."

He was right. She was definitely upset with him. She was upset with herself for believing there could be something good in all this craziness. But she also knew there was no use going through this back and forth all the time. They didn't have the luxury of playing cat and mouse.

"Here's the thing," she said, her throat nearly closing up. They had been dancing around this attraction to each other for what seemed like forever. Her entire high school experience had been defined by the silent looks they'd shared when no one was looking. She'd never had the nerve to tell him how she felt about him, but if there'd ever been a time, this was it.

"What?" he pressed, moving toward her again in the darkness of the farmhouse kitchen. His skin touched hers and this time she didn't move away.

"I have liked you for as long as I can remember," she said. "Probably since the first day I saw you moving into the house across the street when we were eight years old. I didn't fit into your group of friends—or anyone's group of friends, really—so I never told you how I felt about you. I didn't think it meant anything to you, but there were times when I thought there was something between us."

Noah tensed, but in the dark, she couldn't see his face to know what he was feeling or thinking. She was just going into this thing blind.

"And ever since the world fell apart, the connection between us has only grown. It's the worst possible time to try to tell you that I like you, but there it is. I more than like you, and even though the world is a mess, I can't help myself. I'm glad you're still in my life, and I want you to be there for a long time," she said. "Forever, really."

Noah turned toward her. "Parrish—"

"I'm not done," she said, cutting him off. She just needed to say what she needed to say. "If Crash is right about the five of us being connected in some special way, and about our powers being important to the future of the world, then maybe that's all this is, you know? Maybe that's all it's ever been."

"What are you saying?"

"I'm just saying that before we break each other's hearts, maybe we need to step back and think about the group," she said. She felt the sting of tears in her eyes, but did her best to keep it out of her voice. "Karmen obviously has a crush on you. And now this other girl? There was something happening in that shop earlier, whether you want to admit it or not."

Noah backed away, making a strange sound in his throat. "So you think there's nothing special between us?"

"I think maybe there's something special between all of us," she said. "And maybe it's easy to interpret that connection as something more than it really is."

Noah cleared his throat and even in the dark, she could see him run a hand through his hair and turn away from her.

"This is how you feel?"

She didn't know what else to say to him. It wasn't what she wanted to believe, but she had no other explanation. Maybe their attraction all these years had been nothing more than a sense of connection on a deeper level. It was something the entire group shared. It wasn't something special to the two of them, and if she didn't accept the truth, she was just going to get hurt.

"All I'm saying is that it's a tough time to try to decide what any of us are feeling," she said, a lump forming in her throat. "I'm grateful we're all together, but for now, that's all I can be sure of anymore."

Before Noah had a chance to respond to her, the new girl joined them in the kitchen, shining a light right in Parrish's eyes.

"Oops, sorry," she said. "I was coming to make sure you guys were okay. Crash wanted to talk about our plan for tomorrow."

"We'll be there in a second," Noah said.

The new girl turned to go, and suddenly Parrish didn't feel

like being alone with him. She didn't want to hear him say he was relieved that she'd finally started to understand what he'd figured out on his own.

She grabbed the bags of candy. "I think we were done in here, anyway," she said, balancing her flashlight in her arms and following the girl to the other room with a heavy heart.

THIRTY-SIX

THE WITCH

She couldn't hide her smile. She'd overheard the conversation between Noah and Parrish in the dark. Before she'd come into their lives, they'd been well on their way to remembering their past. One kiss would have likely brought their memories rushing back like a tidal wave crashing over them.

In one day, she'd managed to plant that small seed of doubt that would keep them apart and guessing for a while. She was proud of herself. It had been ridiculously easy, and that was just the beginning of her plans to disrupt their relationships and trust.

The others were waiting on the floor of the living room and the witch switched off her flashlight. "Found them," she said.

"Good," Crash said. "Ooh, you guys found candy?"

Parrish spread the candy out on the blankets, stashing the bag of suckers in her backpack. "There was some other food in the kitchen, too," she said. "I put it in bags and set it all on the counters. We can load it up tomorrow."

"Great," Crash said.

"I told them you wanted to talk about the plan," the witch said. She was anxious to hear what he had in store, too. As soon as she knew where they were planning to go, she could let the Dark One know exactly where to find them.

"I didn't want to say anything earlier, because I just wasn't sure I'd be able to get in touch with him with the current state of things," he said. "But I have this friend from a smaller town outside Philly who told me he'd managed to set up a camp in a National Guard Armory there. He was enlisted and went there to help out when things started to get rough. He saved as many as he could and fortified the whole place before it got too bad."

"A safe zone?" Karmen asked.

The witch watched as hope spread across their faces. They honestly still believed there might be such a thing as a safe place left in the world. They obviously had no idea who they were dealing with.

"Kind of," he said. "Not a government place, officially, but he told me they have a lot of weapons and food and water. I hadn't heard from him in a few days, but earlier I got a message from him that they're still doing okay. He said we're welcome to join them if we want."

"But?" Noah asked.

"The only condition is that we help them out when asked," Crash said. "He said that everyone has a job and they pitch in when they're asked to do special assignments like go on supply runs or things like that."

"Sounds reasonable," Parrish said.

"So we're all in?" Crash asked. "I don't want to take us

there if the whole group isn't comfortable with it. I want to make sure we're all on the same page."

The witch considered her options. It was obvious the group wanted to find a safe place to live instead of wandering around in the world. Depending on the security around this place, it might be very difficult for her to plan any attacks that would put the group in danger.

On the other hand, though, letting them feel safe for a while might be a good idea. She would be able to work on her plan to get closer to them and cause them to start doubting each other.

They were also less likely to use their powers when they were with a large group like that. The less they connected with that part of themselves, the better. All she had to do was stall them for a while, just long enough for the Dark One's power to grow. If they were inside a safe zone, they wouldn't stumble on the true fifth accidentally, and they wouldn't go looking for him. Once there, they wouldn't want to leave and risk the kinds of attacks they might find out on the open road.

When Crash had made it around the circle and finally asked for her vote, she nodded in agreement, deciding that above all else, the Dark One needed time. Let them think they were safe and normal, no different from the rest of the humans struggling to survive. Let them think their group was complete and that there was no rush to find anyone else.

"I think it's a good idea," she said. "Even just having this one day out on the road was terrifying. If Karmen hadn't saved us from that group near Baltimore, I don't know what might have happened."

"Oh, that reminds me," Karmen said, her eyes sparkling with excitement. She went to the other side of the room, rummaged in her pack for a second, and came back with both of her hands curled into fists. She held them out toward the witch. "Pick a hand."

The witch frowned. Was this some kind of game humans liked to play? She'd already learned to play some of their card games, but she was worried that her inexperience and lack of knowledge about this world would eventually catch up with her. There was only so long she could play the amnesia trick.

"Which one?" she asked.

Karmen laughed. "You know, pick a hand. Any hand," she said. "Whichever one you want."

The witch studied them both, unsure which was the right choice or why Karmen was asking her to play this silly game. Finally, she tapped Karmen's left hand, hoping she'd done the right thing.

Karmen turned her fist over and opened her fingers to reveal a thin silver chain.

"What is it?" she asked.

Karmen straightened the chain. "I found it at the gas station earlier," she said. "On one of those displays where they sell bracelets with everyone's names on them. I figured since you still couldn't remember your own name, it was time to give you one."

The witch's lips parted and her breath caught in her throat. "You're giving me a name?"

"Sure," Karmen said with a shrug. "If that's okay with you, I mean? Especially if we're going to a safe-zone and we're going to meet a lot of new people, we need something to call you other than 'girl' or 'you'."

The witch turned away, not wanting them to see the tears in her eyes.

She'd been taken in by the Council when she was just a young witch. They had found her roaming the woods near the city, unable to remember her name or how she had gotten there. None of the servant girls were given names by the Council of Fire. They were told they were unworthy, mere slaves with no value or purpose outside of serving the elders.

She had longed for a name her entire life, because a name would mean she had proven herself. She had worth.

"Do you want to try it on?" Karmen asked, holding the silver bracelet out to her.

The witch ran her fingers under her eyes and nodded. Karmen secured the delicate clasp around the wrist on her healthy arm, and when she touched the letters of her new name, she couldn't hold back the rest of her tears.

"Lily," she whispered.

"Do you like it?" Karmen asked.

She nodded and reached out to take Karmen's hand. "I love it," she said. "I don't know how to thank you."

Karmen shrugged. "It was nothing, honestly."

"This means more to me than you can know."

"What was the other one?" Crash asked.

Karmen opened her other hand all the way and held the other name up for them to see. "Rose," she said.

"Flowers?" Parrish asked.

"I guess it sounds morbid, but since we know this virus started from some kind of flower, I thought it seemed appropriate," she said. "Without those flowers, we might not all be together right now."

"Nice, so you named her after the virus?" Parrish said.

"They're still beautiful names," Karmen said. "And we're all somehow linked to this virus, aren't we? It has killed so many, but at the same time, it's made us new people. Like we were reborn."

"It's a beautiful thought. And I like the name Lily," Noah said. He touched her hand and ran his thumb across the letters. "It suits you."

"You think?" she said, unable to hold back her smile. She'd never been treated with such respect and kindness.

"Definitely," he said, meeting her eyes.

"Does it have a meaning?" she asked. "Other than the flower?"

"Purity, I think," Crash said. "They were my mother's favorite flowers."

"I love it," she said, wishing her soul was pure. She wanted to be worthy of her new name.

Crash smiled at her and then clapped his hands together. "So it's settled then. Tomorrow we go to Philly and meet up with these survivors," he said. "And for now, I think it's a good idea if we keep our new abilities a secret. I have a feeling anything or anyone that's different from normal is just going to scare people right now."

"Agreed," Noah said.

"We should probably think about getting some rest," Parrish said. "Who wants to take the first shift on watch? I was thinking we should rotate just in case something happens in the middle of the night."

"I'll start," the witch said. She didn't think she'd be able to sleep, anyway. Not now.

"Thanks Lily," Parrish said.

The witch looked up, gasping at the sound of her new name on someone else's lips. Parrish winked at her and the witch blushed.

I have a name, she thought as her heart fluttered in her chest.

When the others had switched off the lights and climbed under the covers to sleep, she sat in a chair by the window, her feet tucked under her body. She pressed the cool silver chain against her cheek and smiled.

This gesture went against everything she'd believed about the guardians. She'd grown up thinking the Dark One was unjustly punished for her part in the war, and the guardians were wrong for trapping her here in this world.

But what if she'd been the one who was wrong?

She ran a hand along the aching burns that pulsed with a pain she didn't understand. The Dark One said the pain would make her stronger, but hadn't she lived in pain her entire life?

It was unexpected kindness that suddenly made her heart surge with pride and power. She glanced back at the room of sleeping guardians. After a lifetime of feeling alone and ignored, this was the first time she'd ever felt accepted. Needed. These teenagers weren't asking anything of her. They simply invited her into their group without question and promised to take care of her.

It was the closest she had ever felt to having a real family.

But when she looked back toward the window, a servant of the Dark One was watching her, its eyes locked on her face. The zombie didn't move or beat against the window. It simply watched her, reminding her that the Dark One had eyes everywhere.

And that to betray her now would mean nothing less than death.

THIRTY-SEVEN

CRASH

E veryone was sleeping, but he couldn't shut off his mind enough to rest.

Maybe it was the baby upstairs in the crib, or maybe it was the dreams he'd been having lately, but something had him feeling restless.

Finally giving up on sleep, he sat up and looked around.

Karmen was on her stomach on the floor, her legs propped up behind her and a book open on the floor under the lamp. He smiled.

He tossed his blanket to the side and stood up, walking over to sit next to her.

She closed her book and sighed. "Can't sleep?" she asked.

"Not a wink," he said. "You?"

"It was my turn to stand watch," she said.

"It's quiet around here, at least," he said. "No signs of any rotters except the ones we killed earlier."

He didn't mention the baby.

"What are you reading?" he asked.

"Just something I found on the coffee table," she said. "Atlas Shrugged. Ever read it?"

"It's one of my favorites," he said. "Not exactly light reading, though."

"Tell me about it," she said with a laugh.

"I thought you said you didn't like to read," he said. He almost didn't mention it, because he liked the fact that they were carrying on an actual conversation instead of shooting insults toward each other.

"I lied," she said, and he could swear he saw her cheeks turn pink in the dim light.

"Why?"

She shrugged. "I don't know. I guess reading isn't exactly what people expect the head cheerleader to say she likes to do in her spare time," she said. "Plus, I didn't want anyone to start in on the dumb blonde jokes."

"The curse of popularity," he said. He put his hands behind his head and leaned back against the couch. "I was lucky never to be burdened with that."

"I know you're teasing me, but it's harder than you might think," she said, sitting up and crossing her legs under her. "Being pretty and popular isn't as fun as people think it is. People are always watching you. Judging you. Expecting things from you."

"So why give in to it?" he asked. "I mean, I know none of that really matters now, but why play the game if you hated it so much?"

She shrugged again and avoided his eyes.

"You work so hard to keep everyone at arm's length, don't you? Why is that?" he asked, knowing he might be pushing her too hard, but not wanting to let up. He wanted to know more about her. What made her tick? Why was she always so hard on everyone?

"You wouldn't understand."

"Try me," he said.

"My life wasn't as perfect as everyone thought it was," she said, her voice barely more than a whisper. "My dad, he was kind of a monster, to be honest. I guess I was always afraid if I let anyone in, they'd see it and they'd know."

"Know what?" His heart felt like it was about to beat right out of his chest. He'd wanted her to open up to him, but he hadn't expected this.

When she glanced up at him, her eyes were full of tears.

"Can we talk about something else?" she asked, swiping at her cheek.

Crash nodded, understanding everything now. She didn't even have to say it for him to know what her father must have done to her. If the bastard wasn't already dead, he would have hunted him down and killed him.

"My father was kind of a monster, too," he said.

"He was?" She sniffed and tugged at the pages of the book.

"When I was really little, we used to take a trip out of the city every summer to visit his family," he said. He looked around the room of the big farmhouse. "They lived in a place like this. Big and isolated. A real country place. My grandparents bred horses, and I used to love to visit their place. After growing up in a small apartment in the city, it was like visiting a mansion. There were eight bedrooms in their house, and I loved that I had my own space."

He wasn't sure why he was dredging up these old memories, but the moment they'd pulled up to the farmhouse, he hadn't been able to get those summers out of his mind.

"One summer night, when I was five, my parents sent me to bed and sat down to play cards with my grandparents and my aunt and uncle. I couldn't sleep, so I sat at the window looking up at all those stars," he said. "I heard a glass break downstairs and my dad started yelling. Naturally, I snuck down the stairs to find out what was going on. It wasn't really that unusual for my dad to be yelling. He was a mean dude, always shouting and saying terrible things, especially when he'd been drinking. But until that night, he'd never gotten so violent."

"What did he do?" she asked.

Crash took a deep breath, remembering that night like it was yesterday.

"He was yelling at my mom for spilling his scotch on the cards. He called her all kinds of terrible names, but I'd heard it all before. My parents argued a lot. I hated it, but I was used to it," he said. He brought his hands down to his lap and balled them into fists. "This time was different, though. My mom just wouldn't back down. They'd both been drinking and money was tight that year, so they were both overworked and stressed. My mom hadn't even wanted to go on the trip to the farm that year. She'd told him they didn't have the money to take time off, but Dad had insisted, saying he didn't care if they both had to work double shifts, he was going to the country like he did every year.

"Anyway, the argument got out of hand. I remember sitting on those steps in the dark with my hands tightened around the baluster. I had never been so scared in my life. My grandparents were trying to break it up, but my dad was huge. He was one of those big guys that was twice as big as his mom and even bigger than his father. You just didn't mess with him, you know?"

Karmen nodded, her eyes locked on his. Her undivided attention gave him the strength to go on, knowing in his gut she needed to hear this story.

"They just kept shouting at each other, and finally, my dad picked his glass off the table and smashed it against my mom's forehead," he said, cringing at the memory. "She fell to the ground like a ragdoll, and I swear to God, I thought he'd killed her. And he didn't stop there. He kicked her three times in the head before his dad finally managed to pull him away."

"Holy shit, was she okay?"

Crash shook his head. "Would you be okay after that?" he asked. "She spent almost three weeks in the hospital there before they released her. Dad had to go back to work, so he made me leave with him and head back to the city. In my five-year-old brain, I thought maybe I'd never see her again. I thought maybe if I disagreed with him, he'd kill me, too."

"I'm so sorry," she whispered.

"The day my mom came home, they hugged and kissed like nothing had happened," he said. "But after he left for work, my mom came into my room with a suitcase. She told me to pack it as fast as I could and not to ask any questions. I packed as much as I could into a tiny suitcase and she rushed me out to her beat-up old car and drove us out of Chicago as fast as she could. She called in a favor from a friend, changed our names and got a job in D.C. We moved from apartment to apartment, staying with friends of friends for almost two years before she finally saved up enough money to rent her own place."

"Your mother sounds like a very strong woman."

"She was," he said, blinking fast to keep the tears from falling.

"Did the virus take her, too?" Karmen asked.

Crash shook his head. "Cancer," he said. "When I was fifteen."

"Damn. That must have been devastating."

"You have no idea," he said. He didn't like to think about everything he'd had to do to survive when his mom died.

"What did you do without your parents? Did you have any place to go?"

"I followed in my mother's footsteps," he said with a smile. "I was resourceful. I was put into the foster care system for a while, but after I earned enough money, I bought a new identity off a shady guy and pretended I was eighteen. I quit going to school, staying on people's couches until I made enough money to rent that apartment."

Karmen lowered her head. She looked like she was going to cry.

"What?" he asked.

"I feel terrible," she said. "I was so ugly to you and insulting about that apartment. Just knowing what you went through to get that place on your own when you were alone and so young. I'm sorry."

On instinct, he leaned over to touch her arm.

The moment his skin touched hers, a vision flashed in his mind. He was transported to a place where a deep red ocean stretched out as far as the eye could see. The two of them were standing on a shore made of black sand, watching as the fiery waves crashed against the beach and lapped at their bare feet.

She was the same, but different. Older. Still just as hauntingly beautiful. She'd been crying over something, but he couldn't remember what.

Just as suddenly as it had begun, the vision disappeared and he was back in the farmhouse.

He gasped and pulled away.

Karmen's eyes widened. "What just happened?" she asked, her voice trembling.

"Did you see that, too?" he asked. He thought he was going crazy. It had felt so real.

She nodded, her chest rising and falling rapidly with each breath.

"Was that us?" he asked. "How is that possible?"

"I have no idea," she said.

She lifted her eyes to his and he knew her. Not just in this life. In many. He knew it deep in his bones.

"What was that place?" he asked. It couldn't have been real. No ocean on the planet was red like that.

Karmen took a deep breath and shook her head, her face going through a mix of emotions before she settled on a strangely beautiful smile.

"This may sound crazy," she said. "But I think it was home."

THIRTY-EIGHT
THE BOY

The sewers were his only chance.

He'd studied the maps of Manhattan and there was no other way. The streets might be less crowded with those things during the day, but there were enough of them roaming around even in sunlight to make it too dangerous for him.

The subway tunnels would probably be even worse than the streets. It was dark down there, and the boy had a feeling it was one of the places the dead went to hide during the day.

The sewers were the only place he could think of where he might be safe. Even if a few of the undead had found their way down there, there would be enough tunnels and hiding places for him to avoid them if he needed to.

He wasn't looking forward to being alone in the dark down there. He knew it would stink, but he would rather stink and be alive than risk the streets and die.

He wished there was a way to get his hands on a map of the sewer systems, but he wouldn't have even known where to look for one. Some kind of government building? It would be too dangerous even if he knew exactly where maps like that were kept.

His only hope was to go below the surface of the streets and try to follow them as best he could. He could tell just by studying the map that the guardian was somewhere on the island of Manhattan, near Central Park. He had circled a four-block area where he had felt most drawn to her power.

He would have to do his best to get close enough to where she was before he came out of the sewers to search for her. That would be the most dangerous part of his mission. Once he was above ground, he would be in danger of being seen by the rotters. If the Dark One found him, she wouldn't rest until he was killed or captured.

He could end up putting the other guardian in even more danger if he wasn't careful. But he also knew from his dream-talks with the old man that once they were together, their powers would increase. If he could only get to her, everything would be better. He would bring her back to his apartment if he could manage it. They could hide here together until the others found them.

It was risky, but what choice did he have? He couldn't stay here alone for the rest of his life. There was work to be done, and he couldn't do it on his own. He needed them, and they needed him, too.

Did any of them know more about what was going on than he did? Were they searching for him?

He was tired of being alone with his thoughts.

Tomorrow morning, when the sun came up, he would start his journey. He would take his time, sleeping in the sewers if he could, until he got to her.

The boy folded his map and placed it in his backpack. It was just an old Teenage Mutant Ninja Turtles backpack his mom had gotten him second-hand before school started, but he smiled when he looked at it. If the Ninja Turtles could handle living down in the sewers, he could, too.

He knew they weren't real, but zombies weren't supposed to be real either. Human boys weren't supposed to be able to run seventy miles per hour.

But he could.

He finished packing the supplies he thought he might need on his journey. A flashlight and some extra batteries. Food and water. A change of underwear. A black hoodie that was way too big for him, but would hide his face and keep him warm if he needed it.

When he was finished, he climbed into the safety of his dark closet and rested his head against the bag, thinking that before this all started, he had wanted to believe in superheroes.

Now, he had become one.

And out there somewhere, someone was counting on him to rescue her.

THIRTY-NINE

PARRISH

Waves pounded against the side of the boat. It was too small of a boat for such rough waters, but they didn't have too much farther to go.

Parrish looked around, part of her knowing she was dreaming, but another part feeling like it was more memory than dream. She'd been here before.

In the distance, she saw the small strip of land and pointed. Her companions nodded and kept rowing. Crash on one side, Noah on the other. Karmen sat at the other end of the vessel, talking to another young man Parrish didn't recognize.

No, that wasn't exactly right.

She didn't know his name and she was sure she'd never seen him before, but somehow she knew him. But how?

Inside the dream, she couldn't think clearly enough to know how she recognized him, but he belonged there with the four of them. They were a group, and they were almost done with their work. Just one important mission left before they could rest.

The boat finally pulled onto the small white-sand beach,

and Parrish jumped out, the skirt of her dress floating in the water as she helped pull the boat onto the sand.

"This is it," she said.

Her familiar katana was strapped to her back with a strip of tied leather, but she looked so much different than she did now. She was older and dressed in very different clothing than the kind she usually wore.

The others were different, too. If she had to make a guess, she'd have said Noah looked about thirty or thirty-five years old. He wore black pants and a white shirt, his hair long and wavy, tied behind his neck with a black ribbon.

"Do you have the stone?" she asked the young man. He had dark, smooth skin the color of ebony and his eyes were black and beautiful.

He nodded and handed the stone to her.

She stared at it, feeling its weight on her palm even in the dream. She turned it over in her hand, studying the symbols etched into each of its five sides.

A cross. A bolt of lightning. A rose. A spiral. And finally, an infinity symbol. She ran her fingertip over the last symbol, feeling along the grooves as something important clicked into place in her mind.

This is my symbol. It always has been.

"Let's get this over with," Karmen said, climbing out of the boat. "I want to go home."

Parrish caught her friend's arm as she passed. "We aren't going home," she said. "That's why we're here on this island. We can never go home again, don't you understand that?"

"What if I refuse to stay?" Karmen asked, pulling her arm away.

"We brought her here to this world," Parrish said. "It's our responsibility now to watch after the people who live here. We are their guardians now. It's not your decision anymore."

Tears welled up in Karmen's eyes. Her face had aged, but she was still a beauty even then. Her hair flowed down her back almost to her knees, and the wind carried it up like a sail.

"I didn't ask for this," she said.

"None of us did," Parrish told her. "But we cannot argue against destiny."

Karmen closed her eyes and Parrish grabbed her hand. They had been through so much, and it broke her heart to know that for them, it would never truly be over. Someday this world would need them again, so they had to do this one thing that would guarantee they were still around when the time came.

Together, the five of them made their way to the center of the small island. There was nothing more than a few lonely trees on this land, and Parrish knew that after their spell had been cast, it would be impossible for human eyes to ever see or discover it. This would be their place, the keeper of their memories.

She nodded to the young man and he smiled. He pulled a small dagger from his belt and began to draw an outline in the sand. A circle in the center with five lines radiating from it like the sun. At the end of each line, he drew a symbol from the stone.

When he was finished, he put his dagger away and closed his eyes. With palms raised toward the sky, he knelt at the center of the circle. All around them, the ground rumbled and shook. Black stone rose from the sand, filling in the design the man had drawn and making it permanent.

He opened his eyes and nodded to Parrish.

"Take your places," she said.

Each of them moved to their place around the spire, step-

ping onto the pillar that held their symbol. Noah on the cross. Karmen on the rose. The young man on the spiral. Crash on the lightning bolt.

Parrish walked to the center of the spire and placed the stone inside a five-sided hole. It fit perfectly and as it descended into its place deep inside the black spire, the line from the center to each of the pillars lit up with a brilliant light.

All except hers.

Parrish stepped carefully through the sand and stepped onto the pillar with the infinity sign carved inside.

A bright light flashed before her eyes and she opened them, sitting up with a choked gasp.

The dream fell away as quickly as it had come and she was back in the farmhouse, sunlight streaming through the windows.

She squinted and looked up at a smiling Noah.

"Sorry to wake you up, but we need to get going," he said. He studied her and frowned. "Are you alright?"

She shook her head and closed her eyes, wishing the dream would come back to her. She had the feeling she'd been on the edge of discovering something very important.

But all that lingered was the memory of the spire on the beach. The symbols etched into the stone. What did it all mean?

"I'm fine," she said. "I just had a vivid dream, that's all. Where is everyone else?"

"Loading up the truck," he said. He lowered his hand to hers and helped her up.

She stared at him, suddenly remembering the image of him standing on the white beach, his hair tied back and his face older, but familiar.

"You sure you're okay?" he asked.

"I'll be fine," she said. But the memory of the dream lingered long after they'd closed up the old farmhouse and started the journey to the compound. Something about it had rattled her. Something beyond the fact that it had seemed like a memory or that she'd felt connected to the symbols on the stone.

They were a couple hours into the trip when it finally hit her.

She sat up in the back of the Humvee and glanced over at the new girl. Lily.

Everyone in this truck had been there on the beach.

Everyone but her.

PART THREE
THE BETRAYAL

FORTY

CRASH

The drive to Philly was quiet and mercifully uneventful. The roads in some places were clogged with traffic, but it was nothing the Humvee couldn't handle. He'd been driving the whole way, and even though he hadn't gotten much sleep the night before, he was living on pure adrenaline at the thought of what might be waiting for them in Pennsylvania.

He'd convinced Karmen to ride up front with him and they'd talked about their favorite books the entire ride up. She was actually a pretty cool person when she wasn't trying to push everyone away.

They'd grown quiet as they got closer to the city, though.

The idea of a safe place to live was exciting, but there were so many unknowns. How would it change their group? Would they still be able to spend a lot of time together? Or would the bond they'd created slowly begin to unravel?

"Does anyone need a restroom break before we get any closer?" he asked, kind of hoping someone would need to stop.

It was around three and it was hot. He prayed the armory had air conditioning or it was going to be a rough summer ahead.

"I could use a break," Lily said. She stared out the front window and placed a hand to her temple.

Crash's eyes widened. How had he never noticed her hand before now? It had been severely burned, the scars traveling up beyond the sleeve of her shirt.

Had she been wearing long sleeved shirts the whole time she'd been with them? It hadn't occurred to him before now, but he was pretty sure she had, which was strange considering the heat. Maybe she was embarrassed about the scars.

She caught him looking and pulled the sleeve up past her fingertips, her hand disappearing inside the fabric.

He decided not to ask her about it.

"Do you want some Tylenol?"

"Tylenol?" she asked.

"For your head," he said. "The way you were touching your forehead made me think maybe you had a headache."

"No," she said, looking away. "I'm fine."

Crash continued down the road another mile and turned into the first place he could find—a pharmacy just on the outskirts of the suburb they were heading toward.

"My friend said most of the pharmacies had already been cleared out, but we may as well check inside to see if there's anything useful."

Everyone piled out of the Humvee and went through the process of clearing the place out. There were a handful of rotters inside, but it was becoming second nature to kill and move on.

Crash headed to the pharmacy section and jumped over the counter. His friend Tank had been right. Someone—actually, several someones by the looks of it—had already ransacked this place. There wasn't so much as a single pill left behind the counter.

"Find anything?" Noah asked.

"No. You?"

Noah shook his head. "The most useful thing I found was a pack of ballpoint pens and a few spiral notebooks," he said, holding them up. "Parrish and I have both been journaling. I thought I'd see if she wants a couple of them."

Crash smiled. How cool would it be to see Parrish and Noah's journals on the shelves in a bookstore someday, long after this plague had been eradicated and the world had gotten back on its feet? A chronicle of how they won the war against the rotters. It was a nice thought.

When everyone had finished in the bathroom, they climbed back into the Humvee and got back on the road. They were close now, and he couldn't shake the feeling that the whole dynamic of their small group was about to shift. Parrish held the map open to help him navigate through the suburb. Lily sat behind her, her burned hand on her forehead the entire time. Crash wondered if she was really okay.

The drive from the pharmacy to the armory should have only been about fifteen miles, but it took nearly four hours to navigate the clogged streets of the town. The place was a real mess, and he had started to worry that they wouldn't be able to find a way through and would have to resort to hoofing it. He finally found a street that was open and nearly cried for joy when the National Guard Armory came into view.

"Damn, this place is pimp," he said as he pulled up to the gate. It was dark out, but the armory was lit up with floodlights mounted to the sides. He leaned forward to get a better look at the makeshift barbed wire fence his friend had constructed around the building. "No rotters getting in here without taking some serious damage."

"Oh, thank God," Karmen said. "I had nightmares that we'd get here and find it overrun, just like that safe-zone we tried near our house. Also, I have to pee again."

Crash laughed. What would that girl do without modern conveniences like bathrooms?

"It looks secure," Noah said.

"Let me go talk to the guard and tell him who we are," he said. "I'll be right back."

Crash took his gun, just in case, and walked to the front gate. A small guard post had been built up by the fence. It was barely bigger than a small closet, but it was fortified with sheets of solid steel. No way a rotter was breaking through that. Through a small window, he could see someone sitting there, immersed in a Nintendo DS game.

Some guard.

Crash knocked three times, following the instructions Tank had given him the day before. A small slat in the middle of the upper half of the door slid open. A pair of hazel eyes peered out at him.

"May I help you?"

"My name is Crash," he said. "Tank's expecting us."

The slat slid closed and Crash waited as several locks clicked open on the other side. After a short wait, the heavy steel door creaked open and a tall, lanky white guy with shoulder-length, greasy hair nodded to him. He held a plain brown clipboard and a pen.

"How many?"

"There are five of us," he said.

The guy wrote it down on his paper. Man, they were really organized here. He hadn't expected to have to pass some kind of entrance exam.

"And how long have you been together?"

"Well, three of the others have been together since the beginning. They lived on the same street," he said. "The rest of us all got together about a week ago."

"No one in your group has shown any signs of infection or illness?" the guy asked.

Crash shifted his weight. "Do you think I'd really bring sick people into your compound, man? Seriously. Where's Tank? He said we were welcome here."

"Just answer the question."

"No, no one is ill or sick or rotting," he said. "What else?"

"Do you have any weapons with you?"

Crash raised an eyebrow. Was this guy for real? He was wearing a freaking machine gun strapped to his back.

"Yes, we have weapons," he said. "How else do you think we've made it this far?"

"You don't have to get an attitude," the guard said. "I'm just asking the questions I've been told to ask."

"We have lots of weapons," he said.

"I'll need to ask you to surrender them to me now before I can let you inside."

Crash shook his head. "No way. We wouldn't be alive without these weapons. What if the fence is breached? How will we survive?"

"We have children and families inside the walls of that armory," the guard said. "We're not taking any chances with new people. I'm sorry. If you want to come in, you have to give them up."

"And what happens to them then, huh? They become community property? Or we get them back when we're ready to leave?"

"We put all weapons into a secured room for anyone to check out when they're going on a mission outside the compound," the guard said. "We share everything here. Anything you bring inside with you becomes part of the community property."

"This is bullshit," he mumbled.

He hated to give up his guns, but there was no way Parrish was going to give up her sword. Not a chance in hell.

"Can I please talk to Tank for a minute?" he asked.

The guard leaned to the side and studied the idling Humvee. He glanced around and nodded. "One second."

He closed the steel door and spoke to someone on a two-way radio.

A few minutes later, the door opened again and the guard unlocked the main gate. "Pull her on in," he said. "And make it quick. We've cleared out most of the Z's around this place, but more of them just keep coming."

"Then I can talk to Tank?"

"Sure."

Crash nodded and ran back to the truck. He jumped in and waited for the gate to fully open before pulling it through. He parked it next to a row of newer Hummers and a couple white vans, sighing in relief as the gate closed safely behind them.

"What's going on?" Parrish asked.

"They have a few requirements before we can go inside," he said. "Including surrendering all our weapons and supplies."

"Seriously?" Noah asked. "Everything?"

"Everything," he said.

"There's no way I'm parting with my katana," Parrish said.

He sighed. "I know. Hold on, let me talk to my friend first and we'll get this sorted out. Come on."

They left their supplies and weapons in the truck and headed for the main door of the building. A tall, muscled man with shoulder-length salt-and-pepper hair stepped out and smiled.

"Crash? Is that you, brother?"

"Tank?"

"All right!" The man clasped Crash's hand. "We've been waiting for you guys. We were getting worried. We thought you'd be here hours ago."

He hadn't expected his friend to be so much older, but that was one thing about making friends online and in games. Age didn't matter.

"So did we," he said. "A lot of the roads into this part of town are completely blocked off, but we managed to loop around the city and find a path in."

"Well, we're glad to have you. Tell those friends of yours to hurry up and get their asses in here before the Z's get to 'em."

"Something tells me there aren't any rotters getting through that barbed wire," he said. "You've really set this place up, haven't you?"

"Rotters, huh?" Tank said with a laugh. "That's a new one to me. And, yeah we've worked hard to make it safe for our people. I'm glad you guys made it safely. I can't even imagine what it must be like to be on the road. How long were you guys out there?"

"Just a couple days this time around," he said. "There were some nasty fires blowing through D.C. and we had to leave."

He didn't mention the rats.

Crash turned back to his friends and motioned for them to join him. He laughed when Karmen practically skipped all the way to the door and barely said hello to Tank before asking him where she could find the bathroom. A petite woman with one long black braid down her back appeared to show Karmen where to go.

"That's my wife," Tank said. "Kaya. She's good people. If any of you guys need anything, just let me or Kaya know. We've already got some beds set up for you and dinner was just about to start."

"Believe me, that's the best news we've heard all day." Parrish stuck out her hand and Tank took it warmly. "Thanks so much for having us."

"My pleasure."

"There are just a few things I'm concerned about," Crash said. He didn't want to seem ungrateful, but giving up their weapons was a deal-breaker. "We've kinda grown attached to our weapons. We're willing to promise to put them in our bags until we need them, but most of us don't feel comfortable donating them to the community pool."

Tank nodded. "I can understand that," he said. "But you have to understand that this community only works because we're all willing to pitch in. We're all willing to share what we find and what we have. If everyone started laying claim to things they scavenged, we'd end up with a big mess on our hands."

"I'm not saying we won't do our part in here," Crash said. "Anything we find if we go outside the gates is yours. We're willing to share our food and water. But the weapons stay with us. My friend Parrish here has a sword that's been in her family for a long time. It's saved all our lives more than once. I'm sure you can understand why she wouldn't want to give that up."

Tank took a deep breath in through his nose and ran his hands along the belt on his jeans. "Alright, I can accept that," he said. "The weapons are yours, but they don't come into the building until we've built up some trust between our two groups. We don't want to risk any accidents or arguments getting out of hand. Put your things in your vehicle and lock them up. You can take them with you if you go out on a mission or God forbid, anything gets inside the gates, but other than that, keep it to yourself that they're in there. Deal?"

"Deal," Crash said, shaking his friend's hand. "Thanks."

"Now come on in and get settled. Everyone's anxious to meet you."

Crash and the others ran back to the Humvee to lock up their weapons and grab all their bags and other supplies. Once they were all safely inside, Tank locked the door. He was using six deadbolts, which Crash thought might be a little bit of overkill with the fence outside. He liked it. If it were up to him, he'd have overkilled the crap out of this place.

"Let me show you where you guys are gonna sleep, then I'll give you an official tour and introduce you around." Tank led them to a small room that was already set up with five cots, each one with a blanket and pillow neatly on top. Crash was relieved to see they'd still be together, instead of separated by gender. "A buddy of mine owns an Army surplus store. He and his wife brought over the cots and blankets and such. He also brought a few spare pairs of boots if you're looking for some sturdier shoes. They're all different sizes, so you're welcome to check them out and see if any of them fit."

"Thank you," Crash said.

"You said something about food?" Noah asked. "Sorry to interrupt, but I'm starving. We haven't eaten all day."

"Of course, let me show you to what we're calling the mess hall," he said. "It's really just a section of the main room of the armory. "

Crash was impressed. They really had a sweet setup here. It gave him hope that maybe there were other survivors who had grouped up around the country, making the most of it with safety in numbers.

"You guys still have power out here? Or are you guys running off generators?"

"We're lucky to still have power in the whole area," he said. "No telling how long that will last, but we've been stocking up on gasoline for the genny's once it goes out."

Tank walked the group through the main room of the armory, pointing out the different stations they had set up. A medical tent. Entertainment area complete with a TV and a Playstation 4 that a group of guys were playing. The boys looked up and nodded as Crash walked by. They looked about his age, only maybe a couple years younger.

"As soon as the news that people were rising from the dead hit the wires, I put the word out that anyone who wasn't sick was welcome at my place. After about a week, Kaya and I had so many people sleeping in our little house that we had to find something new. That's when I thought about this place. It was deserted, most of the government around here destroyed pretty quickly, so we made it our own. About a week later, we had nearly fifty people bunking here," Tank explained. "Everyone who came brought something with them. Food, water, supplies. One guy came rolling up in a big eighteen wheeler with these metal sheets loaded up on the back. Man, we worked up a sweat that night, welding those sheets onto every weak place in our defenses. We scrounged the barbed wire and fencing from various places around town and constructed that guard shack out front, and we've been locked up inside tight as a drum ever since."

"This is amazing," Noah said.

"Wait, I thought you said you only had about thirty people here now," Crash said, jogging a couple steps to keep up with Tank's big strides.

Sadness darkened Tank's features. "It hasn't all been roses and rainbows, my friend," he said. "We have patrols going out every day looking for more supplies and clearing out the Z's in a radius around our compound here. Sometimes, our guys just don't make it back."

"I'm sorry, I wasn't thinking," he said.

"That's life these days," Tank said with a shrug. "We're all just doing the best we can, trying to survive the best way we know how. We actually have a few guys who just returned from a run yesterday. They got pretty banged up."

"Bitten?" Crash asked.

"If they were bitten, we wouldn't have let them back in," Tank said. "I'm not willing to take that kind of risk for anyone. But they got overrun and had to bust their way through a big window and jump down two stories. They're cut up and bruised. The doctor thinks one of the men's legs might have a small fracture."

"You have a doctor here, too?" Parrish asked.

"She's technically a nurse, but she's a godsend," Tank said.

"I think nurses actually have more practical knowledge than most doctors these days. We're lucky to have her, but the one thing we don't have is medical supplies. We have a few things, but we're already out of antibiotics. Painkillers are getting low. We've already cleared out every pharmacy in the area, but most of them were looted long before we got there. Anyway, if you'll excuse me, I'm going to check on our men and make sure they're doing okay. I hope you guys enjoy your meal. Make yourselves at home."

"Thanks, man," Crash said, shaking his friend's hand again.

Kaya reappeared with Karmen at her side and showed them to the very back of the armory building where a set of long tables had been pushed together in rows, metal chairs evenly spaced along each side. About twenty people stood next to their chairs, paper plates loaded with food on the table in front of them.

Crash and the others went to stand by a few empty spots at the end of the table.

Kaya moved to the head of the group and held up her hands. All conversations came to a halt.

"Thanks for waiting, everyone," she said. "As you know, we've been expecting some special visitors. I'm happy to report that they have arrived safely. We'll make more introductions later, but this is Crash, one of Tank's good friends from before. He's brought Karmen, Parrish, Noah, and Lily with him today."

The group around the tables cheered and a large elderly man patted Crash on the back.

"Welcome, son," he said.

"Before we sit down to enjoy this meal, do we have a

volunteer to say the blessing?"

"I will." A young girl who looked to be about twelve or thirteen raised her hand and Kaya smiled at her.

All along the rows, people joined hands and bowed their heads. The old man next to him reached out and took Crash's left hand. On his right, Karmen held hers out to him and smiled.

"Dear Lord," the girl said, her voice clear in the sudden silence of the large room. "Thank you so much for bringing our new friends safely to us today. We ask that you watch over survivors all over the world. We thank you for giving us the strength and guidance to make it through another day. Lord, we ask that you bless this food we are about to receive and that you continue to keep us safe. In Jesus' name we pray. Amen."

The humble prayer touched his heart more deeply than he expected. Despite his mom often working two or three jobs, she'd always made it a priority to be home to have dinner with him, and she'd always started it off with a prayer similar to this one.

He missed her more than words could express. He'd never been religious, but as everyone around him took their seats, he sent up a prayer of his own, thanking God that his mother had never had to know the world as it was now.

And while he was at it, he thanked God for bringing them to the safety of this place.

There was something touching about this group of survivors taking the time to thank the Lord for their blessings, despite the messed-up state of the world. To his surprise, Karmen gave his hand a light squeeze before letting go. He looked up at her and smiled. Their eyes locked for a long moment before she stuck her tongue out and sat down to eat.

FORTY-ONE
KARMEN

Sleeping on a cot had never been her idea of luxury, but she'd never been so grateful to be sleeping somewhere other than the floor. There were no zombies pounding on the walls. They had power and hot showers. Food.

She'd actually slept a full eight hours without interruption. Other than a beautiful dream about an island with a pristine white-sand beach, she'd been completely out of it.

It was heaven, and she never wanted to leave.

They'd been at the compound nearly a week, and there hadn't been a single breach of the fences. It was safe here.

As soon as she was dressed, she made her way to the main room for breakfast. Parrish was already there, sitting by herself and writing in a journal. Karmen made herself a plate of scrambled eggs—still amazed they were actually getting real hot food for every meal—and plopped down next to her.

"Heya," she said.

Parrish didn't even look up. She just kept on writing. "Hey."

"What are you up to this morning?"

"I think it's called writing," she said.

Karmen glared at her, but instead of her usual snarky come-back, she tried again.

"What are you writing about?"

Parrish studied her for a second before going back to her notebook. "I've been keeping a journal ever since we got on the road. It helps to get my feelings down on paper."

"That makes sense," Karmen said, taking a bite of her eggs. They were warm and fluffy and perfect. "So, what are you doing after that?"

Parrish sighed and closed her notebook. "Why don't you just say whatever it is you're dying to say?"

"Okay," she said, wiggling in her chair from excitement. "I want you to go somewhere with me."

"Where?"

"You see that lady over there? The one with the cute red dress?" Karmen pointed to a middle-aged woman standing by the TV. "She was telling me that there's an outlet mall across the street. A week or so ago, a big group of them went over there and cleared out all of the zombies that were stuck inside. She said we could go shopping for anything we need."

"What do we need?" Parrish asked.

"You know, clothes and stuff."

"We have clothes."

Karmen finished off her eggs and briefly wondered whether chickens could get infected with the virus. "Yes, but all our clothes stink and half of them are covered in blood. The woman was saying they have a Coach store and a Saks Off Fifth outlet over there."

Parrish chewed on her lip for a second, but Karmen could tell she was interested.

"Come on," she said, leaning forward. "The guys are going to be playing with guns all morning. We may as well go have some fun girl time while we still can. Clean clothes? Clean underwear? You can bring your sword if you're worried about safety."

Parrish smiled. "Okay, let's do it."

"Should we ask Lily to come with us?" Karmen asked, looking around for her.

A strange look passed through Parrish's eyes. "Let's just make it the two of us," she said. "For old time's sake."

"Fine by me," she said with a smile. "I'll go tell the guys where we're going."

Getting over to the mall was a piece of cake. Tank's group had routinely done sweeps of the area, and the guard at the gate assured them he'd keep an eye out for them if they needed help.

They walked along the sidewalk in front of the stores, peering at the window displays and talking about what they should look for first. Karmen caught sight of the Saks outlet and nearly jumped for joy.

"Here," she said. "We can probably find everything we want in here."

Karmen opened the door and made a sweeping motion with her hand.

"After you, my dear."

"Why, thank you," Parrish said with a curtsy.

Karmen giggled as they walked inside. She had started to think she might never make it to a mall ever again. After what had happened to her last time she'd tried to go shopping alone back home, she wasn't sure she'd want to risk it, anyway. Knowing there was a safe place to shop right across the street from the compound made her even more convinced they'd made the right decision coming here.

"Where do we even start?" Parrish asked.

"Bags," Karmen said. "I'm obsessed with bags, and they have all the best designers here. Stuff that costs hundreds of dollars. Come on."

Her mother had only given her a small allowance, telling her it wasn't healthy to be so obsessed with material things, but her mother wasn't here, now was she? And everything was free for the taking.

She walked around like a kid in a candy store, running her hand along the leather.

Parrish walked around one of the sales kiosks and pinned a "Sales Associate" tag to her shirt. "Welcome to Saks, how may I help you?"

Karmen giggled and straightened her dirty clothes. "Ah, yes, I'm looking to purchase a bag."

Parrish held her index finger to pursed lips and nodded her head, as if trying to decide on the perfect item for her latest customer. "What type of bag are you looking for?"

"Something big enough to hold a pistol," Karmen said. "And a couple boxes of bullets."

"Hmmm," Parrish said, looking around the store. "Wait, I have just the thing."

They walked to the back wall and Parrish pointed to an array of leather messenger bags and backpacks. Karmen spotted a gorgeous pink cross-body bag and pulled it off the wall. "Valentino," she whispered.

"Yes, that's an excellent choice," Parrish said in her best

snooty-sales-person voice, but as soon as she looked at the tag, she dropped back to her normal one. "Damn. Eight hundred ninety bucks? For a bag? Jeez."

"You can charge it to my credit card," Karmen said, pretending to grab it from her back pocket.

They looked at each other and burst out laughing.

An hour later, they had each picked out new bags for themselves and Lily, several changes of clothes, and shoes Karmen declared were 'good for zombie killing'. It was the first time they had gone shopping together since the summer before they started seventh grade.

"Should we get something for the guys?" Parrish asked. They had moved over to the Gap outlet store, and were browsing through a rack of shirts.

"We can look," Karmen said, thinking back to that summer long ago when so many things had gone wrong. She followed Parrish over to the men's side of the store. "Hey, Parrish?"

"Yeah?"

"Do you remember that summer my parents took us to the Mall of America?"

Parrish threw the jeans she was looking at back on the table. "Sort of," she said. "What size do you think they wear?"

Karmen ignored her question, wishing they could go back to the days when they'd been friends. "I guess we never really hung out after that."

"Nope, I guess not," Parrish said, her bitter tone threatening the fun atmosphere of the morning.

A tense silence followed, but Karmen didn't want things to end like this. Today had stirred up so many memories of the past, when they were close. She wished she could make Parrish understand that she'd had no choice about what she'd done back then to destroy their friendship. "Do you ever wonder why?"

"If I'm remembering correctly, you were a complete bitch to me once school started back."

Karmen folded and refolded the same collared shirt. "I wasn't that bad, was I?"

Parrish moved the hangers on the rack of shirts next to her so fast a few of them fell onto the floor. "What fantasy world are you living in? You completely ruined my life that year. Don't you remember telling everyone that I had lice? Oh, and then there was the fact that you threatened everyone who was having any kind of party that if they invited me, you and the rest of the junior varsity cheerleaders wouldn't come."

"I only did those things because... " she sighed, her voice trailing off. She hadn't meant to ruin the morning. She'd only wanted to talk.

"No, please, tell me what I did to deserve complete social outcast status."

Karmen had pushed the conversation to this point, but now that the moment of truth had arrived, she was nervous.

"Tell me," Parrish insisted. "Please tell me you had some reason for turning your back on your best friend, besides me not being pretty or cool enough for you."

"Is that what you think? That I stopped being your friend because you weren't pretty enough?"

"What else was I supposed to think, Karmen? We were best friends for years, then you get on the JV cheerleading squad and develop some boobs and all of a sudden I'm not good enough for you anymore."

Karmen wanted to tell Parrish the rest of the story, but she was scared. Other than the other night with Crash, she had never told anyone about her father. She'd only sabotaged her friendship with Parrish to protect her. She'd seen the way her father had stood in the doorway of their hotel room, staring at her friend like he'd always stared at her. She would never have been able to forgive herself if she'd let him hurt someone else.

But if she told Parrish the truth, would she be able to forgive her?

Before she got the chance, she heard a shuffling noise to her left. Parrish started to talk again, but Karmen held up her hand and listened. Was there someone in the store with them? The woman in the red dress had told her the mall was totally clear of zombies, but what if she'd been wrong?

A low growl sounded from the shadows and before Karmen's mind could totally register what was happening, a woman jumped at her from behind one of the clothing racks. Her decaying hands wrapped around Karmen's throat and dragged her to the ground. She tried to scream, but she could hardly breathe.

Parrish pulled her sword from her back and cut off one of the woman's hands. Karmen pushed away and crawled forward, kicking at the rotter who was still grabbing at her with her remaining hand.

Karmen turned onto her back and kicked again, watching as the sword in Parrish's hand exploded in flames and came down hard on the woman's neck.

The stench of burning flesh turned Karmen's stomach. "Thank you," she said, coughing and swallowing to get the tightness of fear out of her throat. "How did you do that?"

Above her, Parrish stared at her sword as the flames died down. "I have no idea," she whispered.

"I thought your powers turned things to ice," she said.

"I did, too."

Parrish shook her head and offered her hand. Karmen took it, using the leverage to pull herself up.

"Thanks," she said again, trying to control her wavering voice. The attack had come out of nowhere and she couldn't fight the wave of emotions rushing through her. A sob escaped her lips and she covered her mouth.

"Are you okay?" Parrish asked. "You weren't bitten or anything, right?"

"No," she said between hiccup-like gulps of air. She couldn't seem to catch her breath. It was all just too much. Every time she thought they were safe, something else happened to bring her back to the horror of the world. She wasn't sure she could handle it.

She needed to know she wasn't alone in this, and she hated herself for treating Parrish the way she had all this time. She'd been blind. She hadn't realized how much she desperately needed a friend.

"I'm so sorry, Parrish," she said. "I never meant to hurt you. You have to believe me. I was only trying to protect you. I didn't want him to hurt you like he hurt me."

"What?" Parrish asked, touching her arms. "What are you talking about?"

"My dad," she said, sobbing. Wanting to get it out of her. Wanting to be able to let it go, once and for all. "I pushed you away so he wouldn't—"

Before she could finish, Parrish pulled her close and held her so tight, she could hardly breathe. Karmen's arms wrapped around her friend and they cried together, the weight of their past pain and anger lifting for the first time in ages.

"I didn't know," Parrish whispered.

"We should probably get back to the others," she said after a while, when she was finally able to speak without sobbing. She pulled away from Parrish and wiped her face and nose on a shirt from the rack.

Parrish smiled and raised an eyebrow at the shirt. Karmen shrugged and laughed, her lungs stuttering at the sudden intake of air.

"Hey," Parrish said, touching her arm. "Whatever happened in the past can stay there. We're here together now, that's what's important. And I promise, I'll never let anyone hurt you again."

Karmen nodded, her eyes filling with tears again.

"Come on," Parrish said, picking up some of the bags they'd filled with clothes. "Let's head back so we can try all this stuff on and make the guys insane with jealousy."

Karmen smiled through her tears and linked arms with her old friend, feeling light and free for the first time in as long as she could remember.

"If you're looking for some real firepower, give this sucker a try." Tank handed Noah a semi-automatic rifle. "This here's an AK-47. Russian military grade artillery. With this puppy, you could shoot the head off a zombie from half a mile away. Be careful, though, it's heavy as hell."

To Noah, it was light as a feather.

"Thanks." Noah pulled the gun to his shoulder and looked through the sight.

"Woohoo!" Crash slapped him on the back and held his own gun up in the air. From the looks of it, Crash had chosen a high-powered rifle. Noah also noticed a couple of pistols in his waistband. Someone was enjoying the unlimited firepower of this armory. "Is this the coolest or what? Let's head up to the roof and get in some target practice."

"What's up on the roof?"

Crash lifted an eyebrow and gave him a sly smile. "Why don't we grab the girls and go find out?"

"Don't go far with those guns," Tank said. "Meet me on the roof in five."

Parrish, Karmen, and Lily were sitting on the floor in their temporary bedroom, going through a bunch of bags filled with clothes. Parrish had changed into a pair of tight black jeans and a black tank top. Her long hair was newly washed and fell straight down her back in a way that took Noah's breath away.

"I take it your shopping trip was uneventful?" he asked. When she looked up at him and smiled, his heart did a double-pump.

"Nice gun," she said, raising an eyebrow.

"Guns," Crash said from behind him. "Plural. Now go out there and pick your poison. We're all heading up to the roof for some shooting lessons. If we're going to volunteer for any missions, we need to make sure we all know how to aim for the head."

"There's no way I'm going to use a gun," Karmen said, stuffing clothes into a tan backpack.

"Oh?" Crash leaned against the bedpost. "And how exactly are you going to keep yourself safe for the rest of your life?"

"I'll just use my mind thingy," she said with a shrug.

"Okay, that's fine for one or two, or even a group when you're inside the safety of the Humvee, but we never know what kind of situation we might end up in eventually. How many of those things can you control with your mind anyway? And for how long?"

Noah saw a look of concern cross Karmen's face as she considered this question. "I don't know," she finally admitted.

"The other thing to consider is that if we don't want these guys to know about our powers, you won't be able to use your mind control for a while," Noah said, glancing toward the door to make sure no one was standing in the hallway.

"Then it's settled," Crash said, grabbing her hand and pulling her up from the bed. "Pick out a gun just in case. I'll help teach you how to shoot it."

A few minutes later, the five of them were up on the roof of the armory with Tank as their teacher. "One thing we know for sure is that the rotters are attracted to noise," he was saying.

"Yeah, we learned that the hard way," Noah said, glancing at Karmen. Had it really only been a couple weeks since her screams had attracted a huge group to them in D.C.? It felt like months had passed.

Tank pointed at a hand-crank siren set up near the edge of the roof. "We had this siren installed, gosh, about twenty years ago? Mostly, it was for emergencies like tornadoes or bad weather or whatever. Only used it a handful of times, really. But this baby's responsible for helping us keep the area clear of zombies. See, what we do is crank it up and wait. With the noise this thing makes, any rotters within a two mile radius will head this way, thinking they're about to get fed. Even the ones who were inside, hiding from the sun."

"Then, when they get here, it's like shooting fish in a barrell," Crash said. "Brilliant, dude. That's awesome."

"Crank 'er up." Tank pointed to the siren and backed away. Crash jumped right in and cranked the handle. In seconds, a screaming siren blasted out across the parking lot below.

Noah lifted his hands to his ears. Dang, that was loud.

He scanned the surrounding area. A large warehouse was directly behind them. The mall was across the street. To his left, he could see a gas station and a housing subdivision beyond that. To the right, there was a grocery store. When the zombies started coming, they should be pretty easy to spot with all the open parking lots around. Tank had chosen the perfect spot for his compound. High ground. Easy line of sight. No trees to block the view.

He didn't have to wait long before he spotted the first one. A woman in tattered clothing stumbled toward them from the gas station. She had a terrible limp and her gray hair was matted to her head. Half of her face was already rotted away. Either that or something had been chewing on her.

"Why don't you take this one out, Noah," Tank said, pointing to the woman.

He lifted the AK-47 to his shoulder, lined up the woman's head in his rifle's sight, took a steady breath in then pulled the trigger on the exhale. A burst of bullets shot forth from his rifle and the woman's head exploded. Her body remained standing for a moment, and then slowly fell to the asphalt in a bloody heap.

"Sweet," Crash yelled. "You got one."

"Good shot, man," Tank said, holding up his hand.

Noah slapped his hand and smiled.

"This one's mine," Parrish said. She had also grabbed the same gun as Noah and was aiming at a middle-aged male lumbering over from the grocery store side. It took her a long while to take aim, but when she pulled the trigger, she was dead on. The zombie's face crumpled in a spray of bullets, knocking him back a few steps before he fell to the ground.

It was slow going at first, but Tank kept cranking the siren, and the rotters kept coming. Most of them seemed to wander in from the housing area to the left, which made sense. Noah wondered how many were stuck inside their houses, too stupid to open their own doors to get out.

They took turns with their shots. Karmen missed most of them, but Parrish impressed him with her aim and accuracy. The gun had some major recoil, but once she learned the feel of it, she rarely missed. Crash seemed to prefer the carpet-the-entire-area-with-bullets-and-hope-for-the-best style, sitting on his trigger and waving his gun around until most of the zombies were dead or unable to move. Not very efficient, but it worked most of the time.

Lily was completely out of her element. She had a hard time holding her weapon and couldn't seem to hit her target no matter how hard they tried to teach her.

As for Noah, he was a natural. He never missed, landing a perfect headshot every single time. Tank was starting to take notice, and he wondered if he should miss on purpose, just to make it look more realistic.

"Your turn, Karmen," Noah said.

She took aim and pulled the trigger. The gun kicked her shoulder back and the bullet missed by a mile.

"I can't do it," she said, setting her gun down on the roof. "This sucks."

"It takes practice," Noah said. "Don't give up."

He was trying to give her some encouragement, but apparently Karmen had ideas of her own. A group of four zombies were crossing the street from the mall in a little cluster. Karmen stared them down, and before anyone realized what she was doing, the rotters stopped moving, as if their feet were glued to the ground.

What was she thinking? Not with Tank right there on the roof. Not after they'd all decided to keep their abilities a secret.

Noah tried to distract him by pointing out an elderly man on the other side of the armory, but Tank had already noticed the strange behavior of the group.

"What the hell?" Tank asked, pointing at the small group that was now completely frozen in place on the sidewalk. "What are they doing?"

"Weird," Noah said, trying to act like he had no idea what was going on. "Crank the siren again, maybe?"

He nudged Crash and looked at his friend with wide eyes, as if to say *do something*. Crash took the hint.

"Hey Karmen, don't get so discouraged," Crash said, taking her hand. "I know what will make you feel better."

He stood in front of her and pulled her close to him, planting his lips right on hers.

Noah and Parrish exchanged a worried look, but it worked. Karmen lost her concentration and slapped Crash across the face, leaving a huge red welt on his skin. The rotters started moving again, stumbling toward the armory as the siren wailed.

Crash winked at Noah, who lifted his rifle and took out the group of four with four very precise shots.

Keeping their abilities a secret from this group was going to be a heck of a lot harder than he'd thought.

"Whhat the hell did you think you were doing up there?" she shouted. They were back in their room downstairs, and it had been hard to keep her mouth shut about it for the past half hour. Karmen had put everything in jeopardy for no reason.

"I don't know what you're talking about," Karmen said, sitting on the bed and crossing her arms in front of her chest.

"You know exactly what I'm talking about," she said. "We agreed we weren't going to use our abilities for a while. We don't want to freak these people out. You of all people have to agree we have a good thing going here, right? Why would you risk that? Just because you couldn't take a good enough shot to kill a rotter from fifty feet away?"

Karmen didn't answer. Instead, she turned away and picked up a book, as if she didn't even care that she'd put the whole group at risk.

"We have electricity here. Food. Safety. You were being selfish," she said.

"What's going on?" Lily opened the door and stepped inside.

"We were just discussing Karmen's childish behavior on the roof," she said.

"Why are you suddenly the leader of this group?" Karmen asked. "You can't tell everyone what to do and where to go."

Parrish took a deep breath, trying to calm her anger. Just this morning, they'd had a major breakthrough and Parrish had believed everything was going to be better between them. Why was Karmen stirring up drama now?

"Look, I'm not trying to be anyone's leader. I just want to make sure we stick together," she said. "If we make an agreement, we stick to it. We're guests here and they're being extremely nice to us, but all this can come to an end at any second, and we need to be ready to get on the road as a team. That's all I'm saying."

Karmen didn't offer an explanation for her behavior. Instead, she put her headphones on and turned on her iPhone.

"Maybe you should cut her some slack," Lily said. "You're always causing drama these days."

"I'm causing drama?" Parrish asked, hardly believing what she was hearing.

Lily sat down next to Karmen, a challenging look in her eyes that sent a wave of anger through Parrish's body. Was she intentionally trying to cause trouble in the group?

"Fine," Parrish said. "I'm going to get some lunch. I'll be in the dining room."

She left the other two girls in the room and stomped toward the dining area.

"What's wrong with you?" Crash asked when she sat down next to him at the table.

Kaya had made hotdogs and baked beans for lunch, and it smelled like heaven. Parrish was starving after her busy morning.

"I tried to talk to Karmen about what happened on the roof, but she's acting like a spoiled child."

"And that's any different from her normal behavior?" he said with a laugh. "It'll be okay. I think we covered it pretty well."

"Yeah? Well what about next time? What if we get attacked and she does it again?" She kept her voice low so no one else could hear their conversation, but she didn't even like talking about this out in the common areas. From the way Tank had stared at those rotters, she knew he'd understood something was off. Another instance like that and they'd all be back out on the street.

Crash sighed. "I'll talk to her again tonight when she's had a little time to calm down," he said. "Tank told me he was pretty impressed with our shooting skills and might be sending us out to do a job soon."

Her heart skipped. "A job? We just got here."

He shrugged. "Maybe we shouldn't have done such a good job on the roof," he said. "He told me they could really use some good fighters like us and that he had a job in mind for us. That's all he said, but I don't like the sound of it."

"I don't either," she said. She took a bite of her hotdog, unable to enjoy the warm food under the current circumstances. What kind of job did Tank have in mind for them?

"Don't look so worried," Crash said. "We'll take it one day at a time."

"It's one thing if he sends us out as a group of five," she said. She looked around to make sure no one was paying attention to their conversation. "But what if he sends us out with some of the others from their group? We won't be able to use any of our special talents, and what's worse, we could get attacked again by those things."

"Things?" he asked.

She stared him down, opening her eyes wider.

"Oh," he said. "The assassins."

"We could put everyone who's with us in more danger than they could possibly imagine. We'll get them killed."

He set his hotdog back on his plate. "I'll talk to him, okay? I'll tell him that if we go out, we go together and alone," he said.

"You don't think that will make him even more curious?"

"I don't know, but I'll just have to tell him those are our terms," he said. "I'll tell him we've been working as a group for a while and that we have a system for how to fight together as a group. I think he'll understand that."

"I hope so," she said. "Because I don't want to be responsible for someone here dying."

"I don't either."

She pushed her baked beans around on the plate.

She couldn't stop thinking about the look in Lily's eyes earlier. What was up with that girl?

She wanted to mention her dream from the other night, but she wasn't sure how to bring it up. It kept nagging at her. It had meant something important. Still, she didn't want to raise concerns about Lily if there was nothing to be concerned about. What if she was wrong about her? What if it had just been nothing more than a dream?

"Can I ask you something?" she said.

"Of course."

"Have you had any more of your dreams lately?" she asked. "You know, the ones that tell you about the future? Or about the fifth? Stuff like that."

"A few, but nothing I can make much sense of," he said. "Why?"

"I'm not sure yet," she said. "But I'll tell you when I figure it out. Tell me about your dreams. Anything you remember?"

His shoulders tensed and he made a face.

"What?" she asked.

"It's weird," he said. "I keep having this dream about New York City. Almost every night since we left D.C."

Her heart stopped beating for a second and she forced a breath. "New York? Why?"

"I don't know," he said. "I didn't want to mention it to you, because of your sister and all. But I can't shake this feeling that there's someone there we need to get to."

Tears stung her eyes. She dropped her fork to her plate. "Do you think she's still alive?"

"I honestly can't tell you anything more than that," he said. "I'm sorry."

"What exactly are you dreaming about?" she asked, refusing to leave it at that. "Have you seen a girl with brown hair? Anything about a violin? Or the Four Seasons?"

He shook his head. "No, nothing like that. I haven't seen anyone. In fact, it's almost like I'm seeing the city through someone else's eyes," he said. "And it's just bits and pieces. One night, I dreamed about a small apartment. Definitely not the Four Seasons, because it was really rundown, more like my own apartment was. Another night, I was dreaming about the sewers."

"What do you think it means?" she asked, wishing he had more information.

"I wish I knew," he said. "It doesn't make any sense to me. I thought once we got together as a group—once we found the fifth—everything would come together for me. I can't shake the feeling that I'm still missing something."

Parrish swallowed the lump that had formed in her throat. She had to tell him, didn't she? Even if she was wrong about the girl, Crash needed to know.

"What if you were wrong?" she asked.

He turned toward her, his eyes questioning. "About what?"

She took a deep breath, her heart racing.

"What if you were wrong about the girl? About Lily?" she asked. "What if she's not the fifth?"

FORTY-FOUR

THE BOY

He woke just before dawn and went through his pack again, making sure he had everything he might need on his journey to Manhattan. His hands trembled as he placed the items back into the bag, one at a time.

The weather had delayed him a few days, the rain not letting up for even an hour. But the sun had come out yesterday afternoon and the boy was determined to get his start today, no matter how scared he was.

He'd felt safe in his tiny apartment. Everything was familiar here. He had mostly good memories of this place and worried that once he left, he might never be able to return. What if the Dark One found him before he could get to the others?

So far, he'd only had to fight off one person who had turned. His mother. It had been the worst moment of his life, and he wasn't sure he'd survive having to kill another one. Much less a group of them.

The only weapon he had was a small knife from his own kitchen his mother had used to cut steaks when they'd been lucky enough to have them, which was mostly on special occasions like his birthday or a promotion at work.

His two biggest advantages were his speed and his size. He told himself that if he saw one of those things, he'd run the other way and find a place to hide. It sounded simple in his head, but he had seen what happened when someone got cornered. The zombies might be slow, but they were determined. And when they were in a pack, one wrong move could be deadly.

He pulled on the black hoodie that had been his mother's. It nearly swallowed him, coming all the way down to his knees, but the important thing was that when he pulled the hood over his head, it completely hid his face.

If he kept his face hidden and didn't use his powers unless it was a life or death situation, maybe the Dark One wouldn't know it was him. If she was looking through the eyes of her undead minions, she would see him as just another human child.

She wouldn't be expecting a child.

He wasn't sure how he knew, but he sensed the others were older than he was. Over the past century, something had gotten out of sync with their group, and the boy had continued to be reincarnated later and later compared to the others. He must have messed something up when he'd cast the original spell.

But the Dark One wouldn't know that. She'd be expecting him to be older, just like the others.

With the hood secured over his head, he pulled back the curtains on his window and waited for the sun to rise. He watched as the infected slowly made their way to the shadows and the cooler areas inside buildings, taking shelter from the sun's heat. When the street was mostly empty, he climbed down his makeshift ladder of sheets and clothing and set his feet firmly on the sidewalk in front of his apartment building.

The sewer entrance was only a block away, and all he had to do was get to it without raising any suspicions.

His feet itched to run, but he forced himself to walk at a normal pace, glancing around to make sure none of the zombies had noticed him. The walk to that first sewer grate seemed to take an hour, even though he knew only minutes had passed. This was the most dangerous part of his plan until he got to Manhattan, and he could hardly catch his breath, his heart was pounding so hard against his ribs.

A groan behind him made him pick up the pace. He didn't dare look. He knew what was back there. He could hear its feet shuffling against the pavement.

The boy weaved in and out of the mess of cars parked permanently on the street and kept his eyes on the ground, searching for the entrance to the sewers. When he passed the crosswalk, he knew he was close.

From the sound of it, he had two zombies following him now, and he was thankful for the cars that slowed them down. He picked up his pace and scanned the road. It had to be here somewhere.

Please, don't let there be a car over it.

Why hadn't he thought of that earlier? He hadn't even considered the possibility that a car's tires might be parked directly over the grate. Or if a car was over it, the space underneath it might be too small for him to climb under.

Frantically, he searched the ground, praying for a way out

before those two rotters got any closer. He dared a glance behind him and wished he hadn't. They were closer than he thought, and gaining ground.

If he didn't find it soon, he'd have to abandon his plan and run.

And then she would know. The Dark One would know where he was. She would send all of the rotters in New York after him, and God help him if that happened.

He wasn't strong enough yet. Not without the others. He would die before he even had a chance.

He spotted the sewer grate on the ground between a news van and a fancy white car with tinted windows. The van's tires were just inches behind the grate, but not on it. He sighed with relief and jogged toward it, kneeling down and slipping his fingers into the small holes on top of the manhole cover.

The moment he tried to lift up, he realized the most obvious fatal flaw in his plan.

It was way too heavy. He guessed the cover must weigh almost a hundred pounds. He couldn't even begin to lift it.

Frightened tears slipped down his face as he looked up at the infected heading toward him. Their hungry moans had attracted the attention of several more zombies and now a group of more than seven was heading straight for him.

How stupid could he be? How could he not have thought about how heavy the cover would be?

He lifted with all of his strength, praying it would move, even just a little. But it was no use. The thing was made of thick metal and there was no way he was going to get it to move.

There was no way down into the sewers. He needed to

think of a new plan or run back to his apartment and start all over.

But how long could the guardian wait? Losing another day might mean losing her, and he couldn't risk that.

It was either run or fight, and he was running out of time to make a decision.

His toes twitched with nervous energy. Maybe he should run. It would give him away, but at least he would be alive. He would have a chance.

As his panic grew, a great wind began to blow. The thick, humid air cooled and the boy shivered as he looked up. Debris fluttered around him. Abandoned newspapers. Trash left out after the disease took half the city. Coffee cups.

He stood and leaned against the white car. The breeze picked up until it was so strong, it blew the hood of his sweat-shirt off his head and made him squint his eyes. At first, he had no idea where it was coming from. He couldn't remember ever feeling such a strong wind here in the city where the buildings were so tall.

When he looked at the approaching infected, though, and his heart pumped faster, the wind surged. That's when he felt it. His connection to the weather and the cold wind that was now blowing so hard, his entire body shivered.

He stared up at the tall buildings, watching the dust and debris swirl around him. He had an idea, but it was going to be risky. Potentially deadly. But something deep inside told him he could do it.

He glanced around and finally spotted a metal staircase going up the side of one of the apartment buildings. He took off, running as fast as he could, kicking up leaves and dust behind him. He made it to the ladder in seconds, pulling a large crate underneath it. He stood on the crate and jumped up to grab the bottom rung of the ladder. Quickly, he pulled himself up to the first of the small balconies.

When he looked down, the zombies on the street had reached his hiding place between the cars. They scratched and clawed at the news van, confused about where the boy had gone. Taking a deep breath, he continued to climb.

He'd used the fire escape stairs before when he'd been playing with some friends. His mother had scolded him for going out there, telling him it was too dangerous and he could have been killed.

She would have died if she'd seen what he was thinking of doing now. It was crazy, but it was the only way he was going to get to Manhattan.

He climbed all the way to the top floor and then scooted across a windowsill to reach another ladder that led to the roof of the building. Carefully, he balanced himself on the metal ladder and pulled himself to the very top, risking a look down to see just how high he'd climbed. At least ten stories up, but thankfully none of the zombies could climb.

A noise behind him made him spin around, his heart pumping wildly. The roof was covered with infected. He had assumed no one would be up here, but he could see the door to the rooftop swinging in the wind. Someone must have left it open.

He didn't have time to consider the stupidity of what he was doing. He didn't have time to be afraid. He had to run or die. The Dark One would know him, but he had no choice.

The boy bent his knees and leaned forward, getting into a runner's stance as if he were at the starting line of a great race.

He took a deep breath and connected to the wild wind that whipped around him.

He made sure he had a clear shot from this building to the next and took off, running at top speed, his feet barely on the ground. Panic shot through him as he reached the edge of the rooftop, but he had too much momentum now to stop. This was happening, whether he wanted it to or not.

At the very edge of the roof, he jumped, leaping into the air with the wind at his back, pushing him forward. For a moment, it was terrifying, but as the street below him disappeared and the rooftop of the next building was there under his feet, he realized he was not going to die. He had done it. He had jumped.

There were a few more zombies on the next rooftop, but he didn't want to stop. He wanted to feel that weightlessness again. It was a freedom like nothing he'd ever known. He pushed harder, zooming over the top of the roof and jumping again.

He laughed and let out a loud whoop when his feet touched down on the other side.

He couldn't believe it. Just when he'd thought there was no hope left, he'd suddenly learned to fly.

FORTY-FIVE

CRASH

He found Tank on the roof, staring at the bodies on the sidewalk.

"Hey, man, I've been looking everywhere for you," he said. "What are you still doing up here? Kaya made lunch for everyone."

"Hotdogs again?" Tank asked with a laugh, barely glancing at Crash before his eyes wandered back to the dead bodies. "What do you think was going on earlier? With that group over there?"

Crash swallowed. "What do you mean?"

"I've never seen a group act like that before," he said. "One second they were walking toward us, and the next they were stopped, like someone had flipped a switch and simply turned them off."

Crash shrugged and tried to laugh it off. "Maybe they forgot where they were heading," he said. "They heard the siren, started walking, and when it shut off, they stopped. Who knows what makes those things tick?"

"That's never happened before, though," Tank said. "And I've been on this roof cranking that siren every day for weeks. It doesn't make sense."

"Nothing makes sense anymore," Crash said. "I can't explain it."

Tank shook his head and turned toward Crash. "Sorry, I guess I just let it get to me. I've been watching them, you know? Trying to come up with patterns of behavior. But something like this happens and it throws all my theories to the wind. It's like we can't get ahead. Do you think they're changing again? Evolving or something?"

"Who knows, man. Anything is possible," he said, thinking of the super-zombies. He really hoped his friend and their group never had to see those things in action.

"Anyway, don't mind me," Tank said. "What's up? Did you need me for something?"

"I just wanted to ask you about the job you mentioned earlier," he said. After what Parrish had told him about her dream, they'd come up with a plan to find out once and for all. It was risky, but they had both agreed it was necessary. "I talked to some of my crew, and I wanted to let you know we're ready when you are."

"You sure about that?" Tank said. "You guys just got here. I don't want to send you out so soon if you're not up to it."

"We've been through a lot the past few weeks," he said, and left it at that. "But we're grateful to be here. We want to do our part since you've welcomed us in like this."

"I have to admit, I do have something in mind, but it's dangerous."

"What is it?"

"I told you that a few of our guys were injured the other day, right?"

Crash nodded.

"Well, one of them has a serious infection," Tank said. "We tried some natural remedies hoping it would get better, but so far, it's only gotten worse. Our nurse says if we don't get some antibiotics soon, he might not make it."

"Damn," Crash said. "Where can we find antibiotics?"

"I sent a team out yesterday looking in all the places I thought might be easiest to get to. Nursing homes. Vet offices," he said. "But they didn't have any luck. The places around here had either been cleaned out or destroyed."

"Got any other ideas?" Crash asked, even though he knew Tank must have an idea or he wouldn't be talking to him right now.

"This guy that's sick, his name is Stephen," Tank said. He scanned the area and shook his head. "He's one of my best men, so I sent him on that run thinking they'd be okay. If he dies, I don't know that I'll ever be able to forgive myself."

Crash touched his friend's shoulder. "Look, we're all doing the best we can. You aren't responsible for what's happened to the world."

Tank looked at him. "Stephen's wife is pregnant."

"Shit," Crash said.

"Shit's right," Tank said. "I feel terrible for even sending him out there, but he'd insisted on running that group. And like I said, he was my best man. He'd been on tons of missions and always come back. Cheryl begged him not to go. Said she had a bad feeling about it. But I sent him anyway, and now... well, now he's dying and I can't help him."

"What can we do?"

Tank breathed in. "There's a hospital not far from here," he said. "It's possible there are meds inside."

"A hospital?" Crash asked. "That's going to be one of the worst places for rotters right now."

"I know," Tank said. "Which is exactly why I think it's our best chance. Looters got to the easier places because they were easy. Less risky. But the hospital is a last resort. Most people wouldn't go near it unless they had to, and the chances of them cleaning out an entire hospital without dying first is low."

"Which means our chances aren't great, either," Crash said. "What about driving further out? Checking some of the surrounding towns?"

Tank shook his head. "We've done that," he said. "Over the past few weeks, we've been sending people out on a daily basis, driving to all the surrounding towns in a sixty mile radius. We've already gotten everything there is to get from those places. Anything much farther and it could take days to get back here. I'm not sure Stephen has days to spare."

Crash ran a hand through his hair. He was willing to go on a mission, but damn. This was going to be rough.

"I know it's a lot to ask with you guys just getting here and all, but the way you proved yourselves earlier with the guns has me thinking that you're my best option of getting over there and getting back in one piece. I was thinking maybe Karmen and that other girl could stay here. I could send a couple of my other boys out with you, instead."

Crash shook his head. "No can do," he said. "We'll do this for you, no problem, but on our terms. I'm not trying to be difficult or anything, but we've been together for a while. We know how to fight and how to communicate with each other. We go as a group or we don't go at all."

Tank's eyebrows tensed and he ran a hand across several days' worth of stubble on his chin. "I really don't like the idea of sending those girls out with you when I have no idea what you might find out there," he said. "Now, Parrish, she seems to know what she's doing. She's a real spit-fire, if you ask me, but Karmen? She's fragile, I think. Lily, too. She couldn't hit one of those Z's with a shotgun if it was standing right in front of her."

"I know it sounds odd, but we've got our own system out there," he said. He needed to convince Tank to let them stick together, or the whole thing was off. "Karmen might seem fragile, but she's good under pressure. And she's a lot stronger than she looks. Lily too. And look, this way you don't have to put any more of your men in danger."

"Why are you so eager to take this on right now?" Tank asked.

"Hey, it's the least we can do," Crash said. "This is the only safe place we've heard of, and we're just thankful to be here. If we can help you save one of your friends, we'll do everything we can."

Tank took in a deep breath and shifted his weight from one foot to the other. Finally, he nodded and shrugged his shoulders. "If you think you guys are up to it, I'll pull out the map tonight and show you exactly where you need to go," he said. "You'll need to get up pretty early and plan to set out at first light. It's a bit of a trek over there, and you can't take the Humvee the whole way. There's a bridge about two miles to the east, but it's completely blocked. You can drive up to it, but you'll have to go on foot the rest of the way unless you can find a vehicle once you get over to the other side. I wouldn't count on it though."

"How many miles on foot?" he asked.

"About three."

Crash let out a nervous sigh and rubbed the back of his neck. "Yeah, that's quite a trek. Depending on conditions, that could take us an hour or two by itself."

"Exactly. And once you get to the hospital, I have no idea what you might find. It could very well be overrun," Tank said.

"We'll manage," he said, wondering if this was really worth it. Saving a man's life was important, but if they were just willing to use their powers, Noah might be able fix him up in no time. The problem was they had no idea if Noah's powers worked on infections, or if it would be enough to save this man's life

Besides, there was more to this mission than helping this guy out. They needed to test Lily. They had to know if she was really one of them or not.

Of course, he knew they'd have one heck of a time convincing Karmen that this was something they needed to do. She wouldn't want to leave the compound, but they were going as a group or they weren't going at all.

If Parrish was right about her hunch, they'd be meeting some pretty heavy firepower once they got there, too.

He really hoped she wasn't right.

"If you're sure, then I'll go start getting some things together for you," Tank said. He put a hand on Crash's shoulder. "Cheryl and Stephen are really going to appreciate this. We'll all owe you guys."

"We're happy to help," he said.

"Thank you, brother," Tank said, opening the door to the

main floor. "Have your group stick around for a while after dinner. I'll take you through the route and tell you what I know."

"Sounds good," Crash said. "I'll go tell the others."

He stepped into the main part of the armory and searched for his friends, a sense of doom planting itself in his stomach for the remainder of the afternoon.

"Why are we doing this again?" She was sitting on her bed and wanted to keep it that way. She felt terrible about the way she'd acted up on the roof earlier, and she just wanted to be alone with her music for a little while. Now they were going on some kind of new mission?

"We owe them," Crash said. "They made room for us and are letting us stay as long as we want. Most of the people here don't have any kind of training or skill. They're just regular people trying to survive. We have a better chance of making it back than any of them." Crash sighed. "Look, one of their men is hurt. Dying. He has a pregnant wife here in the compound and she's very worried about him."

"Why don't we let Noah take care of it?" she asked. Even though the news about the pregnant wife tugged at her heart, she didn't want to risk their lives for someone she didn't even know. She didn't mean to be crass, but it was the truth. It was just too dangerous.

"We've been through that already," Noah said. "I'm not even sure I can heal an infection, but even if I could, they would know something was up."

"Yeah, but you would have saved his life," she said. "There's nothing scary about that."

"You have to just trust us on this," Crash said.

"Why us?" she asked.

"Because we're the best ones for the job and you know it," Parrish said. She shut the door after a quick glance into the hallway and lowered her voice. "If we don't go, they'll send another group of their own men, and you know what that means. We can help, and everyone in this room knows that."

Karmen sighed and wrapped her earbuds around her phone. "I don't like this at all," she said. "We just got here. It's the first time I've felt safe since this whole mess started. I don't want to leave."

"Then we need to prove to them we truly deserve to be here," Crash said. "If we do this for them, just think what that will mean. They'll let us stay as long as we want."

She sat up on the edge of the cot. "No, what will happen is they'll realize we're good at this. Too good. They'll send us out on all the tough missions from now on, can't you see that? We won't be any safer than we were when we were on the road."

"That's not true," Crash said. "I think if we do this, it clears us to hang out here for a long time before they would ask anything more of us. Especially if we can help save someone's life. We'll be heroes."

"You'll be heroes," she said, laying back down and grabbing her headphones. "I'm not going."

"You are not about to pull this on us right now," Parrish

shouted. "Not after your little stunt on the roof. If you want to stay, you're—"

"Hey, there's no reason to get upset," Crash said, putting a hand on Parrish's arm.

He met Karmen's eyes and she looked away, embarrassed. She knew she was acting like a child, but she wasn't ready to go back out there. She'd had enough.

"You guys go on to dinner," he said. "Karmen and I will meet you out there."

"Fine," Parrish said. "We'll see you out there."

Parrish shot a dirty look at Karmen as she left and once the door was closed, Karmen sat up and stuck her tongue out at the door.

"That girl really knows how to drive someone insane," she said.

Crash laughed. "You're one to talk," he mumbled, sitting next to her on her cot.

Karmen rolled her eyes. "You're not going to start in on me, too, are you?"

"I understand why you don't want to go, but there's more to this than you know," he said. "It's really important that we go on this mission."

She studied him. His voice was so serious, which wasn't typical Crash. What was he talking about?

"Tell me why," she said. "Why now? Why this mission?"

He sighed. There was something he didn't want to tell her. Or wasn't supposed to tell her. But if he wanted her to go along with this, he better start talking.

"Crash, whatever it is, you need to tell me," she said. "I'm a part of this group, too, and you guys can't just go around making all the decisions, treating me like I'm just some tagalong who's incapable of making the tough calls. What's really going on?"

He stood up and went to the door, opening it just a crack and looking into the hallway. When he shut the door and sat back down, Karmen's heart started racing a bit faster. What the heck was happening?

"Parrish didn't want me to tell anyone else just yet, but I think you're right. You're a part of this group and you have a right to know what's going on," he said.

She swallowed hard. Whatever it was sounded more serious than just going out to find some antibiotics.

"Parrish had a dream the other night. Something about a boat and a small island in the middle of nowhere," he said. "In the dream, we were all there, but we were different. Older, maybe. Kind of like what you and I saw the other day with the red ocean."

Karmen closed her eyes and breathed in. She'd had a similar dream about an island, too. She pulled her legs under her body and fiddled with the end of her shirt. Talking about the visions and the dreams made her uncomfortable, like she wasn't in control at all of what was going on in her own life. Like she didn't even know who she really was.

"In her dream, we were all there. You, me, Noah, Parrish. But Lily wasn't there," he said. "There was someone else with us in the dream. Someone younger. A guy with dark skin."

"What does it mean?" She thought of the strange vision she and Crash had the other day in the farmhouse. It had felt so real, as if it actually happened. Chills ran up her arms.

"I don't know exactly, but Parrish thinks it might mean this girl isn't who we thought she was. That maybe she's not actually the fifth," he said. "And there's a part of me that thinks she might be right."

"Because of one dream?" she asked.

"I've been having dreams, too," he said. "Dreams about New York City. I've had this feeling there's someone there we need to get to, but I can never see them clearly. And the thing is, that's the way I always felt about the fifth when I first started dreaming about you guys. For some reason, I could see your faces and sense that you were close by, but with the fifth, I was never sure."

"But you knew she was hiding in that closet," she said. "You told us that. How else would you have known she was there?"

"I never saw the fifth's face," he said. "What if the fifth is still out there? What if that's why we still don't have any answers about what's going on with us?"

"And it was just some random other person with powers hiding in a closet?" she asked. "I'm not buying it."

"I know it sounds crazy, but I think there's more to this. From the beginning I've had a feeling that once the five of us came together, we'd know what we were supposed to do. I thought it would all fall together like the pieces of a puzzle fitting perfectly into place," he said. "But that hasn't happened. Something's off. Now Parrish has this dream and sees five of us together, but the fifth is someone different? I don't think it's a coincidence."

"What does any of this have to do with this mission?" she asked, kind of wishing she had just agreed to go and not asked for an explanation in the first place.

"What if the attack in D.C. wasn't started by some random assassin?" he asked.

Karmen's breath caught in her throat. "What are you saying?"

"When I first noticed them on top of that building, there was a human up there with them. Creating them. Or at least that's what we think might have happened," he said. "Is it really a coincidence that it was the same building where we found Lily?"

"You're saying you think she's the assassin?" she said. "You can't be serious."

But there was a part of her that wasn't so sure. When Lily had touched her hand in the Humvee back in Baltimore, hadn't she felt something strange? Dark?

And what about the fact that she couldn't remember her own name or tell them anything about her past?

Chills ran through her veins.

"That's what we're hoping to find out," he said. "I know it's risky, but it's the only thing we could think of to be sure. If we go out there tomorrow morning and it's just a normal mission, then we rethink this and come at the dream from another angle. But if the super-zombies are there waiting for us?"

She stood up. "Wait a second, you're saying we're going to intentionally go out there knowing there's the danger that we'll have to face those things all over again?"

"I know it's a huge risk—"

"It's insanity," she said. "Last time we fought them, we barely made it out alive. What if we don't make it out this time?"

"We will," he said. "Karmen, we have to know. And we can't just ask her. If it's true, she'll deny it."

Karmen's hands began to tremble and she pressed them tight against her arms. "This can't be happening," she said.

"She's our friend. She's a part of this group just like the rest of us. She has powers just like we do."

"We don't even know what these powers mean or who else might have them, though, do we?"

She shook her head and ran a hand through her hair. "I can't believe we're doing this," she said. "What if they are out there waiting for us again?"

"Then we'll know," he said. "Karmen, is there anything strange you might have noticed about her? Anything, no matter how small?"

She took a deep breath and tried to think about the past couple weeks since they'd met up with this girl. She stared down at the girl's backpack and her eyes widened.

The cloak.

The night she'd accidentally searched Lily's bag, thinking it was her own, she'd found that weird cloak made of a material she'd never seen before.

"Karmen, what is it?" he asked.

She looked away, shaking her head. "Nothing," she said. Telling him about the cloak wouldn't change anything, and if the girl walked in on them going through her things, who knows what might happen. She kept her mouth shut, but deep down, she knew he was right about this mission.

They needed to know the truth.

"I'll go with you," she said. She pressed her index finger hard into his chest. "But so help me God, if I die out there tomorrow, I'll come back as a rotter and kill you myself."

Crash laughed and stared into her eyes, stepping a little closer than she wanted him to.

"You've got a deal, Barbie," he said. "And by the way, I haven't been able to stop thinking about that kiss earlier."

Anger flushed her cheeks and she pulled away, wanting to slap him again.

"You are such a jerk," she said, throwing open the door to the room. "And if you pull a stunt like that again, you better get used to sleeping with one eye open from now on."

He walked past her into the hallway, but turned before he walked away. "I think next time, I'll wait for you to kiss me," he said. "And believe me, there will be a next time."

He winked and started down the hallway, but Karmen stayed behind. When he had disappeared through the door to the main armory warehouse, she went back into the bedroom and closed the door.

She squatted next to Lily's bag and opened it with trembling hands, wanting to get another look at the strange cloak.

Instead, she found normal clothes. Jeans. T-shirts. A sweater. She pulled them all from the bag, turning it over onto the floor. The cloak wasn't there. What in the heck was going on?

Karmen was sure of what she'd seen that morning in Crash's apartment. She could never forget a cloak like that. What had she done with it?

She looked inside the bag, making sure it was empty. The cloak had taken up most of the backpack, so she knew it was too big to fit into one of the smaller compartments, but she opened the zippered pouch on the side anyway.

She stuck her hand inside and felt around. It was empty except for a smooth stone. Karmen clasped her hand around it and a small shock went through her palm. She drew her hand away and shook it. It hadn't hurt, exactly, but what in the world was it?

She reached in again and took the stone from the bag, turning it over in her hand.

It was a black rock with five sides, a symbol etched into each one. As she turned it over, she gasped when one of the symbols—a rose—lit up with a dim red glow.

Her heart raced as she stared down at the stone in her hand.

What was Lily doing with something like this? Karmen wasn't sure what it meant, but whatever it was, her body had reacted to it. And the stone had reacted to her.

Somehow, she knew that rose meant something to her. She'd seen it before, but where?

She stuffed the girl's clothes back into her bag, carefully setting it against the cot where she'd found it. She slipped the stone into its pocket inside the bag and turned off the light as she went to join the others in the dining area, thinking that tomorrow's outing might be a lot more dangerous than any of them imagined.

FORTY-SEVEN
PARRISH

Still reeling from her argument with Karmen, Parrish sat down at the table and picked at her dinner. She knew she should be eating, but she was too angry. Too scared.

There was something greater and more dangerous at work in this world than any of them realized, and she was sick and tired of guessing at what that might be. Where had this virus really come from? What did their dreams really mean?

She just wanted answers.

The virus has taken everything away from her. Her future. Her family. Her identity. And now it was threatening to take her sanity.

They had come so far and been through so much, trying to find a place safe enough to rest and think through everything. But what if they had brought the enemy along with them?

She looked up at the girl sitting across from her. She looked normal. She was beautiful with her long black hair and pale skin. Other than the fact that she didn't have a zit or freckle on her perfect skin, she looked like any normal teenager.

But what about her past? The rest of them had shared stories about their families and their lives before the virus, but this girl had never once told them anything about her past. Not even her name.

"Hot dogs again for dinner," she said as casually as she could. "Not that I'm not incredibly grateful to have a hot meal, but I was just thinking how much I miss pizza. And Reese's Pieces, oh man, I'd kill for some of those. I've been looking for them at every gas station and pharmacy we've stopped at so far, but apparently everyone loves them, because they've been cleaned out. What about you?"

She stared at Lily, who had just taken a bite of her baked beans and scrunched her nose.

"Who, me?" she asked, swallowing.

"Yeah, we hardly know anything about you," Parrish said. "If you could have any meal in the world right now, what would it be? The sky's the limit?"

Lily shrugged and looked down at her food. "I don't know. I guess I haven't really thought about it."

"Come on, there has to be something," she said. "What was your favorite thing your mom ever cooked for you? Like on your birthday? What would she make for you?"

Lilyl's hands tensed into fists around her plastic silverware. "I don't have a mother," she said.

Parrish finished taking a sip of water and set her cup back on the table. "Damn, I'm sorry," she said softly. "I didn't know. What happened to her? I lost my mom to the virus."

"I never knew her," she said, her tone harsh and bitter. "I'd rather not talk about it."

Under the table, Crash kicked her foot, but she ignored him.

"Okay, but everyone has a favorite food, right? What's your favorite kind of candy?" she asked.

Lily cleared her throat and looked up. "I don't know. Those Reese's things you mentioned. Those are good."

Parrish glanced at Crash and he shook his head. She could tell he didn't want her to push the issue, but she had known Lily wouldn't have a favorite food or share stories about her family or her birthday. There was something definitely off about her, and Parrish was surprised none of them had really noticed it before now.

She was different. Guarded.

And Parrish wanted to know why.

"Mine is Hot Pockets," Crash said. "I could eat those things for every meal, every day."

"Ew, those are so gross," Karmen said, finally joining them at the table. "They're hardly even real food."

"They're delicious," he said. "And I've been surviving just fine on them for years."

"Well, if I could have any meal in the world right now, I'd want to go to Makoto. Have you guys ever been there?" Karmen asked.

"I went once with my dad," Noah said. "They had the best sushi in the city."

Karmen smiled. "I loved their sushi. I always made my parents take me there for my birthday," she said. "And I'd always make them get me a cake from The Cakeroom. I miss that place so much. They had this Hummingbird cake that had bananas and walnuts and the most delicious cream cheese icing you ever tasted in your life. It was to die for."

"I remember that place," Parrish said. "Did you ever try their Nutella cookies? Oh my God."

"Right?" Karmen asked, giggling. "Beats hot dogs and baked beans any day."

"Sounds like you guys are having fun over here," Kaya said, placing a hand on Parrish's back.

She blushed, hoping Kaya hadn't misunderstood their conversation. She didn't want to seem ungrateful.

"We were just reminiscing about our favorite restaurants back home," she said.

"I understand," Kaya said. "Sometimes it gets old having the same meals over and over again, but you'll get used to it."

"These hot dogs are great," Noah said. "Thank you for cooking for us again."

"Anything for you guys," she said. "My husband told me what you're planning to do tomorrow, and I can't tell you how thankful I am that you're willing to go out again so soon. It will mean a lot to all of us if you can find some medicine."

Parrish nodded. "My sister and father were in New York when the virus hit," she said. "I understand what it's like to be afraid you're going to lose your family."

Kaya's face softened and she leaned down to give Parrish a hug. "You poor girl," she said. "I can't even imagine what that must have been like for you."

"It's been hard, but we've all had to face hard things over the past month or so," Parrish said. "If we can help a family stay alive, that's all that matters."

"Eat up," Kaya said, clapping her hands together. "You're going to need plenty of good food and rest if you're planning to be on the road so early in the morning. I'll say a prayer for you all and hope to see you back here safely before dark tomorrow night."

Kaya smiled and moved on to talk to a group further down the table.

I hope so, too, Parrish thought, and looked up again at the mysterious girl sitting across from her.

FORTY-EIGHT

CRASH

Tank spread the map on the table and pointed to a spot he'd circled in red. Crash leaned over him to get a closer look at the route.

"The hospital is over here," he said. "It's about six miles from here by car, but like I told Crash, the bridge is completely jammed up and unless you drive about fifty miles out of your way into more unpredictable territory, your best bet is on foot after you hit the bridge. We had some guys try to drive up north for a better way around to that side of town, but they ran into some large hordes of Z's and had to turn around."

"Does anyone in your group know much about that side of town?" Crash asked. "Anyone who might have gotten a good look at the hospital?"

Tank sighed and studied the map. He pointed to a subdivision a couple blocks south of the store. "One of the men, Jenkins, used to live over in this subdivision. He and his two sons did a pretty good job clearing things out at the beginning before they came here. They said they took care of a lot of Z's over by the hospital, but that they didn't risk going inside."

"We'll do the best we can," Crash said.

"Thank you," Tank said, putting a hand on his shoulder. "This really does mean a lot to a lot of people around here."

"We're glad to help," Parrish said. "Anything else we need to know about the surrounding area? Places we should absolutely avoid, things like that?"

Tank circled an area north of the bridge. "Last time I was out there, this section had a huge population of Z's. There's a group of apartment buildings there, so there were a lot of people living in a confined space. I'd avoid it at all costs if I could."

Crash looked up and saw that Lily was studying the map hard, her burned hand touching her temple. Something tugged at the back of his mind and his pulse quickened.

"You feeling okay?" he asked.

She looked up. "Sure," she said with a wavering smile. "I'm just trying to think about the plan and how we're going to get in and out of that hospital without getting hurt."

"I thought you maybe had a headache or something from the way you're touching your head like that," he said. He glanced over and met Parrish's eyes. "Want someone to get you an aspirin or something?"

"No, I'm fine," she said. She hid her hand inside her shirt sleeve and backed away from the table.

Crash was sure she'd done almost the exact same thing the other day. He was probably reading too much into it, but his nerves knotted in his stomach.

"Well, we all need to get some rest, I'm sure," he said. "Tank, thanks for walking us through the route. I'll set an alarm for five so we have time to get up and get some coffee and breakfast before we take off, if that sounds alright with you."

"Absolutely," Tank said. "Some of the women, including Cheryl, volunteered to get up early and fix a nice breakfast of bacon and eggs to make sure you guys leave with energy and full stomachs. They're packing up some snacks and MRE's for you, too, in case you end up being gone overnight."

"That's very nice of them," Parrish said. "What about cell phones? If the electricity and internet is still working, does that mean phones are, too? That way we could call if something goes wrong."

"I wish," Tank said, shaking his head. "I can't explain why one thing works and the other doesn't, but cell service has been down for a good while now. We have a few sets of walkie talkies you can take, but the signal won't reach the whole way."

"That would be great," Crash said.

He folded up the map and stuck it in his backpack for safe keeping.

"I'm heading to bed," he said. "If you guys know what's good for you, you'll turn in early, too. I have a feeling it's going to be a very long day tomorrow."

He shook Tank's hand and said goodnight to the others, hoping that for once, his dreams would take the night off.

FORTY-NINE
NOAH

Parrish and Crash had explained why they were going on this wild goose chase tomorrow, but he didn't like it at all.

Lily might not be like the rest of them, but it was obvious she'd faced some kind of trauma and had been having a hard time getting over it. She was suffering from amnesia, which really wasn't that uncommon when it came to severe post-traumatic-stress.

Leading them into the unknown as a test to see if she was somehow controlling the super-zombies sounded like a practice in insanity to him.

If they were wrong, they were still putting themselves in danger from the regular zombies out there. They could come across a horde of them and someone could get hurt or killed in the process.

If they were right, they would have to face another group of super-zombies. They'd barely survived the attack in D.C., so why would they willingly walk into another attack?

But Parrish had said it was better that they find out the truth when they were away from the compound, rather than stay here and risk the entire place getting ambushed by those things.

And she was right.

Noah just didn't like the odds. Either way, they were taking themselves away from what had to be one of the safest places in the country and putting themselves back in danger.

He was still hoping he might be able to talk Parrish out of it.

When the others had headed back to the room, he hung back, touching her arm and motioning for her to follow him upstairs.

She glanced toward the others and nodded. "I'll be there in a minute," she said. "Meet you on the roof?"

He nodded and watched as she disappeared into their bedroom. He made his way to the stairwell and up to the roof, amazed at how bright it was at this time of night.

With the electricity still on around town, all the street lights were on. They must have been set on some kind of timer. Floodlights had been attached to all corners and sides of the armory about ten feet apart from one another, the light shining out in all directions.

The shopping mall was mostly dark, but he could see houses with lights shining through the windows up and down the street. Was anyone still alive in there?

He guessed not, since they would have surely realized what was going on here at the armory and come here instead. Still, he liked to think there were survivors all across the country, and maybe even the world, living in their own homes with their families intact. Safe and alive. When all this was over and the rotter population had been eradicated, he hoped those families would be able to rebuild the world.

"What are you thinking about?" Parrish asked softly, coming to stand beside him at the edge of the rooftop.

"I didn't even hear you come up," he said.

"You looked so peaceful just now," she said. "Hopeful."

He smiled. "I was just imagining that there were families in those homes who hadn't lost anyone," he said. "I was thinking how the survivors would be able to rebuild someday, once the rotters were gone."

"Do you think that's really possible?" she asked.

"Some people are immune," he said. "I can't imagine there are many people left who weren't exposed to the virus at all, so that means most people who are still alive can't get sick. If we can find a way to get rid of the rotters that exist now, all that will be left are healthy people, right?"

"That's a pleasant thought. A world without rotters," she said. "I was thinking about Cheryl's baby. She's six months along already, but what happens when that baby is born? We don't know how immunity works. Zoe and I seemed to be immune to the virus, but not Mom and Dad. It could also work the other way around. What if the parents are both immune, but the baby is born with the virus?"

Noah shuddered. He hadn't thought of that at all. He'd only been thinking about the people who were still alive now. Not the ones who hadn't yet been born.

"I guess we hope for the best," he said. The world didn't have much of a future if babies born to survivors weren't immune. Not unless someone was able to find a cure, and he doubted there were many scientists like his father still alive and qualified to find one.

Parrish slipped her hand into his and stared out at the houses.

"I like your version of the future better," she said.

It felt so good to hold her hand. To touch her and feel close to her.

He'd really messed up the other day getting close to Lily the way he did. He'd been entranced by her at the time, but the moment he'd seen Parrish storm out of that clothing store, he'd known she was the one for him.

She was the only one, and she always had been. He just didn't know how to make her see that.

"What did you want to talk about?" she asked.

He faced her and grabbed her other hand. "I was going to try to talk you out of this mission tomorrow," he said. "I thought maybe I could convince you how crazy it was for us to risk everything just on the off chance that Lily had something to do with the super-zombies and the attacks in D.C. and at the hospital."

"Noah—"

"Wait," he said. "Just hear me out."

He shifted his weight and stared into her violet eyes.

"I know I upset you the other day when you walked in on us talking at that store," he said. She tried to pull away, but he held onto her hands and pulled her closer. "I understand why you said the things you said about us all being connected and that maybe you and I aren't any different than the rest of the group, but you were wrong."

Her lips parted and a gentle breeze blew her hair across her shoulder.

His heart thundered in his chest. "I don't know what happened in that store with her, but I wasn't myself," he said.

"I felt pulled in by her, but it was nothing like what I feel when I'm around you."

"You think she cast some kind of spell on you?"

"I don't know," he said. Until now, he hadn't thought enough about it to realize what had really happened between him and Lily. But now, with the doubts and suspicions surrounding her, he had to wonder if there was something more to it. "I don't want you to think I'm trying to put the responsibility of that moment off on someone else, but I wasn't thinking clearly. It was like she got inside my head and made me think I wanted her."

"But you don't?" Parrish asked, her head tilted up toward him.

"No." He shook his head, never more sure of anything in his life. "I want you, Parrish. It's always been you. I don't know what's going to happen tomorrow, but if there's any chance this will be my last night on this earth, I don't want to leave things unsaid between us."

He swallowed, his throat dry from nerves.

"I love you," he said. "I think I always have, but I was too stupid to admit it to myself. What we have is something real, and it's special, and it's different from anything I feel for anyone else. I look out at those houses, and all I can think about is that maybe someday, when all this is over, you and I can find a house of our own and start a real life together. Start a family, maybe, whatever you want. I know this sounds crazy with everything that's going on and the fact that we're young, but I think—no I know, in the deepest part of myself, at the core of who I am and who I've always been—that we were meant to be together."

She smiled, her tears sparkling in the light.

"I love you, too," she said.

He leaned down, wrapping his arms around her as his lips touched hers.

The night fell away and the two of them stood together in a garden of blue flowers. The sun warmed their faces as their bodies pressed closer. Parrish's hands gripped the edge of his shirt and clung to him as if her life depended on it.

He pulled away, cupping her face in his hands.

It was Parrish, but she was slightly older. Her eyes were a deep purple and she wore a white dress that trailed along the grass behind her.

A man stood before them, his hands pressed together and a smile on his face as he stared at them. "A most unlikely union," the man said. "But one that I suspect will last for centuries."

"Thank you, Tobias," Parrish said. "For everything."

"You're welcome, my dear," the man said. "My only regret is that your families couldn't be here to celebrate with you."

"They wouldn't understand," Noah said. "But it doesn't matter. We have each other. That's the only thing that will ever matter again."

He leaned down to kiss her and the vision disappeared. They were back on the rooftop, their bodies trembling as they pulled apart.

"What was that?" Parrish asked.

"I think it was our wedding," Noah said, his breath short and his heart racing.

"But where? When?" she asked. She clung to him, her arms tugging at his shirt just as she had in the vision.

"I don't know," he said. He touched her face, knowing he had touched her this way so many times before. More than he could count, across lifetimes.

"Kiss me again," she whispered, her toes lifting from the ground as her eyes closed.

He pulled her tighter against his chest, running his hands along her back and through her long hair. He had never known a kiss could feel this way. It was like being set on fire, but also like coming home for the first time in ages.

He never wanted to let her go.

Visions passed between them. Memories of a past life together filled with love and laughter and great sorrow and struggle. He saw her in an open field, an army of soldiers behind her, her raised sword alive with flames. He saw them together on a large terrace overlooking a waterfall, the mist cool on their faces. He saw them on a boat in the ocean, looking toward a small island with pristine white sand.

When she pulled away, the visions faded, but he kept his eyes closed, trying to hold onto them for as long as he could. Her chest rose and fell against his rapidly, her body shivering as she gripped his arm.

"What's happening to us?" she asked, her voice breathless.

"I think we're remembering," he said softly.

"Remembering what?"

He opened his eyes and saw her then. The girl he'd known since childhood. A woman he'd known for longer than his mind could comprehend. Her eyes were filled with tears, and in that moment, he loved her more than anyone had ever loved another.

"We're remembering who we are," he said, wiping a tear from her cheek. "Who we've always been."

FIFTY

PARRISH

Parrish woke up the next morning with a new lease on life. She and Noah had spent hours on the roof, talking about the visions that had passed through their minds as they kissed for the first time. She still wasn't sure what it all meant, but she knew that it was real.

Even facing whatever may come their way on this trip to the hospital, she wasn't afraid. As long as they were together, they could face anything.

Her visions of past lives with Noah also made her realize that she'd been right about her dream.

It wasn't just a dream. It was a memory of something she'd done in the past. Something she'd done with her four best friends. And one of them was missing.

Where was the fifth?

The girl who had joined their group didn't belong, and Parrish eyed her as they all got dressed for the day. What was she doing with them? What was her story? And what the hell did she have planned for them today?

Because Parrish knew she had something up her sleeve. Another ambush by super-zombies? Worse?

Whatever it was, they would face it together, and when the time came, they would confront Lily and make her tell them the truth.

Parrish rummaged through the bags of clothes she'd gotten from the mall across the street and smiled. When she'd left her house, she hadn't exactly brought her favorite things along with her. She'd been trudging around in jeans and boots, but when she picked through the clothing at the mall, she'd chosen things that made her feel like the best version of herself. Strange how a simple change of attire could make you feel like a complete badass.

She pulled on a pair of opaque black tights, tall black socks that were thick enough to cover the lower half of her legs and provide some protection from biting teeth, a pair of tight black shorts, and a black tank top with a white infinity sign on the front. She couldn't believe her luck when she'd found it.

She covered the tank top with a black leather jacket. Despite the heat, she wanted something she could pull over her arms as protection when things got real inside that hospital today.

The final piece of the outfit was the perfect pair of tall black leather boots that buckled all the way up to her knee.

She stared at her reflection in the mirror of the shared bathroom and smiled. She felt more like herself than she had in a long time, and she was ready to face whatever came her way.

When she popped back into the bedroom, most of the others were ready to go. She emptied her backpack, reloaded it with essentials like extra bottles of water, ammo, and all the cherry suckers she had left.

She unwrapped one of the suckers, pulled the backpack onto her back, and secured her sword in the makeshift holster she'd created.

Noah's eyes caught hers and he made a show of looking her up and down, before raising an appreciative eyebrow. She popped the candy into her mouth and smiled. Knowing he had her back—that he'd had her back for centuries—gave her an extra boost of adrenaline. Who needed sleep when you had a guy like that for a boyfriend?

"Who's ready to kick some zombie ass?" she asked and headed toward the door. She prayed it wouldn't be long before they'd be back here, a lot of their questions answered once and for all.

FIFTY-ONE

CRASH

It felt good to be back inside the Humvee, even if it was just for part of the ride. Right now, this was the only piece of home he had left.

His hands gripped the steering wheel as he pulled through the gate, nodding at the guard who gave them a thumbs up.

"We appreciate what you guys are doing for us," the guard said. "Come home safe."

"We will," Crash said, and prayed to God it was true.

What were they getting themselves into?

Ever since Parrish had brought up her own doubts, Crash had started to realize just how much all the pieces didn't fit together with this girl. He'd never seen her face in his dreams. He hadn't had the feeling the fifth was close to them at all until that night when they'd found her in the closet. And ever since they'd met up with her, he'd been having the same dream over and over, like he was supposed to find someone else.

At first, he'd thought maybe there was a sixth. That being together had made him remember someone else. But now he knew the truth. They'd never met the fifth. Lily was an imposter.

And now he was leading them straight into a battlefield with the enemy at their side.

He cleared his throat and glanced in the rearview mirror. "Everybody remember the plan?" he asked.

"We've been over it a dozen times," Karmen said. "I think we've got it."

"Just checking," he said with a nervous laugh. "The roads should be relatively clear up to the bridge, but after that we're going into unknown territory."

The sun was coming up in the east, but it was an overcast day, a slight drizzle of rain misting the windshield. Crash really hoped that didn't mean they were going to face a lot of rotters who hadn't bothered to go into hiding this morning.

If they got into too much trouble, they could always just turn around and head back early, right?

The group was quiet during the few miles to the bridge. Parrish sat next to him in the front and any time their eyes met, his stomach tightened. They both knew they wouldn't be heading home early today. They were going to find out the truth, one way or another. Today, they were finally going to get some answers.

So far, the streets closest to the armory were empty of rotters. Probably thanks to Tank's practice of running the siren a few times a day to clear out any undead in the area. Crash knew they wouldn't be quite so lucky on the other side of that bridge.

"This is it," he called, parking in the grass next to a line of stopped cars near the bridge. He turned around and looked at Noah. "Unless you think you're strong enough to move those cars and make a path for us, we're on foot from here on out."

Noah shrugged. "I guess I could try."

Hope fluttered in Crash's stomach as he watched Noah walk up to the first car. He lifted it by the bumper, but could only move it a few feet before he set it down again. He walked around to the other side and put his hands on the undercarriage between the two doors on the passenger side. He lifted and the car toppled over onto its side. Helpful, but not exactly enough space for them to squeeze the Humvee through it.

"This isn't going to work," Parrish said.

"Let's just see," Crash said. "I really don't want to have to take this on foot."

After about ten more minutes of watching Noah move one car, Crash shook his head and climbed out of the vehicle.

"This is going to take too much time," he said. "You'd have to move at least fifty cars to get us across this bridge. It would be dark by the time you were finished. Let's just walk."

"Sorry," Noah said, moving his shoulders in a circular motion and shaking it off. "I tried."

Parrish grabbed his arm and pushed up on her tiptoes to kiss his cheek.

Crash pulled on his backpack, watching as the two of them smiled at each other and exchanged whispers. Well, well. When did this become a thing? You had to be blind not to notice there was something brewing between them, but overnight, it had gone to a full boil.

It was about time, as far as he was concerned.

He glanced at Karmen, warmth creeping up the back of his neck. If only he could convince her that the two of them could have something great, too. Maybe he'd have to corner Noah later and ask him to share his moves.

"Why are we still standing around?" Parrish asked, climbing over the first car. "Let's get moving."

"Right behind you," Crash called.

He climbed on top of the trunk of the first car and turned to offer his hand to Karmen, hoisting her up. She smiled and his heart melted.

Someday.

Lily reached for his hand and he helped pull her up, too. Now that they were away from the safety of the compound, he wished they could just confront her right here. Ask her whether she was the one behind the super-zombie attacks or not. He wanted to know how she'd found out about the fifth and convinced him he'd been dreaming of her, but he knew that there was no point in asking her now. She could deny it, and none of them would be able to prove otherwise.

They had to catch her in the act. It was the only way.

He just hated they all had to risk their lives in the process.

It took nearly twenty minutes to cross the bridge. The cars were packed so tightly, there was nowhere to actually put their feet down on the bridge. They had to climb over the tops, jumping from hood to trunk along the way. And the worst part was that some of the cars still had rotters trapped inside.

"Watch out for that one," Parrish called, pointing to a brown sedan on the far left side. "A couple rotters inside with the windows open."

Crash nodded and helped steer the girls to the other side.

When they had finally made it through the maze of cars, Crash jumped down into the grass on the shoulder and leaned his neck from side to side. He'd been tense all morning and his body was rebelling.

"Maybe we should take a quick break for water," he said. "It's not super hot out today, but we still need to make sure we're staying hydrated. You never know what we might have to fight once we get inside, and we've still got a three mile trek before we get there."

Parrish nodded and pointed to a truck ahead with its tailgate down. "Anyone who needs to sit for a second can sit over there," she said. "The ground looks pretty wet, so I'd avoid that unless you want to be uncomfortable all day."

Karmen sat down on the tailgate of the rusted truck and Crash moved to sit down beside her.

"How are you holding up this morning?" he asked.

Parrish, Noah, and Lily stood to the side, discussing the fastest route to the hospital.

"I'm okay," she said. She shifted and bit her lip. "I'm just scared."

"Me too," he said.

"What happens if we're right? About Lily?" she asked. "I mean, assuming we even survive what's coming."

He glanced at the other group. They hadn't really talked about what they would do if they found out she wasn't the true fifth. "We'll confront her, I guess," he said. "Try to find out why she's doing this and who she's working for. Maybe she knows something about why all this is happening."

"And you really think she'll just tell us the truth?" Karmen asked.

Okay, so their plan wasn't exactly worked out yet, but it was still the best option they had. "We'll figure it out as we go," he said. "Don't look so worried. Our powers are growing. Even if we're attacked, we survived it once. How bad can it be?"

"This is terrifying," she said. "I don't think I'm cut out for all this."

"I won't let anything happen to you," he said, wishing like hell he could take her hand in his. "Come on, let's get back on the road."

She nodded and slid off the tailgate.

They met up with the others and everyone put their drinks away and started walking along the grass on the side of the road.

Three miles to the hospital. Three miles until they faced whatever—or whoever—was waiting for them there.

FIFTY-TWO

THE BOY

Rooftops soared past him. He had no idea how fast he was running now, but it only took him a few seconds to cross most of the rooftops before he was back in the air, soaring high above the streets.

Just ahead, though, he could see that he was running out of room. The next block of buildings were taller than the ones he'd been jumping so far, and he wasn't sure he would be able to make that kind of jump. But if he didn't slow down, he wouldn't be able to stop in time, either.

Should he risk it?

He might have a better chance of doing it now than if he slowed down and lost his momentum. He didn't want to have to go down to the streets again. At this rate, he might be able to get close to the guardian by nightfall. If he switched to having to navigate the streets, it could take days.

He decided to go for it.

He leaned forward and crouched low as he reached the

edge of the rooftop. He vaulted himself across the space, imagining the wind lifting him higher so he could reach the next ledge, but by the time he'd gotten halfway over, he knew he wasn't going to make it.

He risked a glance downward and cried out. He was so high up that if he fell now, there would be nothing left of him but a bloodstain on the pavement.

He stretched his arms, reaching for the ledge that hung over the next rooftop. His body slammed against the brick and his fingertips latched on. Light flashed through his eyes from the blow, but he concentrated on holding on above all else.

He wasn't strong. He'd always been a scrawny kid, fast but small. He tried to pull himself up, but it was too hard. He was barely hanging on and every second that passed seemed to add ten pounds to him.

He glanced down and closed his eyes, pressing his head against the brick. He didn't want to die. Not now.

He looked from side-to-side, searching for the fire escape or a ladder of some kind. He spotted one several feet away and started swinging his body back and forth. With each forward swing, he let go and flew just a little closer to the ladder. It took almost half an hour to go five feet, but when he made it and his fingers curled around the cool metal ladder, he cried for joy.

He hugged the ladder tight and rested his arms for a minute before he climbed to the top of the building.

There were no infected on this rooftop, so he sat down and leaned his back against some kind of air vent. The sun beat down on his dark skin and sweat trickled down the side of his face. He shrugged out of his hoodie and stuffed it deep into his backpack.

Hunger pains twisted his stomach, so he searched for a pack of crackers and his bottle of water.

Everything looked different from up here.

The sun was shining and as he ate, he looked toward Manhattan at the tall buildings that made up the iconic skyline.

He looked toward the area of Central Park. He couldn't see the park from here, but he could feel the guardian's blood pulsing through her veins. She was close. He closed his eyes, a vision of a hotel coming to him. The girl was in a room at the Four Seasons. He could see the sign out front as plain as day. She was there, in a balcony room. If he could make it to a nearby rooftop, he could jump to her balcony and save her.

When he opened his eyes, the vision faded, but the information was burned on his brain. He didn't understand how he knew, but he trusted it.

He finished his meal and sat for a few more minutes, looking out over the city. From here, it still looked like a post-card, windows glinting in the light. The Empire State Building rose above all the rest. It was beautiful and quiet, the air so clear.

But even for all its beauty, there was a sinister silence that sent a shiver down his back. It wasn't supposed to be so quiet here. The city was all about life and movement and noise, but the virus had stolen that.

His mom used to complain about all the traffic and the constant honking outside their building and on the streets. She'd hated that about New York, but the boy would have given anything to hear cars honking and people shouting at each other right now. It wasn't right to hear the city so quiet.

As he stood and pulled the backpack onto his shoulders, he wondered if the city would ever regain its life, or if it would always and forever be a tomb where the only sounds were those of the hungry rotters stumbling from place to place.

FIFTY-THREE

THE WITCH

The three miles to the hospital were quiet, but then, she had known it would be. The Dark One knew exactly where they were headed, and she had commanded her minions to wait for them there, only attacking when the time was right.

Everything was coming together. The Dark One's powers were growing rapidly, and soon she would be able to escape her prison of ice.

Her minions had finally located Parrish's sister, too. The girl was exactly where her sister believed her to be—still hidden away in the safety of her hotel room. The witch wasn't sure why the girl had failed to answer the phone, but it was a stroke of luck for the Dark One. Now she would have the child all to herself, a bargaining chip if and when the time came.

The fifth was in New York, too. The Dark One's servants had spotted him yesterday, leaping and flying across rooftops. He was nothing more than a child himself, several years younger than the rest. And now that he had shown himself, it wouldn't be long before the Dark One put an end to him.

After today, this could all be over.

The witch hated the thought of betraying her new friends, but whenever her devotion wavered, she thought of the Dark One's promise of great power.

A few rotters stumbled out from behind houses or hiding places between cars as they walked, but there were never more than a couple together at a time, and Parrish and Noah took care of them quickly.

"I can't believe how quiet it is," Karmen said. "We've barely seen any of those things out here."

"Tank said some of his buddies cleared out a lot of these neighborhoods a few weeks ago," Crash said. "It shouldn't be too hard to get to the hospital if it keeps up like this."

"We're lucky," the witch said.

They walked along the sidewalk at a brisk pace, anxious to get to the hospital, but the witch wanted to slow down. Lately she'd been having doubts about her part in all this. What if she had chosen the wrong side? What if it was the Dark One who was wrong for wanting to go free and go home to their world?

What if the guardians truly had saved her people from a terrible nightmare all those centuries ago?

She tugged on a strand of her long dark hair and followed behind Crash and Karmen, her feet not wanting to move any faster. There was a part of her that wanted to tell them not to go. They could turn around right now and leave this place. It would be difficult to hide from the Dark One now that she had eyes everywhere, but with her help, they might find ways to survive and stay hidden.

But she knew that if she told them, they would never forgive her. All their kindness would disappear and they would look at her like she was a monster. It had been her who sent those super-zombies after them in D.C. It was she who had told the Dark One about their journey and made sure there were hordes of zombies slowing them down along the way.

And she had told the Dark One about the hospital.

Whatever they faced inside that place would be because of her. She wanted to feel proud of that, the way she had in the early days when she'd been so sure she was fighting on the right side. All she wanted was to be powerful and to be needed.

Her whole life, she had been treated like she was nothing. Nobody. But these guardians had given her a name and welcomed her into their life. Now, she was repaying them by leading them straight to their own deaths.

She knew what waited in that hospital. Nightmare didn't even begin to describe it.

Several times on their journey, as the miles passed, she opened her mouth to tell them the truth, but in the end, she couldn't bring herself to betray her mistress.

When the hospital came into view and the opportunity to warn them disappeared, she held back tears of regret. She had gone too far down this road to turn back now. She had committed her life to the Dark One, and she would have to live with that decision, as painful as it may be.

All she could hope now was that the guardians would go quickly. That they wouldn't feel much pain as the rotters ripped them apart.

Crash stopped on the lawn of the large hospital and clapped his hands together. "Let's get this shit over with," he said.

He set his large duffel bag on the ground and unzipped it. Guns and ammo filled the bag and he took one out and passed it to Karmen.

"I really hope I don't have to use this thing," she said.

"Just so long as you're not pointing it at one of us, you're good," he said with a wink. He held the next one out to her. "Lily?"

She blinked, still not used to her name. After today, would there be anyone left who would ever call her by that name?

"Thanks," she mumbled, taking the shotgun.

Noah stepped forward and grabbed a handful of shells, stuffing them in his pocket. Parrish had her sword and two handguns strapped to her belt.

"Where's the list?" Parrish asked.

"What list?" Lily asked.

"Tank gave us a list of things to get if we made it inside," Crash said, pulling a piece of paper from the pocket of his jeans. "We're supposed to grab inhalers for Asthma, any kind of antibiotics we can get our hands on, painkillers, blood pressure medicine, saline, needles, a defibrillator, and a few other odds and ends."

"That's a long list," Noah said. "Even if we do manage to get inside and not get killed, how the heck are we going to carry all that home?"

Crash patted him on the back. "That's where you come in, my friend," he said with a laugh. "We'll just load you up like a pack horse."

Noah shook his head and ran a hand across his forehead. "Awesome. My life's dream realized."

The witch smiled. She loved the way they all joked around with each other, even in the most terrifying of circumstances. She was really going to miss them.

"I was thinking we should check the ambulances first," Crash said. "We might be able to find a lot of the meds and a defibrillator in there."

"That would be nice," Parrish said. "Maybe we could bypass the hospital completely."

The witch jerked her head toward Parrish. The Dark One's servants were all waiting for them inside. If she didn't get them in there, the Dark One might punish her again. She pulled her injured arm close to her body.

"I have a bad feeling we're not going to be that lucky," Crash mumbled. He looked up at the sky, covering his face with the piece of paper that held Tank's list. "It's about ten in the morning, so if we hustle, we really might be able to do this and be home by dark. At the very least, I'm hoping we can get clear of the hospital and hunker down in one of those houses we passed."

"If we don't find what we need by five this afternoon, I say we leave," Noah said.

"I'll second that," Karmen said, raising her hand. "I do not want to end up stuck in there overnight."

"Let's get to it, then," Parrish said.

The witch hesitated. "Can you wait up just a second?" she said.

The others stopped and all looked at her, squinting in the bright morning sun that had finally burned away the foggy mist of morning.

"I just wanted to let you guys know that no matter what happens today, being a part of this group has meant the world to me," she said. Her words were a betrayal to her mistress, but she couldn't let them die without telling them what they had meant to her. "I know I haven't said much about my past, but growing up, I didn't have a lot of friends. I never knew my parents at all, and the people who raised me didn't think much of me, to be honest. I just wanted you to know that the past couple weeks with you have been some of the happiest of my life. Thank you for that."

Parrish shifted her weight and looked down at the ground. "What do you think is going to happen to us today?" she asked.

The witch shook her head. "I don't know," she said. "But in case we run into any danger, I just wanted you all to know how I felt."

Crash touched her arm. "Thank you," he said. "If things go south in there, I hope you know that we've always considered you one of us. We never wanted you to be anything else."

A tear slid down her cheek and she brushed it away.

"Are we done with the sappy friendship phase of the day?" Karmen asked. "Because I'm ready to get to the kick-ass and get-the-hell-out-of-here phase, if you don't mind."

The witch smiled and nodded. "I'm ready," she said.

The group walked down the small hill to the ambulance bay, and she wondered what her life might have been like if she had grown up in this world instead of her own. If she had known friends like these, would she have felt so broken? So desperate?

The questions were pointless now, because her choice had been made. The path had already been laid out, and there was no turning back now.

But still, she wondered if she'd had lifetimes to try again and again, if in one of them, she might have finally gotten it right.

FIFTY-FOUR

PARRISH

A bead of sweat trickled down her back. The morning had started out nice, but it was getting hotter by the minute. She was melting out here.

"Let's get this over with," she said, tying the leather jacket around her waist.

She held her katana close by her side as she walked toward the bay of ambulances. Even from here, though, she could see that someone else had been here before. There were five ambulances parked near the emergency room entrance, two of which had their back doors open, supplies spilling from the back.

A few dead bodies rotted on the pavement behind the first of the vehicles.

"Doesn't look good," Noah said.

"Let's check them anyway," she said. She pointed to the second nearest ambulance. "Crash, you and Karmen check that one. The rest of us will look in this first one."

She caught Lily's eye.

"You stand out here and watch for any sign of activity. Any movement, let us know."

Lily nodded and clutched her shotgun awkwardly against her body. "I can do that," she said.

Parrish didn't trust her. What was up with that speech she'd just given? It had seemed truly heartfelt, but it put a bad taste in Parrish's mouth.

Did she know something about what was waiting for them in the hospital? Had she set them up?

Parrish wasn't ready to confront her or totally write her off yet, but she was definitely going to keep her eye on the girl. And she was going to be careful every step of the way in that hospital. Any sign of trouble and they needed to run.

Noah hopped into the back of the first ambulance and held his hand out to her. She grabbed it and pulled herself up.

"What exactly are we looking for in here?" he asked.

"Medicine, supplies, whatever we can find," she said.

The inside was a mess. The seats had been ripped to shreds and the gurney was hanging half-in, half-out the back door. Most of the lockers were open and empty.

Parrish checked them all anyway, making sure they didn't miss anything that might be useful, but this one was already cleaned out.

The two of them jumped down and moved to the third ambulance. The doors on this one were closed. Noah grabbed the handle and met her eyes. She lifted her sword and nodded, ready for something to jump out at her.

The doors swung open, but thankfully, no one was inside. This one looked relatively untouched, and a spark of hope ignited in her heart. Maybe they really could avoid the hospital. She didn't like the idea of going in there. It was too big with too many unknown factors. Open the wrong door and there could be hundreds of rotters waiting on the other side.

A few of the lockers opened easily, revealing gloves, needles, sanitizing wipes. She shrugged off her backpack and unzipped it quickly, stuffing everything she could hold inside.

"That's something at least," Noah said. "These others seem to be locked."

She raised an eyebrow. "I thought you had some kind of super strength?" she asked. "You're telling me you aren't strong enough to break a simple lock?"

He smiled and shrugged. "I hadn't thought of it that way," he said. "I'll give it a shot."

Noah pulled on the first locker and the drawer flew open, nearly knocking him on his ass.

Laughter rocked Parrish backward. She doubled over and clutched her stomach. "Maybe that was a little overkill," she said.

"You think?" he asked. He had fallen onto the paramedic's seat, his body completely sideways in the chair. He laughed and when their eyes met, her stomach fluttered. She really hoped last night's kisses were just the beginning for the two of them.

"It's nice to hear you laugh," he said.

"You too," she said softly. "Now get the rest of these lockers open. We're burning daylight."

Noah opened the rest of the drawers more carefully, but most of them were empty. The last drawer had a large bag inside and when Noah unzipped it, Parrish whistled.

"Look at that," she said. There were several bags full of fluid. She dug through them, reading the labels. "Saline,

Valium, Morphine, Dopamine, Glucagon, there are all kinds of painkillers and stuff here."

"Sweet," Noah said, crouching beside her to look through the IV bags. "I don't see any antibiotics, though."

"Are you sure?" she asked. "Would you recognize them?"

"My parents were doctors, remember?"

"Yeah, but you weren't," she teased.

He smiled again, bumping his arm playfully against hers. "I know drugs," he said. "And there are no antibiotics in these lockers."

"What about a defibrillator?" she asked.

He stood and motioned to a small shelf. "I think that would usually go here."

"So it's missing."

"Looks that way," he said. "But this is a lot of stuff. I'm surprised we found so much in one ambulance."

"Maybe we'll get lucky in one of the other ambulances and walk away from this place without ever going inside," she said.

They jumped down and told the others what they'd found.

"Awesome," Crash said. "The two we checked were trashed, but that's a huge find. Good job."

"Let's just hope we hit the jackpot with this last one."

"Yeah, out of the whole list, they need the antibiotics most," he said. "Without those, we may as well be going home empty-handed."

"It's quiet out here," Lily said. "Maybe this place is deserted."

"I wouldn't count on it," Parrish said. "It's hot out here today. They're all probably hiding inside where it's nice and cool."

"And dark," Karmen added.

"Let's check this one out and see where we are," she said.

Noah pulled the doors open while the rest of them watched, weapons ready.

A single rotter in a paramedic's uniform stumbled out of the back, and Crash lit him up with machine gun fire.

Parrish smiled and put her hand on his shoulder. "I think you got him," she shouted.

Crash let off the trigger and laughed. "Sorry," he said. "I freaked for a second there."

"Well, at least now we'll know if there are any rotters roaming around the outside," she said. "When we get inside, though, I think we should try to only use our guns as a last resort. If we see one or two by themselves, it's best to just let me or Noah handle it quietly, I think. The less attention we draw to ourselves, the better."

Crash nodded. "Good idea."

Noah and Karmen had already started searching the ambulance, and when Parrish looked up, Noah lifted a machine from the floor and smiled.

"Is that what I think it is?"

"I hope so," he said. "It's definitely some kind of heart monitor."

"Oh man, that's definitely a defib," Crash said, slapping his hands together. "This rocks. We got nearly everything on the list. Please tell me there are some antibiotics in this ambulance."

Karmen pushed a drawer closed and shook her head. "I don't see any meds in this one. Just some plastic tubing and needles and stuff."

"Shit," Parrish muttered. She closed her eyes and leaned

against the ambulance. The one thing they needed most and it wasn't here. Fate was playing with them.

"Can't we just take these things back and say we didn't find anything else," Karmen said. "I don't want to go inside."

"We can't," Crash said. "Stephen will die if we don't get him some antibiotics fast. It's the most important thing."

Parrish pulled a deep breath through her nose. He was right.

She didn't like it, but he was right.

"So the question now is where do we start?" she asked. "Where are we most likely to find antibiotics? Anyone know?"

"All I could do was a quick search on the internet," Crash said. "Most hospitals have a dispensary or med room where they keep most of the drugs under lock and key. From what I can tell, that's most likely to be close to the ER."

"Crap, that's not good," she said. "The ER's were the worst hit with everyone coming into the hospital in droves. It's too dangerous."

"When I went to the hospital a couple of years ago when I broke my arm, the nurse had some kind of cart she wheeled around that had meds in it," Karmen said. "It had a computer monitor on top and she pulled the drawers out to get the bags out of the bottom. What if we could find one of those?"

"Good call," Parrish said. "Maybe if we start at the main entrance and clear our way through, we'll be able to find a cart somewhere in one of the rooms."

"The med room would be our best bet," Crash said. "Maybe we should at least check the ER first. Like you said, a lot of the patients were quarantined. It's possible the quarantine was in a different part of the hospital. The ER might not be as bad as you think, and if we find the med room, we're golden."

Parrish bit her lip and leaned against the back of the truck. For some reason, they were all looking to her to tell them what to do. She hadn't volunteered to be the leader of the group, but the position had been handed to her.

She wanted to make the right decision here, because the wrong one could be fatal. There were no second chances in the zombie apocalypse.

They were close to the ER's entrance. It wouldn't hurt to at least look inside.

"Noah and Crash, you guys run up there to the doors and see if you see movement inside first," she said. "If it's clear, we'll start here in the ER. If there's movement, we start at the main entrance."

The girls waited as the guys ran up to check. They came back a few minutes later, shaking their heads.

"It's a shit-show in there," Crash said. "We definitely can't start here."

"Then the main entrance it is," she said. "We'll look for the nurse's carts in the patient rooms first."

"And if we don't find one?" Karmen asked.

"Then we move slowly in the direction of the ER," she said. "If we come across large groups, we turn around and try another way. Anyone object?"

No one did.

"Okay," she said, hiking her backpack higher on her shoulders. "When we get in there, we stick together. No one goes off by themselves under any circumstances, understood?"

They all nodded.

"We'll clear as we go so we have a direct way out if we

need it. With a small group, we don't use guns or make a lot of noise," she said. "If we get overrun, we head back out the way we came. Everyone ready?"

"Ready as I'll ever be," Karmen said.

They made their way across the front lawn in silence. The glass door leading into the building glimmered in the sunlight, and as they stepped into the dark hallway, it was like stepping into another world.

Instead of the clean, sanitized smell of a normal hospital, the stench of this place turned her stomach instantly. Dried blood decorated the walls and floors, and Parrish nearly slipped in a pool of it just past the entrance. Noah caught her arm and kept her from falling.

"Thanks," she said, wiping her boot on the rubber mat near the door. "Watch your step, everyone."

"Should we use flashlights?" Crash asked. "Or should I turn on lights as we go?"

"Lights would be good," she said. "But only in our immediate vicinity. Turn them off as we move. Can you do that?"

"Piece of cake," he said.

The fluorescents above their head buzzed as they came to life.

The horror of the hallway looked much worse in the light, but she didn't have the luxury of time to stand here and gawk at it. They needed to move quickly and efficiently. Clearing this place could take hours, and they were burning daylight.

"Noah, you and I will take the lead, clearing out any rotters we come across along the way," she said. "Let's leave the supplies we gathered so far out here by the admin desk so we don't have to carry them the whole way. We'll pick them up on our way out."

They emptied everything out of their packs and stuffed it behind the desk with the heart monitor.

"You ready?" she asked Noah.

He nodded, lifting his bat and walking slowly forward.

This section was mostly just small administrative offices. Parrish glanced inside each door, and when she was sure it was empty, she shut it behind her.

"Why close the doors?" Karmen asked.

"Just in case we missed one," she said. "We don't have time to go inside every room, and we need to be sure the path back out is clear. The doors should slow them down, at the very least."

Karmen nodded. Her shotgun was cradled close to her chest, the barrel pointed toward the ceiling. Parrish hoped she didn't have to use it.

They crept down the hallway, lights going on as they walked and turning off behind them.

They passed the front desk and started down the first of three long corridors.

Parrish listened for any sign of movement or moaning, but the place was eerily silent except for the sound of the lights flickering on and off. Up ahead, the doors to patient rooms were lined up on both sides of the hallway. Some were open and some were closed.

"We'll clear from left to right all the way down," she said. "Crash you concentrate on keeping the right lights turned on and off. I will go into the room on the left while Noah clears the door on the right side of the hall. Karmen and Lily, you stand in the center of the hallway, back-to-back, ready to help if either of us needs it. Ready? Let's clear as fast as we can."

Her heart pounded as she stepped into the first room. It

appeared to be empty. The bed had been turned over and blood pooled on the floor near the window. Bloody footsteps were smeared across the tile, but whoever had made them seemed to be long gone.

There was no sign of a medical cart, so Parrish left the room and shut the door behind her. One down, God knew how many left to go.

Noah came out of the door opposite hers and shook his head.

They moved to the next set of doors, clearing each room as fast as they could. After nearly half an hour, they'd checked the entire corridor and found nothing useful.

"This is going to take forever," Karmen said. "Why don't we each just take a room? It would go so much faster."

Parrish didn't like the idea, but Karmen was right. This methodical search was taking too long. They had to move faster if they had any hope of getting out of here before dark.

"Let's move to the next hallway," she said. "Lily, you stay in the center. The rest of us will each take a room this time."

She touched Karmen's arm.

"Can you handle yourself in a room alone?"

"Yeah, I can do it," she said.

Parrish nodded and led them to the second corridor. They each stood outside a room and when Parrish nodded, they disappeared inside.

This room had two beds in it with a curtain separating them. Parrish blew out a nervous breath and stepped deeper into the room. She reached for the curtain, but just as her hand touched the fabric, a rotter latched onto her arm, its grip so tight it cut off her circulation.

She brought her blade down on its shoulder, severing its

arm from its body in a single slice. She kicked the thing's chest, and as it stumbled backward, she sliced its head off.

The damn fingers were still wrapped around her forearm and she had to set her sword on the bed to pry it off.

Another rotter grabbed her shoulders, pulling her back. She twisted around and reached for her sword, but before she could get to it, Lily brought the butt of her gun down on the rotter's head and it fell to the floor, dark red blood oozing from its skull.

She leaned against the bed to catch her breath. "Thanks," she said.

"No problem," Lily said, out of breath.

Parrish studied her. Had she misjudged her? If this girl had really set them up, would she have just tried to save Parrish's life? She really hoped she'd been wrong about Lily, and that they would make it through the day without trouble.

In the next room, Karmen screamed. Parrish grabbed her sword and raced from the room, her boots squeaking against the floors. A rotter had its hands around Karmen's neck, its jaws open and snapping. Her hand was pressed against the thing's chest, keeping it at arm's length.

Parrish brought her blade down on its skull, slicing it in two.

Karmen gasped and threw her arms around Parrish.

"Are you okay?" she asked. "Were you bitten?"

Karmen shook her head and pulled away, her eyes wide and scared. "I know I should have tried to use my mind control, but I freaked out," she said. "I don't think I can do it unless I can concentrate, and how am I supposed to concentrate when one of those things is trying to choke me out?"

"Maybe this is a bad idea," Parrish said when they all met

back in the hallway. "We need to stay together, no matter how long it takes."

"Look, the carts are big," Karmen said. "I think we should just go in pairs, open the door and glance inside. If we don't see it at first glance, we shut the door and move on."

Parrish nodded, but every part of her felt weary. They'd been here less than an hour and were already on Plan D. They weren't cut out for this, and it was going to get someone killed.

"Okay, Karmen you go with Noah and Lily will come with me," she said. She wanted to keep an eye on her, just in case. "Crash, you stay in the hall and guard us."

This plan worked better than any of the others. They cleared the hall quickly and moved onto the last one in this wing, but had no luck finding one of the nurse's carts.

"What now?" Crash asked.

"We move in the direction of the ER," she said. She pointed toward a sign posted in the hallway.

"Luckily we haven't seen many rotters yet," Crash said. "A handful at best. Maybe most of them are contained to the ER."

"Maybe," she said, but she doubted it. There was no way they were going to be that lucky.

The double doors leading to the next section of the hospital were closed, but there were small square windows at eye-level. Parrish peered inside, but it was too dark to see much.

"Crash, can you—"

"Already on it, boss," he said.

The lights in the next corridor came on. The hallway was trashed, just like the rest of the hospital. Bodies littered the floor, but Parrish watched closely to see if any of them were still moving.

"I think we're clear," she said.

She pushed through the doors and they made their way down the hall toward the nurse's station, stepping over corpses as they walked.

"Which way?"

Noah lifted his shirt and cleared blood away from another sign on the wall. The ER was to the left. More patient rooms to the right.

"Maybe we should split up," Crash said. "I know we said we needed to stick together, but we could be here for hours."

"I think he's right," Lily said. "This place appears to be mostly clear, so if we split up, we can cover a lot of ground twice as fast."

Parrish swallowed a lump of fear. She didn't want to lose sight of anyone, but clearing room by room as a group was taking too long. It was already past noon.

If something was going to happen, wouldn't it have happened already? Maybe she'd been wrong and Lily was not the one who'd summoned those super-zombies.

"Okay, the guys head toward the patient rooms," she said. "Us girls will go toward the ER. If you get into trouble, use the radios. We'll meet back up here if we can. If the way is blocked, just head for the exit."

Noah grabbed her hand. "Are you sure about this?" he whispered. "I don't want to leave you."

"I think it's the only way we're going to clear this place in time," she said. She squeezed his hand. "Be careful."

"You too," he said.

"What about lights?" Karmen said as they started toward the ER. "Without Crash we'll be in the dark the whole way."

"Got it," Crash yelled from the other side of the corridor.

All the lights in front of them switched on.

"Thank you," Karmen shouted back.

"We're quiet from here on out," Parrish said. "And the three of us stick together."

They cleared the rest of the hallway, checking rooms as they went. How could there not be a single nurse's cart in any of these rooms? They probably got locked up in the meds room at the end of each shift, but the hospital had been overrun. Who would have had time to put things away neatly?

They had to find one soon.

At least they hadn't come across any rotters or super-zombies. Maybe she'd been completely wrong about today. Maybe whoever had attacked them in D.C. was long gone, and had been unable to track them when they left the city.

She held onto that hope as they pushed deeper into the hospital, following the signs toward the emergency room.

She figured if they didn't find something in the next few hours, it was time to call it.

After clearing another hallway, they came across a second set of double doors. Parrish tried to see inside, but the windows were covered in blood and gore on the other side. She couldn't see anything.

She pressed her ear to the door, listening for any sound of shuffling feet or groans. After a long pause, she finally took a deep breath and pushed the doors open.

Some of the lights in this hallway were broken, so they only had a dimly lit path through the mess of dead bodies that covered the floors. Most of them were ripped open and the smell of decay hung thick in the air like a fog.

"You've got to be kidding me," Karmen said, lifting the

collar of her t-shirt over her mouth and nose. "This is disgusting."

Parrish grabbed an extra shirt out of her bag and tied it around her face. It helped some, but nothing could protect her from that smell.

"We must be near the quarantine zone," she said. She wondered why there hadn't been any signs warning them to stay out. So far, though, none of the bodies appeared to be moving. These people had been dead for a long time. She stepped over them as best she could, but there were so many.

"We have to be getting close to the ER now," she said. "Keep your eyes peeled for any sign of the meds room so we can get the heck out of here."

"Amen to that," Karmen said.

They'd made it halfway down the long hallway before the tiny hairs on the back of her neck stood up. Something wasn't right here.

"Why are we stopping?" Lily asked.

Parrish looked down at the bodies on the floor. She couldn't explain it, but a sudden darkness had come over this place.

"Something's wrong," she said. "We need to go. Now."

But the moment she turned, every dead body on the floor opened its eyes.

"Do you think we're even going to find anything?" Noah asked.

They'd cleared another five or six rooms, but they hadn't seen any sign of a medical cart. All the cabinets had been opened up, their contents long since gone. "I'm thinking someone got to this place before we did."

"I'm starting to think you're right about that," Crash said. "At least they cleared the rotters out for us, too."

"Let's move faster," he said. "I don't like the idea of us being separated from the girls. Why did we let them take the more dangerous route?"

Crash shrugged. "I think those girls know how to handle themselves," he said. "Maybe better than we do."

"True," Noah said with a laugh. "It's still hard to believe some of the things we can do now, isn't it?"

"You can say that again," Crash mumbled.

They made their way through more rooms, but this whole thing felt like a waste of time. They'd had more luck in the first fifteen minutes back at the ambulance bay than they'd had the past two hours.

"Holy crap, look at this," Crash said.

Noah pushed past him, his heart racing. In the middle of the room, a dead nurse was slumped over a beige rolling cart. She'd knocked the monitor to the floor, but he was sure this was the kind of cart Karmen had been talking about.

"Jackpot," he whispered. "I can't believe we actually found one."

"Let's open this puppy up and see what's inside," Crash said.

The nurse's body was blocking most of the front of the cart. Noah hated to just push her to the floor, but they needed to get into those drawers.

He carefully poked at her body with his bat, preparing to swing if she moved.

She didn't.

He took a deep breath and leaned his bat against the wall. "I'll get her," he said.

He wrapped his arms around the nurse's waist and lifted her onto his shoulder. As carefully as he could, he moved her to the bed and set her down. It wasn't nearly what the woman deserved, but it was better than shoving her to the floor like a piece of garbage.

There were several drawers on the front side of the cart, but when Crash tugged on them, they didn't budge.

"Locked," he said.

"Let me try." Noah reached toward the drawers, but he paused when the radio at his hip came to life.

Static blasted from it and he grabbed the radio and turned it down.

"Parrish? Is everything okay?" he asked. He let up on the side button and listened. All he heard was more static. Dammit, these things weren't working. Why hadn't they checked them earlier?

"We'll check on them in a second," Crash said. "Come here and see if you can open this. Or look for a badge on the nurse's body."

Noah glanced toward the nurse, but the bed was empty.

"Crash, she's gone," he shouted. He reached for his bat, his breath catching in his chest.

Before he could wrap his hands around it, Crash slammed into him and they both fell to the floor. The bat clunked across the tile, out of reach.

Noah scrambled onto his back and reached for his gun, but as the nurse stepped into view, the sight of her brought bile into his throat.

The veins in her arms pulsed as sores broke out across her skin, acid spilling onto the floor. Her jaw unhinged and a set of razor-sharp teeth protruded from her lips as she let out a blood-curdling scream that made every muscle in his body tense.

But the worst of it was that there was no mistaking the fiery red of her eyes.

Whoever wanted them dead had found them.

FIFTY-SIX
PARRISH

"It's a trap," she shouted. She gripped her sword tighter and spun around, searching for an exit, but they were surrounded. The lights flickered, and Parrish prayed for Crash to hang on to whatever power was controlling those lights.

Karmen fiddled with the radio, screaming into it that they needed help, but the only response was static.

The bodies that littered the floor stood, their eyes locked on the three girls standing in the middle of them.

"What do we do?" Karmen screamed.

"Whatever it was you both did back in Baltimore, I need you to do it again," she said.

She looked at Lily, catching her eye for a second. The girl looked just as surprised as Parrish, but she wasn't convinced. Would she help them? Or fight to destroy them?

Her mind raced to find a strategy for survival, but she couldn't think straight. There were just too many of them. If they cleared back toward the door, they'd still have dozens at their backs.

"Come closer," she said as she sliced through the neck of the closest rotter. "Put your backs against mine. I'll kill toward the door. You try to daze or mesmerize the ones behind me if you can."

"I don't know if I can do this," Karmen said. She lifted her shotgun and blasted a hole in the chest of a rotter clawing at her arms.

"You have to," Parrish said, her ears ringing. "You won't be able to shoot them fast enough."

"Take my hand," Lily said.

Parrish didn't have time to turn around and see if what they were doing was working or not. There were so many rotters right in front of her that she couldn't even see the double doors anymore.

She slashed through them as fast as she could, inching forward as each one fell. A dim blue light surrounded her sword.

"Parrish, help," Karmen screamed.

She stuck her sword through the neck of another rotter and kicked him in the chest, pulling her blade out as he fell backward. She spun on her heels, coming around Lily's side and planting her boot in the gut of another rotter.

Karmen had her hands on her head and was shaking it back and forth wildly. If she didn't get her shit together, she was going to get them all killed.

Parrish moved in front of Karmen and sliced down several zombies who had almost reached them on that side, but there was no way she could do this all by herself.

"Hey, I know you're both scared, but we don't have time

for that right now," she said as she fought. "We have to work together. I can't do this alone."

She paused for a second and grabbed Karmen's arm, pulling her hands away from her face so she could look her in the eyes.

"You can do this," she said. "Just breathe."

Karmen took a deep breath in through her nose and nodded, but her eyes were wild with fear.

A rotting hand grabbed Parrish's arm and she gritted her teeth, spinning around to kick the zombie's knee. It cracked and the rotter fell to the ground, its teeth snapping onto the laces on her boot.

She pulled a pistol from the leather strap at her hip and shot it straight through the top of its head.

When she'd created a small space between their group and the rotters behind them, she pushed back through the two other girls and started killing her way toward the doors again. Blood splattered onto her neck and face, but she kept going. Her muscles ached, but she didn't stop for a second.

One by one the rotters fell.

When she spun around again, relief filled her heart. There were at least ten more rotters on that side, but they were standing there, dazed and unmoving. Karmen and Lily were standing in front of them, their hands clutched together at their sides.

Parrish didn't know what to make of it. In her mind, she'd decided that if they ran into an ambush today, that meant Lily was their enemy. But the girl was helping them. That had to count for something, right?

With space to shoot, Parrish aimed her pistol at the rotters still blocking the double doors. She missed a couple times, but was finally able to take three down before she ran out of bullets. She stuffed the pistol back into her belt and raised her sword, stepping over the bodies of the dead as she moved forward.

The doors were in her sights now, only seven or eight still blocking the way, but as she took the last of them down, the doors swung open and a nightmare stepped inside.

Blazing red eyes stared back at her and she nearly fell to her knees with exhaustion and hopelessness.

The man was over six feet tall and built like a tank, his skin stretched over grotesque muscles that were easily three or four times larger than any she'd seen on even the largest body-builder. Dark veins pulsed along his flesh. He stood in the doorway, his eyes locked on the three of them.

Her worst fears had come true. The first two hours had lulled her into a false sense of safety. She'd thought they were going to be okay. Just grab the meds and get home by dark. They could do it.

But it had been a trap all along. They'd been foolish to think that getting back on the road would keep their assassin away.

She'd been with them the entire time. They'd welcomed her into the group with open arms, and she'd led them straight into a death trap.

Parrish backed toward the other girls. She grabbed Lily's burned arm, and the girl shrieked and tried to pull away.

"What have you done?" she asked through gritted teeth. "After all that we did for you, this is how you repay us?"

"I don't know what you're talking about," Lily said. "Let go. You're hurting me."

"Bullshit," Parrish shouted. She was so angry, the tears on

her cheeks fell like lava, so hot they nearly burned her skin. "You aren't the fifth. I wanted to believe you were a part of this group and that you were our friend, but this proves you never were. How could you do this to us?"

She pushed Lily to the ground and the girl stopped denying it. She doubled over, sobs shaking her small frame.

"I'm sorry," she said, looking up at Parrish. She was clutching her arm. "I had no choice."

Were the guys still alive? Or had they been attacked, too?

She prayed they were okay, but right now, she didn't have time to think about it.

"Karmen, we have to run," she said.

"What?" Karmen asked. She must have been so focused on holding the other rotters in her trance that she hadn't yet realized what was going on. She turned toward Parrish and when her eyes landed on the giant near the doors, she unleashed a high-pitched scream that echoed through the halls.

The rotters that had been under her spell woke up and stumbled toward them. They were surrounded by hell on both sides.

"Come on," she yelled. She grabbed Karmen's arm and pulled her through the group of rotters. She hit them so hard, several of them stumbled backward, clearing a small path. One of them managed to grab onto a lock of Parrish's hair and yank her forward. Karmen slipped out of her grip and slammed the barrel of her shotgun into the rotter's head.

Parrish put both hands on the hilt of her sword and started swinging. They had to get through this group to the next set of doors. Maybe they could find a place to hide until they figured out a plan. She prayed the guys were doing better than they were.

"What about Lily?" Karmen said as they pushed through the crowd and ran toward the doors.

"She's the one who brought them here," Parrish said. "Can't you see that?"

Karmen glanced back at Lily, but Parrish put a hand on her arm.

"Leave her."

They broke through to the other side and stopped dead in their tracks. They'd made it to the main lobby of the emergency room, a huge open area filled with more zombies than Parrish had ever seen in one place.

She only got that one brief glimpse of them all before all the lights in the hospital went out.

FIFTY-SEVEN

CRASH

Something hard slammed into him, sending his body flying across the room like a ragdoll. He crashed into Noah and tumbled to the floor, his head smacking against the tile.

Dazed, Crash brought a hand to the side of his head. The lights above him flickered, and he struggled to hold onto his connection with them. A scream pierced the silence, sending a wave of pain through his already throbbing head. Beside him, Noah popped off six rounds of shots from his handgun.

Crash forced his eyes open. His vision blurred, but there was no mistaking the red eyes.

He scrambled backward until his back hit the wall. The machine gun pressed into him. His fear attempted to paralyze him, but he pushed through it, forcing himself to react.

He struggled to grab his weapon and pull it around his body, but his hands were shaking so badly he could hardly find the trigger.

The nurse they'd found slumped over the med cart had been transformed into some kind of monster. Her skin oozed a foul-smelling acid that dripped from the sores on her arms and face onto the floor. The tiles at her feet sizzled.

Pointed teeth that looked like they belonged on a shark more than a human being stretched her lips wide as her mouth snapped open and closed.

The monster lunged toward Noah with terrifying speed, pouncing on his chest and clawing at his arms.

Shit, he couldn't shoot this thing with enough accuracy to hit it without hitting Noah too.

Crash stood and vaulted over the hospital bed, searching for anything he could use as a weapon. His eyes landed on the cracked monitor on the floor by the nurse's cart. He picked it up and swung it as hard as he could at the nurse's head.

She screamed as her head jerked sideways.

Noah rolled over, using the momentum of the hit to push her off his chest. He gripped the edge of the windowsill and catapulted himself toward Crash.

"What do we do?" Crash asked.

Noah leaned down to grab his bat from the floor. He reared back and slammed the weapon into the nurse's head. Her skull cracked and more acid poured through the wound, but it didn't kill her.

Crash finally found the trigger on his machine gun and sprayed the monster with bullets. He had a hard time keeping it steady and ended up unloading half his magazine into the wall just above her head.

The bullets that actually hit her seemed to do some damage, and she fell face-first onto the floor. For one brief moment, he thought he might have killed it, but she pushed up on her hands, attempting to stand.

And she was pissed.

"We run," Noah said. "Go."

Crash didn't need to be told twice. He sprinted from the room, waiting until Noah was clear to slam the door shut. That wouldn't hold her for long, but at least it would buy them some time.

"Which way?" he shouted. If they ran toward the girls, they'd just be leading this thing straight to them. At the same time, if they ran outside, they'd be leaving the girls inside alone.

What if they were being attacked, too? Those damned radios were crap. They should have done a test before they split up, but he just hadn't thought about it. He tried to connect to the signal in his mind, but it was too much to keep the power going and manage it all at once.

"This way," Noah said, making the decision for him as he ran in the direction of the ER.

They'd only made it halfway to the next turn before the nurse's scream echoed down the hallway. The sound seemed to reach inside his mind and twist it. He lifted his hands to his ears and doubled over, the pain so intense he could barely think straight.

When it was over, the nurse was already on them again, her mouth open wide and her red eyes locked on Crash.

Before he could steady his aim to shoot her again, Noah had grabbed his shotgun from his backpack. He blasted the nurse at close range, taking off the entire left side of her face.

Acid spewed from the wound, a single drop landing on

Crash's foot. He screamed as it burned a hole through the top of his boot.

Thank God for steel-toed boots, because he did not want to find out what would happen if that stuff got on his skin.

The nurse fell to her knees for a moment, but wasn't giving up. She crawled toward them, the bottom half of her jaw hanging loose. Crash aimed and pulled the trigger on his machine gun, spraying her with bullets until he heard the click of his empty magazine.

The nurse screamed again, but this time the sound gurgled as acid poured from her throat and cheeks. She lay completely on the ground now, still clawing her way across the floor.

Noah stepped forward and smashed what was left of her head in with his bat, the acid eroding parts of the wood so fast it disintegrated the entire end of the bat before he could pull it away.

Crash doubled over, bracing his palms against his knees and trying not to lose his lunch.

"She was normal when you moved her, right?" he asked. "I mean, dead, but normal?"

Noah nodded. "We need to get to the girls," he said. "I think we just got our answer about Lily, which means the girls are in trouble."

Crash bowed his head, tears of frustration and anger welling in his eyes. He'd really hoped they were wrong about her. This was all his fault.

"Come on," Noah said.

They ran down the corridor and followed the signs toward the emergency room, but there were rotters everywhere. From the looks of it, all the dead bodies that had littered the floors earlier were now up and walking around. Crash loaded another magazine into his machine gun and sprayed the hall-way, taking down ten or eleven that stood in their path.

Noah's bat was gone, so he'd started blasting heads with his shotgun, but they hadn't brought enough ammunition for all this. Crash cursed. He had another duffel full of guns and ammo back in the truck, but it wouldn't do them much good now.

They kept fighting their way forward, but when they rounded another corner, the double-doors leading to the next section of the hospital came into view. The windows were covered in blood, but Crash could hear the moans of the undead on the other side of the doors.

He jogged toward them, but about ten feet before he reached the end of the hall, something leapt at him from the shadows and knocked him to the ground. Pain burned through his arm as something sharp ripped his skin apart.

He couldn't hold onto his connection with the building's power and all the lights switched off.

Anger and fear surged through him. He'd come too far to die here, but if this was the end, he was going to take whatever this thing was with him.

Without thinking, he reached up and wrapped his palms around the face of the zombie who had attacked him. It was another woman, her long hair falling against his arm and face as she hovered above him.

She struggled, clawing at his arm with fingers that were sharp as knives.

Deep inside him, something new awakened, like a flame igniting. He poured that fire into his palms, meeting the zombie's eyes dead-on.

Jolts of high-voltage electricity shot through his fingertips.

The zombie's body jerked and twitched, sparks flying from its eyes and mouth, but he didn't let go. He sat up, lifting the thing off his chest as it bucked against him, cooking from the inside.

He didn't let go until it had burned to ashes in his hands.

"We have to turn around," Karmen whispered, searching for Parrish's arm in the darkness.

"If we go back in there, we have to face Lily and that giant," Parrish said. "But if we stay here, we have to face hundreds of rotters. I don't know what to do."

With the lights out, Karmen feared the worst. It meant that somewhere in this building, Crash and Noah were being attacked. And they were losing.

How had this whole day gone to hell so fast?

She couldn't believe they'd been right about Lily. How could someone from their own group betray them like this?

She remembered the darkness she'd felt when Lily had grabbed her arm that day in Baltimore when they'd come across the huge horde of zombies in the smoke. The strange cloak she'd found. The stone with five sides and strange symbols. All the signs had been there, but no one had realized the horrors she'd had planned for them.

The rotters in the lobby of the emergency room had all

caught on that there was food in the room, and Karmen could hear them stumbling over one another to get to the doorway. They didn't have time to think. They needed to act.

"We stay here and fight," Karmen said. She swallowed a thick lump of fear in her throat and focused on that small flame that lived inside of her.

She could feel the rotters growing closer, their moans growing louder.

She connected to the power inside of her, feeding it with her fear and giving it new life. Dark red flames ignited on her palms, quickly surrounding her hands and spreading a red glow through the room.

The fire didn't burn her at all. It made her feel stronger.

A rotter lunged toward her and she lifted her hands. The flames shot out from her palms, igniting the zombie's tattered clothing. The creature whimpered and fell to the ground near her feet.

"Holy crap," Parrish said, lifting her sword, a smile tugging at her lips. "Okay, then. Let's do this."

Blue flames engulfed the blade as Parrish swung forward, pushing her way into the crowded room. She sliced the heads off six zombies in a single motion, their bodies flashing blue for a moment and then frosting over with a thin layer of ice.

Karmen drew in a focused breath, her jaw tense and strong. She would not run screaming or cower in fear. Ever since her powers had first manifested, she'd been afraid of them, scared that using them meant she was giving up on the old world and her old life once and for all.

But what had her old life ever brought her but sadness and fear?

The new world was terrifying and full of nightmares, but

she was strong here. Together, they could change this world and make it right again.

All she had to do was embrace the part of herself she'd been denying for the past few weeks.

Remembering what she'd seen Lily do to the rats back in the apartment, she brought the heel of her hand up to her mouth and stepped forward, her fingers pointing out toward the next group of rotters lumbering toward them.

She rounded her lips and exhaled, praying it would work for her, too.

The flames billowed out in a cloud of heat, engulfing every zombie in their path. It reminded her of a time when she'd watched her brother and his friends play with lighters and cans of hairspray, except this time, the flames were twice as powerful.

The zombies screamed as they burned, many of them falling to their knees in front of her as they clawed at their own flesh.

At her side, Parrish continued to slice through the crowd, the blue flames dancing on her blade and growing brighter with each kill. Together, they stepped over the bodies of the dead and destroyed the rotters in their path.

But there were so many of them. Hundreds more blocking the exit.

And somewhere in the crowd, a low clicking sound was growing louder. It was almost a growl, but slower and much freaking creepier.

Karmen searched through the semi-darkness, trying to figure out where the noise was coming from. Her eyes locked on a zombie in the middle of the crowd, the red of its eyes piercing through the room.

"There's another one," she shouted. "There, in the center."

"Shit," Parrish said, swinging at another group. "There's too many to fight. If she makes it to us, we're—"

But she didn't have a chance to finish her sentence. The zombie with the red eyes leapt onto the counter at the nurse's station, and then jumped halfway across the room, knocking Parrish to the ground.

Karmen screamed and ran toward her friend, but a rotter who had fallen grabbed her leg and pulled her to the floor. Her head smacked against one of the waiting room chairs, and she nearly lost consciousness.

She was aware of the fingers clawing at her jeans and the blood now dripping through her hair and across her temple, but she had to struggle just to keep her eyes open. Parrish had dropped her sword, killing the blue flames that had provided so much light to the room, and now Karmen's own flames had gone out. She couldn't focus enough to bring them back.

She pulled her way forward, using the bodies of the dead to crawl across the floor to her friend. The only light in the room was from the revolving door at the entrance to the ER, but the windows were grimy from so many rotting hands clawing at them for the past few weeks. Still, it was enough to see the teen boy with his hands wrapped around Parrish's neck.

The boy opened his mouth and long tentacles slithered out, snaking their way toward Parrish's face as she screamed.

The rotter that held Karmen's leg tugged and pulled her backward. She rolled over and kicked it as hard as she could, severing the hand from its wrist. As soon as she was free, she scrambled to her feet, nearly tripping again over the bodies that carpeted the floor.

She regained her balance and jumped forward, grabbing the boy's waist and pulling him off Parrish. She fell onto her back, the zombie struggling against her chest. He was stronger than she expected, but she had him around the waist and she wasn't letting go.

"Kill this thing," she shouted.

Out of the corner of her eye, she saw Parrish reach for her sword and stand up, but the tentacles from the boy's mouth were now snaking through his hair toward Karmen. She nearly fainted at the sight of them, desperate not to ever find out what those tentacles would do if they touched her.

Parrish stood over them and plunged her sword into the boy's neck so far that the tip of her blade touched Karmen's cheek. Thick blood poured onto her neck and shoulders as the thing twisted and twitched, grabbing at the blade. Karmen wiggled out from under it, and when she was able to stand, she started kicking at its head over and over until it stopped moving.

"How many of these things do you think there are?" she asked.

"I can't even begin to guess," Parrish said.

Karmen breathed in and out, reconnecting with her power. She focused on the anger pumping through her veins. She focused on the fire that fueled her soul.

She set her sights on the dozens of rotters left on the other side of the ER, and once more, her hands turned to flames.

"Come on," she said. "Let's kill the rest of these, find the guys, and get out of here before we have to find out."

FIFTY-NINE
NOAH

The moans of dozens of rotters echoed through the hall behind him.

Noah spun around, but without the lights, he couldn't see where they were coming from.

"Crash, we could really use some electricity right about now," he said.

"I'm working on it," Crash said. "I'm not feeling so good."

Noah tore off his backpack and searched inside for his flashlight. When he flipped it on, Crash was dusting ashes off his jacket. His arm was bleeding pretty badly.

"Here," Noah said. He handed Crash the flashlight and placed his hand on top of the wound. He closed his eyes and breathed deeply, letting a healing energy pass from him to his friend. Crash's arm frosted over slightly, and the bleeding slowed.

"Wow, you weren't kidding about that," Crash said. He flexed his hand and nodded his head. "Thanks."

"The lights? We need to find the others, and I think we've got some zombies on our tail."

Crash reached out to place his hand flat against the wall. A few seconds later, the lights flickered on, but went back off.

Noah reloaded his shotgun, the moans growing louder around the corner.

"Come on, man, we gotta hurry."

"I'm doing the best I can," Crash said.

Noah blasted the head off a rotter as it turned the corner. It fell in a bloody mess on the floor, but more followed. He shot again, taking four more out before he had to stop and reload. He could just barely see them in the dim light, but it was enough.

Crash finally pulled through and the lights came on.

Noah unloaded the shotgun again, and the dead bodies seemed to slow the rest down for a second. "Let's keep moving. Maybe we can brace these doors closed and keep them back."

Crash nodded and pushed through the double-doors, but what they found inside was ten times more terrifying than a group of rotters.

A towering beast of a man stood at the other end of the hallway, its hand on the doors leading into the ER. Noah pumped his shotgun and aimed directly for the man's head. The pellets ricocheted off the zombie's skin and embedded into the drywall.

Noah's heart skipped a beat. If bullets wouldn't touch this thing, what the hell were they going to do? He had a feeling the girls were on the other side of that door, and he wasn't about to turn and run, but they were going to have to go through this beast to get to them.

The zombie turned toward them. He balled his hands into fists and lifted his foot to stomp hard against the tile floor.

The ground beneath them shook. A picture fell off the wall and shattered, scattering glass across the floor. Noah crouched and pressed his hand against the wall for balance until the earthquake subsided.

"Pile the dead bodies against the door to keep the others from getting through," he said. "I'll see if I can handle this guy."

Crash got to work, dragging bodies and piling them up in front of the door.

Noah dropped his shotgun and peeled the backpack off his back. He didn't need anything slowing him down right now.

The giant zombie walked toward him. It was slow, but the ground shook slightly with every step it took. Noah had no idea how to fight something like this, but he had to try. He had to get to Parrish and make sure she was okay.

He took in a deep breath and focused everything he had on summoning his strength. If he was strong enough to lift a car, he could deal with this guy. Maybe. Fear tightened in his chest.

He gritted his teeth and ran full force toward the beast, leaning his head down and barreling into it with his shoulder. The beast stumbled backward, but got its footing and pushed back, tossing Noah into the air. His head slammed against the wall and he fell to the floor in a daze.

Struggling, he pulled himself up and tried again. This time, he reared his fist back and punched the zombie in the gut. It was like punching a reinforced steel door, his knuckles cracking against it.

The beast grabbed him by the waist and lifted him off the

ground. Noah struggled to get free, but had nothing to grab onto except the man's wrists. It wasn't enough. The zombie threw him across the room. He crashed into the pile of zombies at the double-doors.

Crash reached to help him. "Are you okay?"

"I think so," Noah said, stretching his shoulder out. "I can't seem to hurt this thing."

The beast walked toward them again, and with each step, the ground shook, the ceiling raining dust down on them.

"Maybe we could try to run past it?" Crash said. "He's slow. If we could just get by him, we'd be in the clear."

"It's just going to follow us," he said. "We need to put an end to it."

"How?"

"I'm thinking," he said.

He wished Parrish were here. Her sword might be able to do a lot more damage than a gun. Wherever she was, he prayed she and Karmen were alright.

And what had happened to Lily? Was she still with them?

He had to focus.

"Every monster has a weakness," Crash said. "It's a rule of thumb in gaming. Even the most impossible boss fight has a trick to it."

"This isn't a video game," Noah said.

"No, but it applies in real life," he said. "We just have to figure out what it is."

"Yeah, in the next thirty seconds or so," Noah said. "No problem."

The beast was nearly to them.

"That thing you did to my arm," Crash said. "The frost.

Can you use that on him? Freeze him, maybe? That might at least give us some time."

"I don't know," Noah said. "I can try."

Noah reconnected with his healing energy. It seemed like the opposite of what he needed to be doing, but he was out of options.

He breathed in and when he let his breath out, it was cold as ice. When he looked down at his palms, a light blue frost had covered them. Amazed, he lifted his eyes to the giant beast of a zombie.

He ran straight for him, but this time instead of punching him or hitting him, he dropped and slid across the floor. The zombie reached forward, expecting to grab him. The momentum of the motion made him stumble off-balance as Noah slid past.

He quickly stood and placed his palms flat against the zombie's back, pushing all of his healing energy into the thing. The light around his hands grew so bright, he had to squint and turn his head away.

The energy poured through him in waves, pulsing as it flowed into the beast's body. The man fell to his knees and then dropped forward on his hands. He let out a loud rumble of a roar as the light flowed through him and a layer of ice formed across his flesh.

Noah pulled his hands from the man's back and stumbled two steps back, steadying himself against the wall. A massive headache exploded behind his eyes.

But he didn't get a chance to rest. He'd thought it was over, that the beast was down, but a loud cracking noise forced his eyes open. The beast broke through the ice and wrapped a hand around Crash's throat, lifting him from the ground. He threw him against the stack of bodies and Crash's eyes closed.

Noah screamed and ran toward the beast, focusing all his strength on taking this thing to the ground.

But the beast stood and turned, lifting Noah like he weighed nothing. He pulled back and threw him across the room.

Noah soared through the air, terror gripping his heart as he slammed against the double-doors. He felt something crack and then, as if someone had turned out all the lights, his world went black.

SIXTY

PARRISH

An earthquake shook the hospital.

Parrish stumbled against a group of rotters, hands tangling in her hair and dragging her to the ground. One zombie leaned over her, its mouth open, ready to bite. She raised her sword straight through its chin, not stopping until it came out through the other side of its skull.

She yanked the sword down and rolled over as the zombie fell to the floor where she had been.

"What was that?" Karmen asked.

"I don't know, but we need to finish these off and go find the guys," she said.

She stood and sliced through the heads of five zombies, knocking the last of them to the ground.

She wiped the blade of her sword against the back of a rotter and stared at the carnage. They had killed hundreds, but there would be more. She was sure of it.

"Let's go," she said.

She ran back toward the doors leading to the hallway,

prepared to face Lily and the behemoth on the other side, but something sailed through the doors just before she reached them.

"Noah," she cried. She fell to the floor in front of him, her hands shaking in terror.

In that moment, all her memories of their lives together flashed in front of her eyes. Everything that had come back to her when they'd kissed the night before was there. If he was dead, she would have nothing left to live for.

She pulled his head into her lap and stroked his hair, her tears cascading onto his face.

He was still breathing, but he'd been badly hurt. Her head snapped up, realizing what must have happened. She had run from that beast, leaving him there in the hallway for Noah and Crash to find. This was her fault.

She leaned down and kissed his forehead. If he didn't wake up, she would never be able to forgive herself.

The floor shook and through the half-open doors, she saw the giant beast lumbering toward her.

Parrish shrugged out of her backpack and propped it under Noah's head. She stood, steadied herself against the wall and lifted her sword. Just when she'd been feeling weak and thought she'd reached a point where she couldn't possibly go on, a new light had switched on inside her. Power and strength coursed through her veins.

She would not let this beast hurt anyone else.

The beast stopped just short of the door, his eyes locked on hers. He tightened his fists again, and as his mouth opened, Parrish shouted for Karmen to hold onto something.

The ground lurched beneath her feet, debris falling from the ceiling. She crouched low and waited it out. When the earthquake had passed, Parrish steadied herself and stepped forward.

Rage boiled her blood. She wasn't going to wait for this thing to come after her. She was just going to take it out before he even realized what hit him. He was going to pay for hurting Noah.

Parrish moved her sword to her right hand, switching her grip so that she could pull the sword back behind her head, the blade facing forward. New flames engulfed her sword in a burst of light. Blue and red danced together against the steel as she ran toward the beast.

She had no idea if she could kill this thing, but she was certain this was who she was. This was who she had always been.

And if this was going to be the end of her, she was going to die trying to protect her friends.

The beast lifted his arms to shield his body, but Parrish used that to her advantage. She leapt into the air, grabbed his arm with her free hand, and catapulted herself up and over his head. She somersaulted, tucking her legs close to her body and spinning through the air.

She landed softly on the tile floor behind him, pulled her sword back, and plunged it straight into the base of his neck.

The giant beast straightened and stilled as a thick layer of ice formed around his massive body. As the ice reached his head, he took one last gasp of breath. She planted the heel of her boot against the man's back and pushed, using the leverage to pull her sword from its body.

Somewhere deep inside the block of ice, a red glow flickered and grew, exploding in a burst of light that shattered the zombie's body into a million burning pieces.

She fell to her knees, exhausted. Was it finally over?

A hand touched her shoulder and she spun around, sword ready.

"Whoa, there, warrior princess, it's just me," Crash said. His arm was bleeding and his head seemed to be bruised, but he was alive.

"This is the last time we ever go into a hospital," she said with a laugh, her voice still a little shaky.

"You'll have no complaints from me on that one," Karmen said as she fell back against the wall and slid down to the floor. The flames on her hands had disappeared and they were trembling violently.

Parrish stood and used a trash can to prop open the emergency room doors. Noah's body was lying half-in, half-out of the room, his eyes still closed.

"Noah," she whispered, kneeling at his side. "You have to wake up. We need to get out of here."

She kissed his forehead and ran her hand across his bloodied cheek. If they had to, they would carry him out. Now that the ER was clear, they should be able to just walk out. She wasn't sure what time it was, but it wasn't dark yet. They needed to go now if they were going to find a safe place to hide for the night.

"Parrish," Karmen said, backing away. There was an edge to her voice that filled Parrish with dread.

She stood and faced the figure standing near the exit on the other side of the emergency room.

"You should have gone," Parrish said. "Or did you come to do your own dirty work this time?"

Lily's face was flushed, tears running down her cheeks.

"I don't have much time," she said. "I know you can't

possibly understand why I did what I did, but I need to tell you something important."

"I don't want to hear anything you have to say, traitor," Parrish said. "You almost got us killed today. You lied to us. You betrayed all of us."

"I know, and believe me, I wish I could go back in time and make this right, but I can't," Lily said. "I made my choice, and I can't change it. The Dark One is coming for me now, and when she finds out I've spoken to you, she'll punish me more than you could ever imagine."

Chills ran down Parrish's spine. "The Dark One?"

Lily shook her head and swiped at her cheeks. "I know you don't understand what's happening yet, but you will," she said. "I think you've all already realized it, but this is not your first lifetime. You have been alive for centuries, reincarnating over and over again, bound by a spell to protect this world in case the Dark One ever awakened. You've lived here for a very long time, but you are not of this world."

"I don't understand," Parrish said.

"The Dark One threatened to overthrow our world a long time ago. When you couldn't defeat her, you banished her here, locking her in a prison of ice deep inside the earth," Lily said. "She was powerless for centuries, but I messed up. Once in every lifetime, your mentor—a prophet named Tobias Prague— comes to check on you. He passes through a portal to make sure the spell is still in place and that the magical seal you put on this world is working as it should. A few weeks ago, when he opened the portal, I followed him, thinking I would use the information I learned to gain power in my world. When I came through the portal, I killed him."

Parrish listened to the story, not believing that after all this questioning and searching, it was the enemy who was finally giving them answers.

"I didn't mean to kill him," she said. "I was scared. This darkness overwhelmed me, and I couldn't fight it. Before I knew what was happening, my dagger had plunged into his stomach. As he died, he begged me to find you. To warn you, but the Dark One promised me so many things."

Lily sobbed, every once in a while glancing back at the doors, as if she expected someone to come through at any moment.

"My actions created a crack in the magical seal you created long ago, allowing the Dark One to grow a single rose. A rose that infected the first human and spread through the human world, killing millions. With each death, the Dark One grows stronger. I pledged my life to her, believing she would give me something I'd been wanting my entire life. Power. Recognition. A sense of purpose."

"You caused all this," Parrish said. "All of this is your fault."

"Yes. I did this," she said. "But by the time I realized how wrong I was, it was already too late. I can't stop what the Dark One has already set in motion, but you can. Parrish you are stronger than you could ever imagine. There are not many of your kind. Those who wield both sides of the power are extremely rare in our world. You must find the fifth. You must go to the Island of Memories and remember the guardians you once were. You are the only ones who can stop her now. Not just to save what's left of this world, but also to save the people in mine."

"Why are you telling us all this? How do we even know we can trust anything you say?"

"Because I owe you this," she said. "I didn't tell you my name because no one had ever given me one before."

She touched a finger to the bracelet on her arm.

"You are the only friends I've ever known, and I will go to my grave knowing I betrayed you," she said. "But it's my hope that I can help you find the fifth and save your sister."

Hot tears welled up in Parrish's eyes and her breath caught in her chest. "My sister?" she whispered. "My sister is dead."

"She's alive," Lily said. "But the Dark One knows where she is. She plans to use your sister against you. You have to go to New York and find her before the Dark One does. You'll find the fifth there, as well."

Lily glanced back toward the doors and shivered.

"I don't have much time left," she said. "I know you won't believe me when I tell you I'm sorry, but I am."

Behind her, the doors to the ER burst open and two rotters seized her by the arms and dragged her backwards.

"Take this stone," she shouted, struggling against the zombies. She reached into her pocket and threw something toward them. Parrish grabbed it, turning it over in her palm.

"Take the stone to the island," Lily said. "It will help you to remember. It will help you find the fifth."

Lily disappeared through the doors, her screams still echoing through the building long after she was gone.

Parrish let her head fall into her hands.

Zoe was alive. She'd been alive all this time, still waiting for Parrish to come rescue her.

They had to get to New York. Somehow, they had to find a way to get to her sister.

"What did she give you?" Crash asked.

Karmen stepped forward and touched her hand to the

stone. "I saw it in her bag earlier this morning before we left," she said. "There are symbols carved into each side. I think each mark belongs to one of us."

Parrish turned it over in her hands. Four of the symbols lit up, but the fifth remained dark.

They had to find him. They had to rescue her sister. But first, they had to get out of this hospital.

She secured the stone in her backpack and fell to her knees at Noah's side. She placed her hands on his face and his eyes fluttered open.

A sob escaped from her lips and she leaned down and kissed him. "I love you," she said.

He smiled and ran his fingertips along her jawline. "I love you, too," he said. "Is it over?"

She nodded. "I think so," she said. "Can you walk?"

She and Crash helped him to stand.

"I think so," he said.

Noah wrapped his strong arms around her. He kissed the top of her head and hugged her so tight she was afraid he was going to crack a rib.

"We never split up like that again, okay?" he said.

She nodded against his chest, her tears soaking into his shirt. "Yeah, that was a dumb idea," she said. "Is everyone okay?"

"I'm bleeding all over the place, but other than massive claw marks on my arms, I think I'm going to be fine," Crash said.

"I'll look at it again when we get out of here," Noah said.

"Did anyone actually find any damned antibiotics?" Parrish asked. "Because if we walk out of this place without them after everything we just went through, I'm going to scream."

"We found one of those med carts in one of the rooms, but I'll be damned if I'm going back in there now," Crash said.

"Wait," Karmen said. "Look."

She pointed toward a well-lit room visible behind the nurse's station.

Parrish laughed, tears of joy and disbelief falling onto her cheeks. "The meds room," she said.

Karmen jumped over the counter of the nurse's station and pushed through the doors toward the meds room. "It's locked," Karmen said.

Crash leaned over the body of a dead nurse on the floor at Parrish's feet. He grabbed a badge clipped to the front of her scrubs.

"Try this," he said, tossing the badge to Karmen.

She slid the badge through the scanner and the door clicked open.

Karmen clapped and let her head fall back. "Thank God," she said.

Parrish smiled and pushed the door open. "Look for any name that ends with 'cillin'. Like Amoxicillin, Penicillin, whatever."

"Here," Noah said.

The glass case holding the antibiotics was locked, but Parrish slammed the hilt of her sword against it and it shattered. She pulled the bottles of pills and all the IV bags out of the case and stuffed them in her bag, grateful for this one thing.

Banged up, bloodied, and bruised, the four of them made

their way to the exit, pushing out into the amber light of sunset.

There was no sign of the girl and no rotters waiting for them. They had survived a great battle and come out stronger for it. As they searched for a house to sleep in for the night, Parrish cried tears of happiness, her arm linked with Noah's.

She still didn't understand everything that had happened, and there was still a great journey ahead of them but they were alive. Zoe was alive. And for now that was enough.

Because where there was life, there was hope.

SIXTY-ONE

THE WITCH

"Zoe, sweetheart, I'm a friend of your sister's," the witch said. She knocked again, waiting for the girl to open the door.

She hated that the Dark One had sent her to do this task, but she was helpless to fight against the wishes of her mistress. She had strayed, and the Dark One had punished her, just as the witch knew she would.

She trembled, remembering the way her body had burned. At times, she wasn't sure she would survive it, but the Dark One wanted her to live. She wanted to make sure the witch would never forget the consequences of betrayal.

She lifted her hand to the door again, the silver bracelet jangling on her ruined arm. Her entire body was ruined and burned now, her beauty taken from her. She waited, hot tears falling against her cheek.

But the girl didn't come.

Frustrated, knowing this was her last chance to please the Dark One, the young witch placed her ear against the door.

She listened for any sign of movement inside. There was no telling what that child had been through in the past few weeks. She could be comatose in a corner somewhere, barely able to hear what was going on outside the door.

If she had to, she would tear it down. One way or another, she was getting that little girl and taking her somewhere Parrish could never find her. She hated herself for this, but she would never risk being tortured again. She would rather die.

There were no sounds on the other side of the door. With the throngs of undead moving this time of night all around the city, this suite at the top of the Four Seasons was one of the quietest, most sheltered places there were. Zoe had been lucky.

"Zoe, please open the door. I'm here to help you." The worst kind of lie, but she had no choice. It was her life or the girl's, and the witch had plans for her life. She had chosen her side, and she intended to see this through.

When the child didn't answer, the witch turned to the beast of a man behind her and nodded.

She stepped out of the way just before the zombie ran, shoulder-first as hard as he could, toward the door. Wood splintered and cracked, but there was no scream inside.

She had expected a scream of horror.

The zombie moved, his eyes red and vacant. He had been a man once, but now he was nothing more than a vessel. A servant of the Dark One, like so many millions out there now. Like her. It was her only purpose now.

The guardians were strong. They had survived so much, but the war against them had only just begun.

And if they somehow managed to reunite with the fifth, this little girl would help defeat them. Where there was love, there was weakness. She had learned that lesson the hard way.

The witch crawled through the hole in the door and looked around. It was dark, but she sent a conjured orb of light along the edges of the room, searching every nook and cranny where the girl might be hiding. The suite had a large living area and a separate bedroom. So many places for a small child to hide.

Sheets and comforters were piled on the floor, creating a little nest where the child must have been sleeping at night. The room smelled of feces and urine.

There was no sign of the girl now, though. Where could she be hiding?

"Zoe?"

The door to the bedroom was blocked completely. Every piece of furniture light enough for a child to move on her own had been pushed in front of the door, and the smell of decay just beyond it told the story of what she had been protecting herself from.

Her father. Parrish had mentioned he was here with the girl. He had died and risen as one of the Dark One's servants. The witch could hear him in the next room, shuffling around.

She was about to instruct her two minions to clear the area in front of the door when something caught her eye near the window.

She moved quickly, increasing the power of her light.

Her orb moved around the edges of the room and the witch's eyes followed it, searching for the girl. She had to be here somewhere. Hiding like a smart little thing. Not trusting anyone who wasn't Parrish.

But when the light shone on the large window that took up most of the outer wall of the suite, the witch's heart stopped beating for a full five seconds. She couldn't breathe or move.

All she could do was stand in the middle of the large room and stare at that window, her body trembling in fear.

There, across the entire center pane of glass, low enough a child could reach it, was a symbol drawn in blood. A spiral, the symbol for air.

The witch collapsed to her knees, unable to take her eyes off the glass. Tears rolled down her burned face. She had failed her mistress, and she would be punished again.

This was the symbol of the fifth guardian.

Somehow, he had gotten to her first.

T he boy held his hand out, motioning for Zoe to join him on the roof. She was frightened and pale, but she seemed to trust him.

He wished he could tell her everything he knew, but couldn't find his voice. All he could do was lead her, but they needed to move quickly. The Dark One would be searching for them soon.

Carefully, tears shining in her eyes, she placed her hand in his.

He helped her onto the roof, the night air cool against his skin.

"It's been so long since I saw anyone alive," she said. "Where are you taking me?"

He gave her a small smile, wishing he could tell her that everything was going to be okay. Only, he couldn't promise that to her. All he could do was try to keep her safe.

He'd been wrong about who she was. She was not his leader. Not one of the guardians at all. But somehow, she carried the blood of a guardian in her veins. Blood that had protected her from the virus and given her the strength to survive this long.

And she wore the leader's sign—an infinity symbol—around her neck.

He wished he had more time to ask her about herself and what she was doing in that room, but they were running out of time. She needed to follow him now, or it would be too late.

He held up his index finger and reached into his pocket, taking out a small spiral notebook. In a child's hand, he wrote one word.

Home.

She met his eyes and shivered in the dark. "It's cold up here."

He pulled his black hoodie from his bag and helped her put it on. She was a little taller than he was, and a few years older, but the sweatshirt was still way too big on her. She looked so fragile and scared.

The boy held out his hand and nodded, encouraging her to come with him.

Zoe stared at him, and then looked out across the rooftops of the city.

"How will we get there?" she asked. "I don't understand."

The boy smiled. After two days of jumping rooftops, he'd gotten much better at it. So good, he barely needed to touch the ground anymore.

He wrote something else in his notebook and showed it to her.

We're going to fly.

Her eyes widened and she stared at him, shaking her head. "That's impossible," she said.

He offered his hand again, tucking the notebook back into his pocket.

The girl trembled, wrapping the hoodie tighter around her small body. She stared into his eyes, as if trying to decide whether to believe him.

The boy lifted his arms into the air, his hands glowing with a dim blue light.

All around them, the wind picked up, blowing Zoe's hair all around her face. Her eyes widened, and she spun around, her mouth open in awe.

"Are you doing this?" she asked.

The boy smiled and nodded. He raised his arms even higher, and another gust of wind blew over the rooftop.

Zoe giggled, her eyes full of wonder.

He secured his bag—making sure the girl's violin was safely tucked inside—and walked to the edge of the building to stare out over the dark city. Millions of rotters staggered in the streets below, but there were survivors out there somewhere, too. People like the two of them, finding their way to each other against all odds.

He wasn't alone anymore, and soon the others would come for them. The war against the Dark One had just begun, and they would need each other.

Zoe moved beside him and, very slowly, slipped her tiny hand into his.

Together, they flew across rooftops, soaring into the night toward an uncertain future.

A future that now held the smallest promise of hope.

ABOUT THE AUTHOR

Sarra Cannon is the author of several series featuring young adult and college-aged characters, including the bestselling Shadow Demons Saga. Her novels often stem from her own experiences growing up in the small town of Hawkinsville, Georgia, where she learned that being popular always comes at a price and relationships are rarely as simple as they seem.

Sarra owns her own publishing company and has sold three-quarters of a million copies of her books. She currently lives in Charleston, South Carolina with her programmer husband, her adorable redheaded son, and her beautiful daughter.

Love Sarra's books? Join Sarra's Mailing List to be notified of new releases and giveaways!

Also, please come hang out with me in my Facebook Fan Group: Sarra Cannon's Coven. We have a lot of fun in there, and I often share exclusive short stories and teasers in the group. Join now.

Want more? Come join us LIVE three times a week on my YouTube channel.

Connect With Sarra Online:
www.sarracannon.com

www.ingramcontent.com/pod-product-compliance
Lightning Source LLC
Chambersburg PA
CBHW051936240626
47153CB00005B/1512